SHADOW
DREAMS

ELIZABETH MASSIE

SHADOW DREAMS

LEISURE BOOKS NEW YORK CITY

A LEISURE BOOK®
May 2002
Published by

Dorchester Publishing Co., Inc.
276 Fifth Avenue
New York, NY 10001

ISBN 0-8439-4999-6

Visit us on the web at www.dorchesterpub.com.

*To Brian Hodge,
for the many years of friendship,
the many miles traveled from Mt. Vernon to
Waynesboro and back, and the offer of
limeade on a particularly bad day.*

CONTENTS

I Am Not My Smell

The moon is a chalk rock, hanging in the sky in the black of the night and the blue of the day. It is there because it has room there; it is comfortable there. The moon is not its light, though some would say it is. The moon is a big round body with a purpose which I don't understand but don't need to understand.

I am a woman with a bad foot. My foot was crushed last month by a passing car on Ocean Front Boulevard. I didn't get out of the way fast enough and it was run over and now my foot is dying. It is purple and fat and aches when I move it. I have washed it in the salty surf when no one else was around. I have pressed on it to pass the pus but it is still dying.

The boardwalk along the beach is where I live. I scour the rusted barrels in the sand in the blue of the day and curl up under the lip of the walkway in the black of the night. I have room here, but I am not comfortable. My swollen and pounding foot smells very bad. My body is covered with old sweat from my arm pits to my ankles and new sweat from each new day, but I am not my smell. Some think I am. I am a body with a purpose which I just now understand.

Last week I found two wonderful things. One was a brand new tee-shirt in the trash outside Surf Side Souvenirs. I clawed it out before the manager chased me away and threatened to call the police. It was tight but I ripped it up the sides and pulled it on over my sleeveless blouse. The other treasure was a dog. I named him Sunshine.

A dog has never been a treasure to me before. In fact, when I first found Sunshine, I thought he was ugly and gaunt. He growled at me and snapped, but I offered him some french fries I'd found in the dumpster behind Dairy Queen, and he calmed down. And then he sniffed at a small gash in my bad foot and began to lick. This amused him, or pacified him, I'm not sure which. His ears went up and his tail began to wag. It didn't hurt me at all. I shut my eyes, sitting there behind a beach bench on the boardwalk, and let Sunshine lick my swollen, dying foot. I squeezed on the foot, letting it drain for him. Sunshine licked. I pretended I was having a massage from the Man I Love.

As I sat, not bothering any of the vacationers, a child with a red ball cap leaned over the back of the bench and said "Mama, look. That's gross!"

The mother, face all painted and plucked, also looked over the bench seat. Her face registered my smell and then my foot. She contorted. "Disgusting."

I said, "In the Bible, Lazarus let the dogs at the gate lick his sores." But the mother and child were gone already, off in a hurry down the sandy walk and they didn't hear what I had to say.

Sunshine nipped my foot then, a love bite like cats give to their owners, and licked some more.

The dog had bonded with me, and we stayed together. I had little to feed him; I barely can keep up with the demands of my own growling belly. But we slept together and he would lick my foot and ease the heaviest of the throbbing. His hair was warmer than the grit of the ground under the boardwalk lip. He smelled, too, but a dog is not his smell. Even the richest of people know that. They laugh at a smelly dog and excuse him because they love him and because he is not his smell. He is a body with a purpose and they understand.

The Man I Love came out to the beach several days after I found Sunshine. The Man wore his yellow swim trunks and an unbuttoned red shirt that billowed in the breeze and let me see his tan chest and black chest hair and little pink nipples. He comes to the beach once a week, on Saturdays. Therefore, I know he is a working Man. A good Man who is a sane Man. A sane man can hold a job.

I haven't held a job for two years, since I was twenty three. Am I insane? I don't understand insanity, or if I am insane. But I know now that I have a purpose. If sanity is purpose, then I'm sane. My purpose is dreadful, but it is as sure as the beauty of the Man I Love.

The Man I Love is sane and good. He walks with his chin up and he stretches out to the sun and sea before settling down on the rolls of beach sand. He smiles even when no one is looking at him.

I watched him from my shadows under the boardwalk, but Sunshine trotted across the hot sand and sniffed at the Man's crotch. The

Man laughed and pushed Sunshine back a little, then petted him on the head.

"What a good dog," he said.

Sunshine wagged his tail and didn't growl.

"If you were a little healthier," said the Man. "I'd take you home with me. Go on, now, boy." He pet the dog again, and Sunshine just stood and wagged his tail until the Man shed his shirt and went for a swim in the waves.

Sunshine came back to me. I sat in the shadows, my bloated foot resting on a mound of sand I'd made, and rubbed the dog's head. The dog's nose was wet and probing, first on my hand and then back to my foot. What a wonder to pet something the Man had pet.

As I ran my rough fingers through the dog's fur, I began to understand my purpose. I began to realize why I existed.

My heart hammered, and the painful rhythm echoed in my foot.

I slept restlessly that night. A barb was in my chest, cutting with each breath and making it feel as though blood were seeping out to my stomach. I was nauseous, but swallowed it down as I stroked Sunshine.

The next day was Sunday. A lot of people come out on Sunday, even more than Saturday. The sun, in its purpose, was bright and hot. The moon held its position at a distance. It was white and faint.

I moved along the boardwalk. My good foot was bare. My bad foot was wrapped in a rag that had once been a beach towel left behind on the sand by a careless family. Pain sang with each step, hitting high notes when the weight was on the ball of my bad foot. Sunshine trotted along, hoping, I suppose, to be given more french fries or to have the chance at my foot again.

The Dairy Queen was busy. Gaily striped inflated floats were propped up against bike stands. Customers ate inside in the air conditioning and outside at the umbrella-shaded tables. I stood beyond the low chain fence, watching the people eat. Dusty sparrows fared better than I; they flew freely among the tables to gather the scraps. Vacationers watched them with smiles. But I was gawked at by those who noticed me. Their stares held me back behind the chain fence.

To the rear of the restaurant was the Dumpster. I limped around and waited until a pock-faced boy had emptied a container, then I dug inside. Sunshine sat at my feet and waited, chin up. I found some ketchup-covered buns for him. For me, there were chunks of cheeseburger and a third of an apple pie.

I went to a small tree and slid down to eat. I studied the beef beneath the bright orange varnish of cheese. A cow had its purpose. If the cow knew it, would she be distressed? Or in knowing, did a cow embrace life for what it was? The meat was cold.

As I licked grease from my fingers and Sunshine nosed into the towel to get at the fluid from my foot, I saw a flash of open white shirt. My head turned, and there, not ten feet from me, was the Man I Love. He was fumbling in his shorts pocket for his wallet. Seeing his nipples, my own grew hard. I wished I could have licked them like Sunshine licked my foot. I wanted to give them a love bite, and not have the Man push me away because of my smell.

Sunshine ran to the Man. The Man didn't see the dog coming, and when Sunshine jumped up and wagged his tail, the Man stumbled back. Sunshine dropped down and the tail-wagging increased.

"Hey, boy, you're back?" he said.

Sunshine's whole body wagged. I thought, if I was the dog, could I make the man like me enough to take me home? I sucked my fingers and scratched at a sweat-inspired tickle on my stomach.

"You ugly old thing," he said. He rubbed Sunshine vigorously beneath the gangly, whiskered chin. "What do you want from me? You're a mess, now get away."

Sunshine's claws clattered on the concrete of the sidewalk, a happy dog's dance.

"I can't take home an old, skinny dog. Sorry, pup. Vet bills aren't something I want to get into." The Man I Love squatted down and played with Sunshine's ears. My own ears tingled, imagining the sensation. "Now get. You made my hands stink." He laughed, sniffing his hands. Sunshine's body wiggled with joy.

The Man left, wiping his hands on his shorts, certain to wash them once he was inside the Dairy Queen. But certain not to think the dog was bad because he had a smell.

Sunshine came back to me, sat on his haunches, and dipped his tongue to my foot. I pushed him aside and went back to the Dumpster. Beneath mangled Styrofoam, I found a half a fish sandwich. I took it to the tree, slid down, and worked my fingernail into the gash in my foot. It hurt, but the sharp, rough edge of the nail tore the gash into a substantial hole. Sunshine watched. I stuck a small piece of the meat into the hole.

"Sunshine," I said. I pushed his nose to the hole. He sniffed, licked, and then gave my foot a bite. It was gentle at first. I gathered handsful of grass to each side of me. "Sunshine," I said.

Sunshine licked, then bit again, this time harder. A pain that was not the pain of infection drove up through my ankle into the calf of my leg. I sucked air through my teeth. The grass in my fingers ripped from the ground. "Sunshine," I whispered. The dog began to chew, working for the fish in my foot. Blood and clear liquid oozed out between Sunshine's working jaws. Bright stars prickled the edges of my vision.

Not here, I thought.

My foot jerked away from Sunshine. He whined softly, then reached for the running wound again.

"Not here," I said. I put the rest of the fish sandwich down the front of my tee-shirt and tucked the shirt into the waist of my shorts. Then I pushed up from the ground, holding low, thin branches of the tree for balance. My weight was on my good foot, and I was afraid to shift.

A young couple, arm-in-arm, walked by me. The girl wrinkled her nose and nudged her boyfriend. He frowned in my direction and said, "This place wants tourists, they should keep the trash out of public view."

I wobbled; my bad foot caught the brunt of my weight.

A groan scrabbled up my throat and whistled through my lips.

It took me a very long time to walk back to the boardwalk.

The railings of the steps to the beach were hot and welcomed. They eased the burden on the bad foot and allowed me to slide down to the sand. Sunshine keep by my side. His tail didn't wag. He was all business. That was as it should be. I crawled beneath the lip of the boardwalk, then under the steps where the sand was wet and dark and white ghost crabs scuttled about as if it were night.

I eased down onto my butt. My lips were dry and my throat full of the sand of my soul. I wedged my good foot against the back of the bottom step to hold me in place when the real pain came. I pet Sunshine on his gaunt, fur-covered dog skull, and then pulled the fish sandwich from my shirt.

Dogs, I'd heard once, had germ-killing saliva. That was why they could lick their own wounds and not get ill. That, I supposed, was why the dogs who licked Lazarus' sores didn't die. That was why I knew I could feed Sunshine and make him healthy, and then the Man I Love would take the dog home with him.

Through the slats of the steps, the vacationers cannot see me, but I can see them. I can see the hairy legs of the men and the shapely legs of the women as they descend to their temporary paradise by the ocean.

Happy people, oblivious to the crabs and the ugly dog and the stinking woman beneath the steps.

I poke more of the fish sandwich into the gash in my foot. Sunshine nuzzles, licks, then chews. My eyes squeeze shut against the razor-screams of my foot. I feel the hot blood rush out onto the cool sand and the rhythmic stroke and pull of the dog's teeth.

Sunshine might not eat all of me. He will lose interest after a bit and will go off after a Frisbee or a toddler, looking for a playmate. I saw a black and white documentary once, a long time ago. A Nazi dog chased down a Jew and mauled him, but even a trained Nazi dog did not eat a whole Jew. The Nazis had to give the man to the wild pigs to finish.

But what I give Sunshine will be plenty, more than I could ever salvage at one time in a dumpster without being chased away. And what I give him will be my end. My bleeding is profuse. Even a towel-rag could not stop it.

My teeth clench and I search out through the step slats for the moon. I can't find it, but I know it is there. The chalk rock in the blue sky, the meaning of its existence a mystery.

I loosen one hand long enough to cram in more fish. My foot screams the agony of the crucified, offered for a higher purpose.

Sunshine will blossom and be fat and full and healthy and go home with The Man I Love. I will be part of it. I will be pet even as the dog is pet and loved even as the dog is loved. I will lick the man's chest and pink moon-nipples even as Sunshine does.

I howl into my shoulder and grab the steps.

Sweat pours from my flesh, thick and sour. My breath on the air is that of a corpse in the grave.

But the smell of my blood is sweet.

Sanctuary of the Shrinking Soul

The panic first hit Rachael on the anniversary of Katie's death. Rachael stood in the middle of town, her finger on the crosswalk button, her face scrunched beneath the large hood of her brown wool coat. The air outdoors was frigid. Rachael's brown hair was tucked behind her ears beneath the hood, but a single strand was loose, and it beat against her mouth like a frozen insect. She jabbed the button. Cars hissed by on the street. Rachael was not thinking of her daughter Katie. She was, instead, hoping that for once she would get to work on time.

And then it came; an electric charge, a sudden and painful stopping of the heart and a surge of lightning charges to her arms and brain. She was knocked back two steps from the curb. She collided with an old man and small boy and, mumbling terrified apologies, turned and pushed through the door of Jefferson National Bank, then stood in the corner with her arms wrapped tightly about herself.

Customers at the various tables and teller stations turned and gawked, but at that moment she could not care. She just stared back with wide eyes, pulling deeper into the corner, her arms squeezing harder, the back of her hood digging cobwebs out of the corner.

'Smaller,' she thought, not knowing why the thought was there or what it meant. She closed her eyes and the bankers were gone but in their place, on the shades of Rachael's eyelids, were dark figures standing as if in a fog. She could not see their eyes, but could feel them smiling horrid smiles. Rachael felt the panic pull her blood and spin her nerves into an inwardly spiraling current.

'Smaller,' she thought. The figures in the fog opened their dark mouths as if to echo the word.

And then the panic abated. Not suddenly as it had come, but slowly, hesitantly. It eased on her heart and the ends of her nerves, then vanished, leaving Rachael sweating in the corner. The figures melted and were gone. Rachael held her breath, afraid to move should it return. But it did not, and there was nothing irregular at that moment but a spasm in her foot where she had twisted her ankle.

Rachael blinked at the bankers. No words were spoken.

She looked away, then slipped out the door and out into the winter morning.

There was a single red rose in a cheap crystal bud vase on Rachael's desk in the shipping office at C.J.'s Building Supplies. Rachael dropped her purse onto the desk, frowning at the flower, then hung her coat on one of the secretaries' hooks. She sat and took the day's stack of bills and receipts from her tray. Annie O'Gorek, who shared the office with Rachael and one other secretary, and who, since Rachael's employment eight months ago, had been the only one at C.J.'s to be civil to Rachael, entered the office and put her coat up beside Rachael's.

"Hey, lady," Annie said. "I see for once you've beat me to work. Nothing like a little winter tail wind to pick up the old speed, huh? Been here long?"

"About a minute," said Rachael. "This close to Christmas I don't need paper pile-ups. I don't need to give everyone else in this place new reasons to discuss me over their coffee mugs."

Annie sat at her desk next to Rachael's. "Cut it out. You have no more paper work than Judy or I do. Quit thinking about those other assholes. You're a good worker. You've proved that many times."

"And what does it get me? Dirty looks and wisecracks."

If it was going to ease up, wouldn't it have by now?

Annie sighed. Rachael knew what she was going to say, but she did not stop her. It was nice to hear. "Screw them, Rachael. So your Dad owns the place? So he gave you a job. I'm glad he did. You're a good confidante. I can complain to you and it doesn't get any further. You bring candy to work." Annie grinned. She was a graying blonde with glasses, thirty-seven, older than Rachael by four years. Rachael thought that at this point in her life, Annie was the only person she loved.

Rachael let her lips relax in a half-smile, then picked up her ballpoint pen. "So where's Judy?"

"Out sick, I heard at the front. So it's just you and me today, Poncho."

Rachael then looked again at the bud vase, and at the red rose stuck in it. She waved a hand at it. "This thing has got to be for Judy. She's got more boyfriends than a dog's got fleas. Why the hell is it on my desk?"

"Is there a card?"

Rachael leaned over and saw a small envelope beneath the vase. "Yes."

"Why don't you read it?"

"Judy'd pitch a fit if I read one of her lust notes."

Annie said, "Read it."

Rachael grunted, then lifted the vase and removed the envelope. In black ink was printed, "Rachael Brandon."

A buzz began at the base of Rachael's throat.

"I had it sent," said Annie.

Rachael coughed around the buzz. A heat blossomed in her heart and her jaws tightened.

"It's been a year since, well, it's been a year. I thought a rose might help cheer you up a little. You don't talk about it much. You don't talk about it at all. But I thought maybe this would be . . . nice."

In a second, the buzz became a swarm of bees, clotting Rachael's air passage and causing her to convulse.

"Rachael?"

The heat in her heart exploded and spun outward to her arms.

Annie flinched. "Rachael, are you all right?"

Rachael's fingers reached out for the vase and clamped about it. Her eyes filmed over. She could not see Annie anymore. But in the haze were figures, figures of young men, grinning. She could feel cold grass about her, and she smelled the strong tang of alcohol.

"Rachael!"

"Smaller," Rachael gasped, and with the word, she pulled the vase into herself. The rose stem broke and the flower fell at an angle. Rachael shut her eyes, struggling against the force which tried to consume her. "Smaller now." And she closed in around the vase. Her forehead fell to the desk top, her feet drew up beneath the seat of her chair. Both hands took the vase and squeezed. From deep in her darkness, the foggy figures laughed at her.

"Shit, Rachael, what is wrong with you?" Annie's voice was terrified and distant.

The heat was pain. Rachael's chin ground into her sternum; the glass vase dug through the loose weave of her sweater, bruising her flesh. She fought the will of her muscles. Yet her muscles were stronger than her will.

And then the vase shattered. Glass fragments shot out between her fingers and bit into the skin of her palms. The bottom of the vase fell to Rachael's lap and then to the floor. Blood ran down the sweater sleeves. The heat in her body subsided with the flow of the blood. Rachael slowly lifted her face. Annie was on her feet, staring with a stricken expression.

"What the Christ?" she cried. "We've got to get you to a doctor!"

Rachael held her hands over her desk and dropped the remaining bloody glass chunks. She looked at the cuts on her hands.

"Rachael, did you hear me?"

"No," said Rachael, and she felt dazed and foolish. She swallowed hard. "Please, Annie, I can fix this up. I don't need a doctor. I don't know what happened. I haven't had much sleep." She looked at her friend. "Please. I don't know. But I can fix it. I'm sorry."

Annie shut the office door. She fished for a small first aid kit in her desk drawer. "This isn't much, but it should do, as long as you don't need stitches. Do you need stitches, Rachael?"

Rachael shook her head and gingerly took the kit.

Annie said, "Let me help, it's the least I can do. I feel like it's my fault. I shouldn't have mentioned today."

But Rachael shook her head, and clumsily bandaged the wounds herself. She couldn't understand what had happened to her. She felt bad, having given her friend such a scare. But soon a peaceful, familiar dullness fell over her mind, and in less than fifteen minutes, she was dating bills to go out in the lunch time mail.

It was dark when Rachael got home. The beagle was on the front porch, whining to go inside. Rachael worked the key into the lock, taking care of her hands, although the wounds had been less deep than they could have been, and by tomorrow, Band-Aids would be all she needed. The door opened and she and Sallie went inside.

The house was large, a two-story Colonial with all the extras, the house she and her ex-husband Martin had built together. They had been married for seven years; now they had been separated for seven months. Martin gave her the home, and he took his vast income and the car to a neighboring city.

The foyer light flicked on and Rachael dropped her purse to the floor. She patted Sallie on the head. The dog whacked her tail back and forth across the Persian runner.

"I suppose it's dinner time," Rachael said, although her lunch was still heavy on her stomach and she did not feel like eating. She and Sallie retreated to the kitchen in the back of the house, and Rachael pieced together a meal of cold vegetables, sandwiches, and limeade. T.V. trays were set up in the rec room, and Sallie, full of scraps from Rachael's preparations, lay down on top of Rachael's right foot and thumped her tail into dreamland.

Rachael punched the remote control and local news came on the set. Then she picked up her sandwich. At first she thought it was the cuts in her hands beginning to pull, and she worried that she might have needed stitches after all. Her fingers tingled and cramped, and then curved into trembling claws.

"Oh, my God," she began, and Sallie opened her eyes and watched.

Heat exploded in her arms and body again, and she was afraid. Her fingers flinched and jerked, fighting to crush the bread. Rachael fought back. The cuts strained, stretched, and popped open beneath her bandage. Blood oozed afresh through the white gauze wrappings.

"Sallie!" she cried. She thought her fingers would break themselves on their own accord if she did not give in to them.

And so, with a wail, she did. She let her fingers fold, let the silly sandwich be crushed into dough. With a groan, her arms drew inward then, and her neck bowed down, and as she folded tightly, the relief came.

'Smaller,' came the word to her brain. And the word felt right. The word felt safe. She drew her knees up, knocking the tray to its side and spilling the vegetable sticks. She stayed folded, her muscles no longer aching but reveling in the tight confines they had imposed.

And then the heat passed. Rachael slowly unfolded.

She looked at the destroyed sandwich and at the food on the floor. She left the room and went to the den, because it was smaller, and it felt better.

She dozed, and dreamed of nothing as she had for many months, then awoke to the burring of the phone. She answered on the third buzz, then reached down to bury her fingers in the short, soft hair of Sallie's face. Sallie sighed a heavy dog-sigh.

"Rachael, it's Martin. Just wanted to call and see how you're doing."

Rachael had to clear her throat to find her voice. "I'm fine, Martin."

"How's Sallie?"

"Just great."

"Job okay?"

"Sure. Of course. Working for my father is a breeze. Especially when the other co-workers believe he gave me the job because I was a poor little abandoned wife who needed something to do with her time."

Martin didn't say anything for a minute. Then he said, "You know that's not why he gave you the job."

"Then he gave it to me for therapy after the accident. I don't need therapy. I've handled it well if you ask me."

"Rachael . . ."

Rachael felt sweat building on her neck. She wanted to hang up and go to bed. "Why the hell did you call?"

"I told you. To see how you're doing. I thought that today, especially, you might be feeling particularly sad."

"And why is that?"

Martin made a loud sound of astonishment. "Rachael, don't pretend you don't remember."

"Katie," said Rachael. "Of course I remember. You were visiting your parents. Katie and I were in the car, going to a P.T.A. meeting. There was ice and we slid. We hit that tree on Katie's side. I survived. Katie didn't."

"How can you be so detached? She was our daughter!"

23

"I loved her. She's gone. That's the way it is sometimes." Her hands began to pull. She put the free hand to her face and felt the rough material of gauze. She squeezed the receiver, thinking for some reason that it was too large. It would be better if it weren't so large. Everything around this damn house was too large.

"Rachael, I wish we could talk. You don't ever mention her name. It's not right. It isn't healthy."

'Much too goddam LARGE!'

And then the panic came full force, clubbing her in the gut. A flash of horrendous heat, a smell of fire, knocking her breath away. She doubled over, folding in on herself, trying to ease the fear by becoming . . .

"Smaller," she said harshly.

"Rachael?"

"Smaller!" She felt the word pushing her in and she went with it this time. She allowed herself to pull inward, moving toward that tiny core of her center. 'Compacted', she thought. 'Compressed. Diminished.' There were grinning, evil men, leering at her. Laughing at her, their faces painted with the reflection of a roaring fire. Laughing in the fog of some distant night. She pulled down further.

"Smaller!" Rachael screamed. "Smaller, smaller!"

"Lord!" roared Martin. "What the hell is wrong?"

Rachael's body contorted and folded even more. Away from the fire, away from the dark figures.

And then something happened to Martin's voice. Rachael did not know at that moment that she had pulled the cord from the phone, because she was in the comfort of her smallness.

And it was not until she came from her trance that she·found Sallie with her paws tangled in the cord and her lifeless tongue hanging out. One set of Rachael's cramped fingers were buried deep in the dog's eye sockets. Blood was crusted on the back of Rachael's hand and dried on the dog's muzzle.

Rachael wept, then hid the dead dog in the cellar and went to sleep in her closet.

She took a cab to work the next morning, because the thought of walking as she usually did frightened her. Things outside were too big, too open. She hurried inside C.J.'s Building Supplies and did not even stop to get a pack of candy from the machine for Annie. Annie and Judy were already in the secretaries' office.

Dropping her purse on her chair seat, Rachael tried to lift the edge of the desk. It was very heavy, and barely moved.

"Help me?" she asked Annie.

"What do you want to do?" Annie put her pen down.

"I want to move the desk. I don't think I can work in here anymore."

"And why the hell not?" Annie tried to joke. "Do I smell bad or something?"

But Rachael could think of nothing but moving to a smaller space. She had considered it all the way to work in the cab. There was a tiny storage room just down the hall. Only folders and file cabinets and boxes. The manager could just move all that shit to where her desk was now. What could it matter?

"What can it matter?" she said aloud.

"I think we have to talk," said Annie. "Something isn't right."

"I can work in there," said Rachael, picking up the stack of bills that had been waiting for her on her desk. "What can it matter?" Then she looked and saw that the bills were crushed in her hands, balled up into a tight wad. They looked better like that, all crushed up and small. She threw the wad onto the floor.

Annie came around and took Rachael's arms. "I think you might need a day off. You've not taken a day off since you began work. Maybe you need some time. What do you think?"

Rachael's fingers clamped around Annie's forearms. She saw her friend's eyes pop as the fingernails bit into skin. But Rachael could not stop. She needed at that moment to bring Annie in with her, into the safety of the smallness. To have Annie with her, so she would not be alone. And then Annie jerked away and slapped Rachael in the face.

"Damn it, Rachael!" Annie was not only frightened now, she was furious.

"Take a fucking month off, why don't you?" said Judy.

"Annie?" Rachael said softly, feeling close to tears. "I don't . . ."

"No, you don't, do you?" said Judy. "Just get the fuck out of here."

"In a way, Judy's right," said Annie. "Please take some time off." Her voice was frosted with fury.

And Rachael did. She went home and locked her door and stayed in her closet until night, when the phone rang.

Rachael thought it might be Annie on the phone. It took twelve rings to get out of the closet and to the telephone beside the bed. As she reached for the receiver, she felt a rush of agoraphobia. Why had they ever built a bedroom so large, and a house so huge?

But it was the paperboy's mother on the phone; she was ticked. Rachael hadn't had any money when the boy had come to collect the past few weeks. The mother said her son would be over in twenty minutes. Rachael hung up and changed the wrinkled work clothes she had worn all day in the closet. She put on the tightest clothes she could find because they felt safer, then went cautiously downstairs.

When the doorbell rang twenty minutes later, she opened the door to find the paperboy on her stoop. His bike was parked against one of the trees in her front yard, and he had the pad of receipt tickets in his hands. He obviously wasn't happy, but he pulled on a forced, business-like smile.

The last thing Rachael thought of before she fell inward again was that the paperboy was too tall. A paperboy was supposed to be a little boy. A paperboy should be smaller.

She slept in her closet, pressed into the far corner beside the shelf of shoes. She came out to eat and to work on the house, but most of the time she could not face the hugeness of the rooms and the vastness of the ceilings above her. When she slept her sleep was dreamless as it had been since Katie's death, but when the panic came, she saw with increasing clarity the men in the fog, and smelled the alcohol on their breath and heard with more volume their obscene laughter. Then she would pull herself inward even more tightly and hide.

Sometimes the phone would ring and she would ignore it.

Several times she answered. Once it was Annie apologizing for her harshness, and wondering how much more time Rachael would take off. Once it was a saleswoman, wanting Rachael to come to MagnaView Mountain Resort to claim her free set of stainless steel flatware and bonus salad tongs. To Annie, Rachael was polite but evasive. She wanted to see her friend again, but she was afraid to make her angry. Of the MagnaView Mountain Resort saleswoman, Rachael asked the size of the resort. When told it was the largest one in the state, Rachael hung up.

And then on the third night, Martin called. He said he wanted to see her again.

"I know you have reservations about working at your father's establishment," he said. "We both know he gave you the job to help ease you through the rough times. But that doesn't degrade what you are doing. I admire your stoicism. But if it isn't what you'd hoped for, call him and tell him thanks but no thanks. Rachael, I would be happy to help you out financially until you find something more suitable."

"Why?" The phone was cradled under Rachael's chin as she talked. In her hands was one of her favorite books, which she methodically tore into small bits, crushed, and let fall to the floor. By her feet were other books, more work she had done.

"You may have demanded that I leave, but I still care for you."

"That's a joke," said Rachael. Then suddenly, she sat bolt upright. "That's . . . a . . . joke . . ." she said, feeling the oddly familiar words on her tongue, and feeling nauseous.

"It's not."

"No," said Rachael, but not to Martin. "The men said that. They said, 'That's a joke.' I don't know why, but they did." Sweat broke out in beads on her lip.

"Rachael, what do you . . ." But Rachael hung the phone up and Martin was gone. She crawled under the bed, which was the closest small place, trying to escape the memory of the young men in the fog. The panic swirled around her head as the dustballs swirled about her body. The men in the fog had said "That's a joke." They had said, "Smaller, compacted, condensed, crushed." And they had laughed. Their laughter made her sick. Who the hell were they? And from when did she remember them? Tears mingled with the sweat of her face as she tried to burrow into the hardwood floor. Splinters chewed her skin. And then she fell into blessed sleep, free of thought and substance.

It sounded like angels singing. Chimes drifted into the nothingness of Rachael's sleep, and caused her eyes to open and sensations to return. She listened from beneath the bed. Chimes. Singing. No. It was a bell.

She touched a smarting, splintered spot on her chin. The bell rang again. It was the front door. Rachael wriggled out and had to still her heart before she could go downstairs to answer the door. She had not been outside in a week. She had not been downstairs in two full days.

Slowly she went down, stepping over the work she had left scattered in the hall and on the staircase. Her hand trailed along the wall, leaving a smudged streak of grime. She had not bathed this week. The dirt felt close and safe.

She stopped at the front door and peered through the narrow window to the side. It was Martin. He was holding a bunch of pink flowers. Rachael opened the door.

At first Martin was smiling, but when he saw Rachael the smile vanished. "My God, Rachael, what's happened to you?"

Rachael said, "Come in."

Martin hesitantly stepped into the house. His eyes fell to the work Rachael had left all over the floor. "Did someone break in? Did someone rob you? Have you called the police?" But when he looked up, Rachael had wandered into the living room and was standing near the piano. He hurried to her, flowers dropping to the floor. "Rachael, come out of the house with me. You look bad. Were you hurt? Please come . . ."

Rachael lifted a brass candlestick from the piano top, and with a smile she smashed it into Martin's brain. After he fell, she continued to smash his head, making him smaller.

Rachael did not come out of the closet anymore, but drank bottled water she had brought from her pantry and voided in the corner in a Kenny's boot box. Not eating was good because it made her smaller. The panic came more frequently now, but she welcomed it because it took her out of the stench of the closet and into a deeper and more certain smallness. The laughter of the men in the fog, and their obscene words were louder and clearer with each panic; the smell of their alcoholic breath stronger and the open, fire-silhouetted amusement on their faces was sharper, but she let herself flow down and away from them into the comforting tininess. She kept tools with her, for when awake and alert, she proceeded to work on whatever was on the floor and shelves in the closet with her.

There was no sense of time, only of space. So when the closet door opened, Rachael did not focus at first on the face that peered in in horror. It was not her father. It was not Martin. It was not a man from the fog. It was a woman.

"Rachael," said the woman.

It was Annie.

"Annie!" Rachael tried to reach upward, but her arms hurt and she could do no more than spasm. But Annie was here. And that was a wonderful thing.

Annie made long, sickened sounds, turning to vomit on the bedroom floor outside the closet. Then, wiping her mouth, she took one step into the closet and knelt down. She said, "Rachael, there's a dead boy in your kitchen."

Rachael thought, then said, "The paperboy."

"He's been beaten to a pulp."

"I made him smaller. He was too big, Annie."

"All your dishes are smashed. Your furniture, too.

"Books. Glass. It looks as though everything has been destroyed."

"Crushed," said Rachael, and in the back of her brain one of the men in the fog laughed and said, "Crammed, squashed, diminished, smaller." "Yes," said Rachael. "It's all smaller now."

Annie heaved, and jammed her hand into her mouth. Then she said, "I saw Martin downstairs. He's dead, too."

"Smaller," said Rachael.

"Tell me," said Annie.

"There are men," said Rachael. "They laugh at me. They're drunk. I don't know who they are. I have to get away from them. I have to be smaller to get away."

"Who are they?"

"I don't know. I don't want to know," said Rachael.

"Tell me."

Rachael blinked, and on the backs of her eyelids were the men. They were dressed nicely. One had a bottle of something, and he waved it at the others with him. There was a reflection of fire on their faces. Fire from an overturned automobile, a vehicle crashed into the trunk of a very large tree.

"Tell me," said Annie.

"I don't want to know! Leave me alone!" cried Rachael, and her eyes closed and she saw the men. From somewhere outside the scene, she felt Annie take her hand.

Rachael was in the car. It was night time, and the car had hit a tree. They were in the country, and there was no one to help. There was smoke from the engine, and all she could think of was getting out. She popped free of her seat belt, and stumbled out into the high weeds at roadside. Her head reeled. She crawled away behind the car toward the road, trying to cry for help. And then she realized that Katie was still in the car. She could hear her daughter's strangled cries from the crushed side of the automobile.

"Annie!" cried Rachael, but she could not open her eyes to the closet. Annie did not let go of her hand.

Then a car pulled off the side of the road. A car full of young men. They staggered out as if drunk. They did not see Rachael in the weeds, but they went over to the car. She knew they would save Katie, thank God.

The men stared in through the rear window. One took a long drink from his bottle and quoted some garbled piece of bizarre poetry. These men were from the university, Rachael understood then. Young men, men of letters, men of literature. Drunk, yes, but educated. Concerned. She whispered "thank you" as together they wrangled the car from the tree and set it down. Rachael could see the top of Katie's head and could hear her groans more clearly. Fire wisped from beneath the hood. The men's faces were set aglow with the light.

And then one of them said, "Look, my friends. If I had a thesaurus, I could come up with many adjectives."

A chubby man leaned in through the broken glass of the passenger's window. 'Be careful,' Rachael thought. 'Move her out slowly.' But the man laughed and said, "I'll say 'compacted.' "

A second tipped his head and said, "Compressed."

"She seems 'diminished'," said the one with the bottle.

"I'd say 'crushed'," said the chubby man.

"Not a synonym," said the one with the bottle. He moved to the window and studied Katie.

" 'Squashed,' then," the chubby man said.

"Car's gonna blow," said another man, his words slurred and slow.

" 'Squashed' is not a synonym, either. You are all hopeless," said the bottle-man. "I would give you 'smaller.' "

36

The others nodded, laughing. "Smaller," they chorused.

"Car's gonna blow," repeated the man.

And then the bottle-man reached into the window, and Rachael thought, 'Finally, oh thank God, these insane men will save my daughter.'

The bottle-man lifted the bottle and brought it down on top of Katie's head. Glass shattered. The child slumped out of view.

"A new word, brothers," he said. "Synonyms for 'dead.'"

"Well done!" shouted one. "Now that's a joke!"

The young men choked on laughter and stumbled back from the car. With a whoosh the whole automobile was engulfed with the blaze.

"Katie!" screamed Rachael.

"Rachael!" cried Annie from beyond the fire and the weeds and the drunken men in the fog of night.

"Katie!" And Rachael's eyes flew open. "Smaller! Compacted! Crushed! Dead!" And Rachael grabbed a hammer from behind her and slashed it at Annie's face. Annie whipped backward and the hammer grazed her ear. "They made her smaller!" The hammer swung again, wildly, catching Annie on her shoulder. "I want to be with Katie! I want to be smaller!"

Annie grabbed for the hammer but it crunched into her cheek and she screamed. Rachael cried and brought it up and back for another blow. "Come with me, Annie!" But Annie fell forward then, and knocked Rachael against the closet wall. The hammer was tossed free. Beneath Annie's weight, Rachael's ribs broke.

Rachael lay panting. Annie stared, stunned, between her friend and her own blood on her hands and chest. Rachael reached up and tugged weakly at a plastic laundry bag that hung around a silk dress.

"What?" asked Annie hoarsely.

Rachael looked her in the eye, and tugged on the laundry bag. "Smaller," she whimpered.

"No, Rachael," said Annie.

"If not this, what of me then?"

Annie said, "Please, no."

"What of me, then?" said Rachael softly.

Annie stood and took the bag from the hanger. She paused for a moment, but the slow nod from Rachael made her continue. She wrapped the plastic about Rachael's head and face. Rachael bowed down then, pulling the plastic tighter and tighter, making a clear and ungodly cocoon, becoming smaller and smaller and smaller. Annie kissed the top of Rachael's plastic enshrouded hair, and watched as her friend made the final descent into smallness.

Snow Day

The rusted swings in the backyard jangled in the frozen wind, lashing out against the swirls of white, tangling with each other and then loosening and drooping for a moment before picking up the fight again. There was an empty doghouse next to the swing set, but the dog who had lived there had died a few weeks ago, and the chain lay like a steel snake across the snowy ground.

Marnie sat on her bed, one hand against the window sill, one hand on the transparent plastic Mama had taped across the trailer windows to keep the cold out. It was still cold inside, though. The winter air found flaws in the walls and flooring, and Marnie and her mother could often see steamy tendrils of their breath as they ate their supper or sat watching *Wheel* in the living room.

"Marnie, you think you gonna stay in bed all day you got another thing coming." It was Mama. She was in the kitchen, slamming things around. Her ride to work couldn't get through the half-foot of snow on the road, and so she was stuck at home. Likewise, school buses could not travel the routes and risk the safety of the children, and so Marnie was stuck at home, too.

"You hear me?" Mama shouted.

"Yes'um," said Marnie. She leaned down and found the socks she'd kicked off the night before and slipped them onto her feet. The socks were stiff and cold, but Marnie tucked her feet up under her and they began to warm up.

An old newspaper blew by the trailer in the white wind, rolling end over end like the dismembered wing of a dead bird. Marnie watched until it rolled out of view. The wind shifted direction, and the window was suddenly pelted with thick clumps of flakes.

Yesterday, the kids in Marnie's second grade class had been excited. The weather had called for a winter storm warning. There was anticipation in the school; even the teachers had whispered to each other with happy winks.

Marnie had thought, *Please don't snow.*

She had stayed awake until long after Mama had gone to sleep on the sofa. She had looked up at the sky from her bed, and looked for stars. But the sky had been heavy and gray, like the smoke over Mr. Grandy's trailer when it burned up last year. And at two in the morning, it began to snow.

"Get your rump in here, Marnie," called Mama. "You got chores to do and I ain't calling you again."

Marnie slipped from bed, pulled on her jeans and a thin sweatshirt, then padded down the short hall past the bathroom and Mama's bedroom to the kitchen. Mama was sitting at the kitchen bar, her elbows on the counter, her fingers caught up in uncombed hair. Her head turned toward Marnie. One side of her lip went up.

"You know we ain't gonna get you them new shoes now, with me being off work today. You know they fire me and we'll have to live in a tent or cardboard box like them homeless people on T.V."

Marnie looked at the floor and said nothing.

"You know that, don't 'cha?"

Marnie nodded, and wondered if there was something else she should say.

Mama said, "Look at me when I talk to you, little girl."

Marnie looked up at her mother. The woman made a tsking sound, shook her head, then looked away. "Seen my cigarettes?"

"No, ma'am."

"You been smoking my cigarettes? You smoke 'em and I'll have the skin off your hide, you hear me?"

Marnie nodded.

Mama dropped from the stool, went into the living room area and patted the top of the end table. She got on her knees and looked behind the sofa, swearing.

"I think that's them by the T.V.," Marnie said softly.

Mama stopped and looked at the T.V. "Who put 'em there?" she demanded. "You put 'em there?"

"No."

"Johnny put 'em there?"

Marnie shrugged.

"Don't you shrug at me. I can't hear a shrug."

"I don't know if Johnny put 'em there."

Mama came back to the kitchen bar, got on a stool and lit a cigarette. She drew in on the cigarette, closed her eyes, and swayed her head slightly, as if there was music inside the darkness that only she could hear.

Marnie opened the refrigerator door and looked for milk.

There was none. She shut the door and got the box of Honey Comb from the cabinet and took it to the sofa. Sitting, she opened the box, took out a handful of the dry cereal, and put it into her mouth.

Mama turned back around and looked at her daughter.

Mama wasn't old. She was twenty five on her last birthday. Most of the time she had light brown hair like Marnie, but right now it was dyed jet black like a snowless night sky. The makeup she'd put on last night for Johnny was still there this morning, only it seemed to have walked across her face some-time between then and now, leaving traces of lipstick on her cheek and mascara on her temple.

"You don't get no crumbs in that sofa, Mar-nie." The cigarette jabbed the air, punctuat-ing each word. "I get so sick of cleaning up after you I just wanna puke."

Marnie closed her legs together tightly to catch any cereal bits that might not make it to her mouth.

Mama went back into her bedroom. Mar-nie punched the remote control, and the T.V.

sputtered into life. She flipped over to cartoons. An animated mouse mother was tucking her animated mouse baby into bed and singing a song. Marnie felt her stomach cramp as the mouse mother gave her baby a big hug. She wondered if the baby mouse was afraid of the mother's hug. Marnie changed the channel to *Good Morning America*.

Half an hour into the show, Mama came back into the kitchen, a flat glass bottle in her hand. She wore her tight black jeans, a low-necked pink sweater, and her brown heeled boots. She lit another cigarette, and then scratched her remade face. "You gonna have to make this school day up, don't think you won't," she said. "You get out a couple days and it's gonna go into summer and then we ain't going to the beach with Johnny. You hear me?"

"Yes, ma'am."

Mama paced back and forth from the living room to the kitchen. She kept going in front of the T.V., cutting off Marnie's view, but the girl said nothing.

"Ought to cut teachers' pay when they don't work. Cut it right down like mine getting cut down since I can't get to the store." Mama stopped pacing, pulled back the stained shade on the front door window to look at the snow, then flung it back into place. She snorted, sucked on her cigarette, then took a drink from the bottle.

"You like them teachers, Marnie?"

Marnie swallowed a mouthful of cereal. She wished there was milk to wash it down. She said, "They're okay."

Mama sat down by Marnie on the sofa, and Marnie edged herself away, hoping Mama wouldn't notice. Mama turned full-face to Marnie, and her breath was that of ashtrays and alcohol and boredom.

"Why you like those teachers?" Mama asked. "They say bad things 'bout us, you know that. They lie about us. I pay their salary, you know."

Marnie put the box of cereal on the end table and drew up her feet. Mama moved closer, and her lipsticked mouth twitched in a small smile that made Marnie's heart kick painfully.

She thought, *I want to go to school*.

Mama put her arm across the back of the sofa behind Marnie's head. Marnie leaned forward, pretending she was reaching for the remote control.

"I don't mean to yell at you, baby," said Mama. "You know I love you and I just don't like nobody saying nothing bad about us. Nobody can tell us what to do. They ain't got no right to do that."

I want to go to school I want to go to school I want to go to school.

Marnie picked up the remote control. She hoped her mother didn't see how much it was shaking. "I can shovel the sidewalk," Marnie managed. "Then maybe you can go visit Julia up the road. I'll do my homework while you're gone. I'll do the dishes, too."

Mama didn't hear this. She said, "Johnny and me, we love you. We show you we love you, too, in our special way. You know we love you, don't you, Marnie?"

It felt as though a piece of cereal came back up into Marnie's windpipe, and she could hardly breathe. She looked at the door, and wondered what would happen if she tried to run out. She looked at the T.V., and wondered what it would be like to be in one of those show families where nobody ever wanted to run out.

No not now please not now stop snowing stop snowing.

"It's our special, secret way," said Mama. She leaned in very close now, putting her hand on top of Marnie's hair and then moving her hand down. Mama placed a little kiss on Marnie's cheek, then her neck. "You know that. You know to never, never tell secrets, don't you, Marnie?"

47

Elizabeth Massie

Marnie closed her eyes and squeezed them tightly enough to see swirls on the inner lids. Swirls like that of colorful, dancing snow that was never cold and never kept kids out of school.

But there was no music behind the closed eyes.

And the snow outside the trailer kept up for another ten inches, and school was closed for the week.

Dibs

It was the little bloodied mole, cut up underneath the riding mower, that made Molly Branetree remember. She sat on the seat of the rumbling Wheel Horse and stared at the lump of raw rodent for a moment, sickened on the one hand, and intrigued on the other. Sweat slid down the inside of her shirt and she rubbed at it through the cotton.

"Kiwanisani," she said, and then she laughed out loud, a baffled yet humored sound. She turned the engine off and removed her dark glasses. The mole's red viscera glinted in the July sun. Red like body paint in a bright July moon.

"Old Princess Kiwanisani, I can't believe I remembered," Molly said. "And the date is right, too, isn't it? How do you like that? Not so far gone in my old age, after all."

She hopped from the mower and covered the mole with handfuls of cut grass, then stood and looked over at the house. Her husband Randy was at a community softball game with Christopher; her daughter Lorna was earning credits for a Cadette badge at her troop's Girl Scout yard and bake sale. It was Saturday, and she had nothing planned except to mow the yard. What could it matter if she held off until Sunday afternoon?

"Yeah, and what good would it do if I went?" she muttered. The camp was at least an hour and a half from her home in Hensford, and she had no idea if the place even existed anymore. She felt sure she could find the location; the twisting, graveled routes through the mountains had been such a part of her childhood and adolescent summers. She still had occasional dreams about treks along those cool, narrow roads. But what could upholding the old promise do, other than give her a piece of worthless nostalgia and a lawn full of grass yet unmowed?

Molly parked the mower in the garage and wrote her family a note, which she stuck to the refrigerator with a Pizza Hut magnet. No later than midnight, she promised.

She drove her Sunfire west, feeling an exhilaration of foolishness as she went. She turned on the radio, hoping to hear one of the greats from twenty-five years past. Something by the Supremes, or Emerson, Lake, and Palmer, or even the Carpenters. But it was Pearl Jam on the waves, so Molly shut it off. She contented herself with singing "Close To You" to the tune of the air conditioner.

The camp had been named Camp Kiwanisani. Farty name, she and her friends had all agreed, but who could argue when it was the Sacred Ground on which Princess Kiwanisani of the Chihonqui tribe had laid down her life to save her blessed home and people? Of course, Molly's camp friend, Charlene Meadows, who had written to Molly as a pen pal for a full two years after Molly's last summer at camp, had done some research and discovered there had never been a Princess Kiwanisani, or even a Chihonqui tribe. Such was life, Molly had learned. You believe some things for a while, then you go on to others.

The road dipped and swerved, then twisted up along the first ridge of the mountains. Molly had picked up a case of Bud from the Seven-Eleven, and it thumped smugly on the car seat. The shadows of thick trees strobed the pavement before her. Squirrels raced across the road ahead of the car, but Molly didn't slow down. It wasn't that she wanted to hit them, but if this had been twenty-five years ago, she would have given the animals a run for their money.

When the odometer kicked over fifty-two miles since she'd left home, Molly eased on the accelerator and began to watch the left side of the road more carefully. Having checked an old road map at the Seven-Eleven, she had estimated the campsite to be no more than fifty-five miles from Hensford. She knew she could be wrong. She knew the camp could have fallen prey to the Park Service, or have been bought by a private hunting club, or worse, a land developer. But she had to see, regardless. Even if they were plowing for a future ski resort, Molly would straddle a bulldozer and renew her years' old vow to the spirit of Kiwanisani.

Because of the drunken blur through which she and her camp friends had spent that evening, Molly couldn't remember the exact words of the pledge, but she did know she'd promised her soul to the Princess twenty-five years from the date, all for a night with counselor-in-training Danny Freed and his luscious body. The group had slathered on coatings of red war paint and done some kind of dance and had laughed until they puked.

Molly drove three more miles, her hopes beginning to dwindle as she passed curve after curve and saw nothing which indicated the old camp road.

But then it was there, a dirt drive off the paved road, marked only by an old chain strung from the trunk of one tree to another, and Molly's memory cried out "Yes! That's it!" She grinned and pulled her car over. Wrapping her fingers about the steering wheel, she leaned forward and stared. Even without a sign, she knew that this was it. She hopped out and unhooked the chain's simple S hook.

As she dragged the chain aside, watching the round, smooth links scrape through dead leaves, she thought of something else from camp twenty-five years ago. She thought of glasses.

Thick, horn-rimmed glasses.

Who had worn thick glasses? Then she recalled the little twit, the girl four years Molly's junior, who hung around with the older kids at camp. But why had Molly and her friends tolerated this? She couldn't remember. It had been too long.

The Sunfire took the dirt road. Molly began to identify things. Trees, timelessly standing in place; the stream, now lower but much the same, the wood and concrete bridge still covered with elaborate etchings from the penknives of so many past campers. "Rudy loves Anne." "Martha and Paul, TLA." "Jody hates Rick."

Across the bridge was the clearing. Molly steered the car off the side of the pathway and stopped. She climbed out and gazed about her, smiling and reeling with a glorious sense of wonder and return.

It was beautiful. Even though weeds had obliterated the ball field, and the large wooden dining hall was now a vine-ridden, weather-bowed structure, it was beautiful. It spoke to the wild and free girl still inside of Molly, longing for excitement and adventure. The sounds were still here, the sounds of camp even without the campers. Cicadas, tree frogs, crickets, birds, wind. Molly collected her case of beer and her transistor radio and crossed the weedy clearing.

At the edge of the woods, she found flat concrete slabs on which the large tents had sat, tents which held six cots and six campers each. To the west side of the clearing was Unit One, for boys under twelve. Unit Two to the north held tents for the older boys. Unit Three, to the south, was for girls under twelve, and the older girls were housed here in Unit Four on the east. Girls like fifteen-year-old Molly Branetree and Charlene Meadows and the other nameless and face-less memories who shared swim time and meal time and chore time and sneak-out-on-the-last-night-of-camp-to-drink time.

Molly worked the cooler more securely on her hip. She stepped onto the briar-covered path which led away from Unit Four and into the deep woods. There was a snap beneath her foot, and she glanced down. It was merely a stick, and she picked it up and threw it into the weeds. Someone had stepped on the twit's glasses, she remembered. The kid had gone blind for two days until her parents had sent another pair. Of course, it hadn't been an ac-cident. The girl had been a walking joke the other kids liked to play on each other.

Picking her way down the path, Molly watched for the spot where she and her friends had held their last night beer binge. In only a matter of minutes, she was on it. Funny, she thought as she pulled a beer from the cooler and sat on a moss-covered log, it had seemed so far away from the campsite when they were kids. She popped the tab and took a long swig.

Mid-afternoon became late afternoon. Molly listened to the radio, which picked up nothing but a distant country-western sta-tion. Butterflies and wasps joined her vigil, then flew off to other appointments. Several chipmunks gave her hard looks with small brown eyes before skittering beneath the locust thicket. Shadows shifted shape, and stretched long and deep. Molly grew mellow.

And then there were footsteps on the path, and Molly jumped up, her heart lurching to her throat. A tall, lean woman in white windbreaker and jeans appeared through the trees.

"Jesus!" said the woman, her eyes widening in pleasure. "Molly?"

"Charlene?" Molly nearly dropped her beer. "Is it really you?"

Charlene Meadows grinned and strode forward, taking Molly in a firm embrace. "Good Lord, I can't believe you remembered to come. I can't believe you even found this dump. I thought I'd be here alone."

"Hey, it's not a dump," Molly chided cheerfully, offering Charlene a beer. "It's memories. I had to try to get them back. I had to feel it again, for some reason. I miss this place, don't you? I miss the way I was. Corny, right? But you must, too, or you wouldn't have come."

"Princess Kiwanisani's got dibs on your soul, you promised her," said Charlene. She chuckled. "Twenty-five years ago tonight. That's all I can remember. We were so damned drunk. And it was so damned long ago."

"True," said Molly. "The bummer is that after all my promises, I can barely remember my good time with Danny. Did I have fun?"

Charlene sat on the log. She shrugged. "How do I know? I was drunk, too."

"The wonders of youth."

"Tell me," said Charlene. "Who else was in our band of deviant females? Was there a Phyllis?"

"I don't know. Did she wear glasses?"

Charlene shook her head. "Beats me."

Molly thought a moment. "You know, except for you and the twit, I have no idea who else was here."

"Doesn't matter," said Charlene. "We remembered. Now, when does the spirit of the Indian princess come out to get you?"

"Did I promise we'd do that ghastly dance again?"

"I don't know."

Molly took a drink and burped. "Then let the bitch wait," she said, and they both laughed.

They drank Molly's beer. They talked about the past years, filling each other in on college, careers, marriages, separations, therapists, and children.

They were startled out of their chat by a shuffling through the leaves on the path. A bulky figure appeared, swinging a plastic Kroger bag. "Look at this!" roared the figure. Charlene gasped and held her beer can in front of her for protection.

"It's Bigfoot!" Molly cried, her head already buzzing from the beer. "Charlene, we're dead!"

"Molly!" shouted the figure. "Don't you remember me?" Charlene and Molly stared.

"Rachael Ralston. Come on, now, it's only been twenty-five years. Shit, you remember to come out here on the anniversary of the grand event and yet you don't remember me? I'm the one who stole the beer from the camp director that night. Honey, I'm insulted."

Molly stood, almost stumbling, and gave Rachael's pudgy hand a squeeze. "Of course I remember. You put on a little weight is all."

Rachael looked down at herself. "A little! I own a motel, ladies. I clean it, manage it, and cook for the little restaurant. Best food for miles about. I'll give you two the address. You'll come let me cook for sometime."

"Sure," said Charlene. "But only if you have the recipe for that godawful campfire stew."

"Campfire stew, yeah, I remember that," Rachael grinned. "All the leftovers of the week thrown in with some semi-cooked hamburger. Yum."

Rachael sat on a rock beside the log. She had brought her own beer in her Kroger bag, and the three toasted each other. Darkness found the gathering, and fell upon them with a softness that went unnoticed. Soon, Charlene squinted, and got up to gather twigs and logs for a campfire.

" 'Slick chicks.' That was us," mused Rachael as she watched Charlene moving in and out of the trees, collecting the firewood. "Unit Two might have beat us at the archery shoot, but we killed them on the relay swim."

"What a memory," marveled Molly.

Then Rachael said, "I guess we all made it except for Paula." Oh, shit, Paula, that was the twit, thought Molly.

Her stomach lurched and for a reason she could not pin down, she knew it wasn't the excess beer.

Charlene came back and dropped the stack of wood. She made a lumpy pile with the smaller tinder, then held a Bic's flame to it. "Who you talking about?" she asked.

"Paula," said Rachael. "Danny Freed's little sister. Molly was nice to her so she could make a good impression on Danny. You and I went along with it, us being such good friends and all. But it was hard. She was a freak."

Molly thought of the chain links, the snapping stick, the dead and bloody mole beside her riding mower. "Glasses," she said. "Paula wore glasses."

"That's right," said Rachael. "Thick suckers. She couldn't see her nose without them."

"Christ, yeah," said Charlene. "The little creep. The one in Unit Three who we let hang around with us. The one all the kids hated."

"They were always stealing her glasses," said Rachael. "She was an asshole," added Charlene. She blew on the tinder and it smoldered, then caught fire. She raked some larger sticks on top and sat back. "Paula deserved what she got. Always creeping around and peeping in people's tents. Staring at us in our underwear. Killing mice and birds with utensils she took from the dining hall, saying they were vermin we needed to be rid of. I hated being around her. But Molly here insisted."

"She was here with us that night, wasn't she?" asked Molly. She licked her lips, but they felt dry. "When I made that pledge to Kiwanisani?"

"Yeah," said Rachael. "I don't think she drank any beer. But I do remember you, Molly," she added, almost choking on her brew. "You took off all your clothes and bowed to the moon, telling Kiwanisani she had dibs on your soul if you could have one good night with Danny Freed."

"And we danced," said Molly. "Chihonqui war paint on our bodies, and we danced before I made the pledge."

"God, yes!" shouted Charlene. "War paint!" She sat on the log and scratched her forehead. She kicked the cooler over and several beers rolled out. She clawed one up. "Where the hell did we get war paint?"

Molly shrugged. "Stole it I guess. Like everything else that night."

"But you kept your stinking soul for twenty-five years," said Rachael. "It's time to pay up, sister." She reached over and grabbed a handful of Molly's shirt. Molly giggled and pushed her off.

"I'll do it, just wait a second." She stood, dropped her near-empty beer can onto the ground, and, fumbling with her buttons and zipper, she stripped. She knew the night air was cool, but she was well-warmed on the inside. Kneeling on the ground, she pushed back her hair and got into a barely balanced position on one knee.

"Do it, Molly!" cheered Charlene.

Molly stuck her tongue out, then raised her folded hands to the moon. "You have my soul,

61

you greedy spirit. Thanks for the good time with Danny! I hope it was good. I don't really remember!" Then she fell, shaking with laughter, into the dry leaves beside the camp-fire.

" 'Slick chicks'!" crowed Rachael.

And steps sounded on the path, out in the night shadows. Molly rolled over, leaves in her hair and on her butt, and looked at her friends. She felt her bowels tighten, felt the beer in her system try to turn back in her veins. She wrapped her arms about herself.

"Who is it?" Charlene called out.

The steps grew louder. Molly glanced at Rachael, who was frowning. "You got a gun?" she whispered, and Rachael shook her head.

"Hi, there," said a voice. In the dark, the face was indistinguishable, but the glow on the glasses was not.

"Good Lord," said Rachael. "Speak of the devil. It's little Paula Freed, as I live and breathe."

Paula came closer, her features outlined by the faint light. She was skeletal, her face hollow and aged, too much so for a woman of only thirty-six years. She wore a heavy cable knit sweater even on this summer evening. On her feet were white canvas shoes. She stopped by the fire, and slowly lowered herself to the ground. She stared across the fire at the others. Molly gathered her clothes and scooted to the log.

"So, Paula, I see you have a good memory, too," said Charlene. "But you have to know that we are just here for a little reminiscing. I found out there was no such person as Princess Kiwanisani. Hope this doesn't disappoint you too much."

"No soul to claim," said Rachael. "Just some beer and some talk." She burped, then coughed.

Paula nodded. She crossed her arms slowly and her thin mouth worked in a tiny spasm. Yes, still the weird asshole she was back then, thought Molly. Wonder what she's done these past twenty-five years? But Molly didn't really want to know.

"Hey, Paula, how about a beer?" asked Charlene, winking at Molly.

Paula shook her head.

"You didn't drink back then, either, did you?" asked Rachael.

Paula shook her head.

Molly worked her legs into her jeans. She hated being around Paula. This was fun until she showed up. What the hell did she think, that the group would welcome her? She had no tie, other than being witness to a stupid teenage escapade. Paula had nothing to do with the pledge or the dance.

"Hey, Paula," Rachael said. "How's old Danny boy these days?"

"He's better," said Paula.

"Better than what?"

"Than he was."

"Oh," said Charlene. She looked at Molly, and couldn't contain it any longer. She laughed, a slow, slurred rumble. "Sure you don't want a beer, Paula? We're all about flying now, and you'll be left on the ground."

"No," said Paula. "I'm just waiting."

"For what?"

"For dibs."

"I told you," said Charlene. "There is no Kiwanisani. Molly's foul soul remains her own."

Paula rubbed her knees and said nothing. Behind her glasses, her watery eyes seemed to twitch, flickering from face to face through the campfire's glow.

Suddenly Charlene was waving her beer can in the air. The liquid splashed boldly and hissed in the fire. "Hey, speaking of dibs, I remember something. After you made your promise to Kiwanisani, we all made vows to each other. Promises of secrecy, shit like that. We gave each other things to seal the promise."

Molly slipped on her shirt and fumbled with the buttons. They went in the wrong holes but she didn't try to redo them.

"So what did you give?" asked Rachael.

"I don't remember." Charlene squinted her eyes and looked up at the sky beyond the trees. The stars were faint under a moving cover of clouds. Then she looked down at her hands. "A ring," she said. "That was it! I gave the beaded ring I made in crafts to you, Rachael."

"Of course," said Rachael. "And I traded my handcrafted leather wallet. The one with the horse head and all those tiny cowboy boots on it. God," she said. "Do you still have it?"

"Oh, yeah, right," said Charlene. "It's the talk of my office. They all envy me so."

Rachael snorted, got beer up her nose, and hawked onto the ground. "Goddamn. Who's gonna drive me home?"

"What about you, Molly?" asked Charlene. "Other than promising your soul to our Indian spirit guide, what did you give as a token of silence?"

Molly was watching Paula, who had taken off her shoes and was beginning to trim with a pair of nail clippers. Sick, Molly thought, looking away. "What? I don't know. I don't think I gave anything to anybody."

"Sure you did. We all did," said Rachael. "I traded with Charlene, and you traded with . . ." She stopped and looked at Paula. The fire popped. Glowing ashes spit into the air. "Oh, shit," Rachael said. Her mouth drew up in disgust.

Molly glanced at the younger woman.

"Oh, shit," echoed Charlene.

Paula was not trimming her toenails, but the flesh of her little toe, clipping away pieces. Blood poured onto the dirt. She did not grimace nor moan nor make comment, but she bent over her work like the campers had over their latest piece of craftsmanship. She paused for a heartbeat to wipe a hair from her mouth. It left a red streak of war paint.

"What the hell are you doing?" asked Rachael. She stood up, but the beers kept her from standing straight. One arm waved the air. "What the hell is the matter with you?"

Paula did not answer, but continued to clip. And then she pulled a pair of wire snips from the pocket of her pullover sweater, and worked on the bone. With a jerk and a snap much like the breaking of the stick on the path, the toe came off in Paula's hand. She held it up for the others to see.

"Psycho," whispered Molly. Her stomach cramped and twisted. "Psycho bitch."

"Damn it, you're gonna bleed to death!" cried Charlene. "No," said Paula. She jammed her feet back into the white shoes. The one did not stay white for long. She shifted her body, and held the toe out toward Molly.

Molly leaned backward on the log, her chest constricting.

"Man, this is too fucking weird," said Rachael. "Too fucking weird. I got to go home, ladies. Sorry, this is the end of the party."

"You were right, Rachael," Paula said slowly. "Molly didn't trade that night. We didn't have the chance. You'd done your dance and made your pledge, and then you ran off to meet Danny before we could make our trade."

Molly's head rang. She put one hand behind her and felt the ground, trying to find a stick large enough to strike Paula if she came closer.

"Hey, Paula," said Charlene. "So how is old Danny?" The fear in her voice made it slide upward like the nose-pinched Cub Scout rendition they used to do in the song, "We're All Together Again." This time, no one found the humor.

"I already asked her," said Rachael. "She said he's better."

"Than what?"

"Than he was."

"Than he was," nodded Paula. The toe was still in her hand, an offering.

"What does that mean, he's better?" Molly found a stick. She gripped it to test its strength. It broke, and she dropped it. Damn!

67

Her head spun. She wished she hadn't had so much to drink.

"He never married," said Paula. "He was handsome, you know. Women, girls, even some men, always after him for you-know-what. Just like you, Molly."

Rachael wobbled around the fire, but as she crossed beside Paula, heading for the path, Paula was on her feet. Rachael stumbled back a few feet. "Hey, there, Paula, to each her own but you're too freaky for me. I'm leaving."

"No, you aren't," said Paula. "We made dibs. We aren't finished."

"We're grown-ups now, Paula," said Charlene. Her words were slow, slurred. "Adults. We made vows as kids, but as adults, we can keep it or not keep it however we want."

"You all made fun of me, I remember," said Paula. "Laughing at me. Breaking my glasses. I couldn't see for two whole days. I remember."

"We were kids," said Charlene. "We're adults now."

"I'm going," Rachael said. She took a step, but Paula lashed out with her fists and drove the big woman to the ground on her butt. Then Paula stared across the fire at the others. The light glowed in her glasses, twin devil fires. The blood streak on her cheek was now black. The toe jabbed the air like a bizarre piece of chalk in an angry teacher's grasp. Her voice was controlled, deep, and intense.

"We made dibs."

Charlene began to laugh. She slid off the log into the dirt, wheezing and chortling. "I'm just dreaming all this shit!" she said. "What a trip! Goddam!" Then she leaned over and threw up on her feet.

Paula stared across the fire at Molly. Molly stared at the toe. "I watched you and Danny, you know," Paula said. "After the ceremony. After the vows. I went to the counselor's tent and called him out for you, saying you'd found a wounded fox in the woods and wouldn't he come help? Remember?"

"No," whispered Molly.

"Danny followed me here, where you waited for him. Then I left the two of you to your business. Remember?"

"No."

Molly's hand grabbed again at the ground behind the log, but came up with only ash and pine needles and leaves. Nothing big enough to use against this insane woman.

"I was only eleven," said Paula, sliding her empty hand into her sweater pocket. "I wasn't old enough to understand at first what you wanted with my brother. I thought it was going to be harmless, until I saw you and him, groping in the leaves with no clothes on. I had my new glasses, I could see. I thought it would just be playing. Until I saw his little . . . thing . . . get big and hard, until I saw. . . ."

Rachael pushed herself back up. "I'm getting the hell out of here." As she stepped forward again, trying to move around Paula, Paula jerked her hand out of her pocket and shoved it at Rachael. With a grunt, Rachael went down onto her knees.

"Stop that!" shouted Charlene. She sat in the leaves by the log at Molly's feet, her trembling index finger pointed at Paula. "Who the hell do you think you are, you little shit? We can stay or leave as we want."

Paula said, "No one's going anywhere. I want my dibs."

"You can't stop us!" said Charlene.

"Oh, no?" asked Paula. "You're all drunk. Drunk like you were at camp. I can stop you. Now. I want my dibs."

Molly forced her feet underneath her and stood. She had children, she could rationalize with craziness. "Paula, there is no Princess Kiwanisani. Do you understand that?"

"I know that," said Paula. She licked her lips. The toe in her finger glistened with slick, drying blood.

"Good," said Molly. "Then the dibs isn't valid, don't you see? Come on, throw down that toe and have a drink. It'll take the pain away."

On the ground, Rachael gasped, "Molly, help me." Molly looked at Rachael. She slowly rolled over onto her back, her hands clutching her chest. She had been stabbed. "Oh, my God, Rachael," hissed Molly. She tried to stand, but Paula came around the fire, now brandishing something in both hands. In one, the toe. In the other, a sharp knife with a orange wooden handle and the initials CK. Camp Kiwanisani. Molly remembered this knife. It had been used by the camp cooks for slicing beef. Each camper had to do capers, and one day it involved helping the cooks. This was a stolen camp knife, like the other forks and spoons Paula had taken.

"Dibs," Paula said.

Charlene, still seated and swaying, suddenly reached up, grabbing Paula's sweater, trying to jerk her down. But Paula just as swiftly drove the knife into Charlene's neck, and the woman went back into the leaves, her hands at her throat, gurgling and spouting blood.

Molly pushed herself back off the log. She hit the ground and turned over, mouth in the grit and sticks. Get up, get up! her mind screamed. But her body was in another dimension. Her legs pulled up under her, and her palms went down. She pushed. She went up, but something crashed into her and drove her back down. Her face turned against the ground, and she saw Paula standing there. Molly couldn't see the woman's face in the shadows with the fire to her back, but she could imagine it.

Lips tight. Big thick glasses soot-covered now. Eyes tiny behind them, unblinking.

Molly whispered, "Let me go, please."

"Danny said that," said Paula. "He kept on with those women, just like he did with you. I watched him through his bedroom keyhole when he was still at home. I watched him through his apartment window when he was old enough to move out. You spoiled him, you ruined him, letting him do what he did to you. He was bad. He said, 'Let me go, please.' Yes, he was bad. But now he's better."

"What do you mean?"

"Better, like Charlene and Rachael. Better and gone, like those vermin we had to deal with at camp. The rats, the chipmunks, the mice."

Shit shit shit shit. Molly tried to crawl forward, but Paula's foot on her back kept her still.

"I want my dibs," said Paula. "You said you wanted a night with Danny. You promised your soul to Kiwanisani. I knew even then there was no Princess. But we traded, you and me. I said you could have a toe. I said it was worth what you would give me."

I don't remember!

"I promised a toe. You promised me eyes."

What?

With a sharp movement, Paula shoved Molly over onto her back. She could see black tree branches overhead, with soft clouds and occasional stars. Then, Paula's face was in the center of the view. There was a knife at Molly's throat.

"Eyes," said Paula. "You made fun of me for my thick glasses. All I wanted was good eyes, so you wouldn't make fun."

Paula!

"I want my dibs, that's all. You promised."

"NO!"

"Dibs," said Paula.

As Paula took her dibs, Molly screamed. And the scream was that of a tortured soul, lifting to the sky, offered to an ancient Indian princess for a single night of pleasure in the rough grasses and twigs of a long ago camp night.

Assault

The rumbling on the gravelly, dusted road out past the field caused the little girl to start, wide-eyed, and then drop from the sycamore into the alfalfa and run, panting, through the high gnarls of grass toward the house. She did not yell, but whispered to herself the words that drove her forward across the field and up the hillside to the white house.

"Blackers," she said. "Blackers, blackers."

Her arms worked before her in a swimmer's strokes, parting the grass and shooting forward. Her legs, toughened by a summer's length of play in weeds and briars, slipped unaffected through the dense, sharp blades. Breath rushed in and out through her mouth.

"Blackers, blackers," she said. She neared the house, skirting the corner of Mother's squash garden and ducking beneath the whirling rags pinned to the clotheswire.

"Blackers! Blackers!"

There was a whoop from the hen barn, and Ralphie stumbled out, tripping over the caned rake he held. He righted himself and ran for the house.

"Blackers, Jimmy! Ginny seen blackers! Hurry!"

Jimmy appeared at the edge of the smoke-house behind the hen barn. Fear had tightened his face, making him look younger than seventeen, making him look vulnerable. The older brother dropped the sack of meat he was carrying and bolted after Ralphie and Ginny.

Ginny was the first on the porch. She hurled herself through the battered screen door. Ralphie and Jimmy followed. Mother met them, dishrag in hand, in the foyer.

"My God, what's the matter?" she said.

Jimmy slammed the front door closed, heaving his weight against the splintering oak. Ralphie twisted the deadlock. Ginny, leaning over to catch her knees and her breath, sputtered, "Blackers."

Mother's fingers parted and the dishrag fell to the hall floor.

* * *

They hid in the kitchen, the safest place, the only room in the house that had windows totally obscured by thick holly brush. If there had been a second floor the family would have gone there, but as it was, there was only a narrow attic crawl space, and, as Mother said, the family would surely suffocate if huddled together there for any time. Ginny squatted beneath the kitchen table, her arm hooked about the neck of Sandy, the family's golden retriever. Every so often, Sandy would whine and twist her head to lick Ginny's face, but Ginny would jerk Sandy's head back by a finger beneath the collar, and Sandy would straighten.

Ralphie and Jimmy sat with their backs against the cabinets beneath the sink, each a near twin of the other, with Jimmy's creased and scarred hands one of the few distinctions between him and his younger brother.

Mother sat in the space between the stove and the refrigerator, twisting her dishrag around her pinkie.

The family listened for the blackers. As Jimmy had locked the last of the windows in Ralphie's bedroom, he had heard their sounds in the driveway. He scuttled to the kitchen, holding low at the waist in case one might already be clawing at the front door, trying to see in, trying to get in.

They stayed in the kitchen, and they waited, listening, breathing in shallow, airy gasps.

At first there was the thumping on the porch and front door. At the first bump, Ginny winced and Sandy started up on her noisily clacking nails. Mother leaned over and pulled Sandy down, then touched Ginny gently on the cheek. Ginny nodded and tried to smile, but the corners of her mouth merely jumped as if in a spasm.

"It will be all right," Mother mouthed, and Ginny nodded again.

Ralphie's lower lip drew in between his teeth and the corners of his eyes twitched.

The thumping outside began to move; there were grunts and shuffling sounds rounding the opposite side of the house. There was soft picking at the window screens, and then silence. Ralphie's lips came free of his teeth. There was a spot of blood where the skin had come off.

The rear door in the back hall crashed and jangled on its hinges. Ginny jumped and hit her head on the underside of the table. Jimmy grabbed Ralphie's arm and burrowed his fingers deep into the flesh. The door knob twisted, squeaking and grating. The door held. The knob was released.

"They won't get us," Ginny whispered to Sandy.

Jimmy held up his index finger, motioning her to be silent.

Ralphie looked at the little knick-knack shelf by the pantry. On it was a photo of Daddy, lovingly preserved in a cover of Handi-Wrap. Often Ginny would glean the fields for wild flowers and put them on the shelf by Daddy's picture. In memory.

The holly branches scraped the kitchen window, playing the screen like an angry child playing a harp. Ginny buried her face in Sandy's fur. Mother's head came up; her silent prayer worked on her lips. "Protect us from our enemies. Foil the demons who seek to destroy us."

Grumbling noises tangled within the holly, trying to work to the window. The branches pulled away and then were hurled toward the screen, gouging the woven wire.

Ralphie kept watching Daddy's face. Daddy's shrine.

Daddy, who had been taken by the blackers almost two months ago. Daddy, who had never come home again.

The holly branches shivered, and then became still.

Mother looked up from her prayer. Jimmy's fingers loosened on Ralphie's arm; Ralphie patted Jimmy's hand reassuringly.

It sounded as though the blackers were going away.

Mother tilted her head, angling her ear to catch the sounds through the closed window. The shuffling was fainter; it moved from the house to the driveway.

Jimmy licked his lips and looked questioningly at Mother. Mother shook her head, waiting. Ginny wiped tears on Sandy's yellow coat.

They listened. They held still.

"They're gone," said Ralphie, turning to his mother.

Mother held up her hand, frowning and listening.

Ralphie and Jimmy and Ginny remained quiet. Finally, Mother lowered her hand and wiped it on her hip.

"All right," she said. Her shoulders drooped, her lids fluttered. "They're gone."

Ralphie stood, offering a helping hand to Jimmy, who took it and hoisted himself to his feet. Ginny crawled from beneath the table. Sandy began pacing the kitchen in frantic ecstasy. Mother stretched upward and gave Sandy a healthy pat on the rump.

"Thank God," said Mother. "Thank God for His protection."

Ginny and Ralphie and Jimmy nodded in solemn agreement.

Mother clapped her hands together. "Get those windows, Jimmy, before we cook to death."

Jimmy tugged open the kitchen door and went into the foyer. He approached the foyer window carefully, just to be certain that mother was right. He leaned slowly toward the glass and peered out from the bottom corner.

And then there was a crash on the front door, and Jimmy hurled himself backward onto the floor. He jammed his fist into his mouth to hold back the scream that hammered in his throat. He held without moving, hoping that the blacker would not see him.

The door was hit again, with less force, and then the guttural grunting grew fainter as it moved off the porch. Jimmy pressed his cheek to the floor, praying and listening. There was motion on the driveway, gravel crunching and scattering, and Jimmy knew, with certainty, that the blackers had left. The family was safe.

Ginny's face appeared at the kitchen door. "Jimmy?"

Jimmy rolled over and sat up. "They're gone now, I heard them on the road."

Ginny and Ralphie and Mother stepped from the kitchen and helped Jimmy unlock the window and let in the meadow-sweet summer air.

"I hate this goddam job," said Barbara as she steered the ungainly black agency car to the side of the road. "I don't think it would be so bad if I did food stamps or support, or even foster care. But protective services is too much. I can't deal day after day with abused children. I can't try week after week to visit families who aren't ever home." She looked back over her shoulder at the distant white house beyond the alfalfa field.

"I know they're home," said Sam. "I think it's time we got a court order and got into that place."

"I hate confrontation."

"Then you're in the wrong profession," Sam said coolly.

"That family has been through some weird shit. For Christ's sake, the father was convicted of slaughtering an elderly neighbor for Christmas dinner. The police found the remains of nine other bodies in the garden. I don't exactly call that your normal family situation."

Barbara put her forehead on the steering wheel. "I know."

"We've got to keep close tabs on the kids, Barbara. The mother seemed oblivious to the peculiarity of the situation. When a father with such a strong, abnormal hold on his family is removed from the home, the kids are often lost and quite confused. We owe it to them to make sure they're getting along. To make sure they recover as much as possible."

"You're right."

"Chin up," said Sam.

"But you know," Barbara said as she steered the black car back onto the road. "I need a vacation."

"Don't we all?"

"You'll get a court order for me?"

Sam put his feet up on the dashboard. "All you had to do was ask."

Mother took the foyer rug out to the porch and shook it over the railing, scattering dust into the sunlight. Ralphie raked the last of the soiled hay from the hen barn and tossed it into the wheelbarrow for a trip to the comport pile. Ginny pulled herself back into the sycamore tree, singing, "Who's afraid of the blacka-blacka-blackers?" Jimmy plopped the sack of meat onto the kitchen and slit the bag open with a carving knife. He rolled the meat out and admired Ralphie's hunting skills, which were nearly as good as his own now. Ralphie had had to hunt as far away as Elkton County, but what he'd caught was a prize. The woman was large and plump. She had been trussed and portioned and smoked to near perfection.

Jimmy put the knife on the table and went out to call Mother because cooking was women's work.

What Happened When Mosby Paulsen Had Her Painting Reproduced on the Cover of the Phone Book

Mail was in.

Elliott Mitchell stepped out onto the front stoop, pleased and shocked, as he usually was, at the cool roughness of the concrete beneath his bare feet. From the mailbox he pulled assorted flyers and bills, several final notices, and two copies of the new phone book, wrapped in brown paper. Elliott flipped through the collection, taking mental notes of the exciting variety of places from where the mail had come and filing this information away in the hungry places of his mind.

Washington, D.C. Chicago, Illinois. Pueblo, Colorado.

If there had been an atlas in his home like there had been in school, he would have looked them up. But the names themselves were intriguing enough.

He moved back into the house. His feet found the familiar, sticky warmth of the worn living room carpet. The cats peed here, and food from Elliott's mother's tray were spilled here. Elliott couldn't keep up with it all anymore, and so the cats continued to pee and his mother's trembling hands continued to knock portions of her dinners onto her lap and onto the floor.

Elliott dropped the stack of mail onto the top of the console television. He moved into the small kitchen. The windows were closed and locked in defiance of the cool May air. Orange flowered curtains hung, dead weights against grease-iced window glass.

There was a two-liter Dr. Pepper in the refrigerator.

Elliott took a long swing from the bottle.

"Ellie?"

Elliott's stomach fluttered. He turned toward the call. A drip of cola caught in the corner of his mouth then slid to his chin.

"What, Mom?"

"Can't hear my set. Come turn it up, honey."

Elliott put the drink back and closed the refrigerator door. On the door, held by an eclectic collection of magnets, were some of Elliott's best school papers from seventh grade. A spelling test, "A+!" A letter written in social studies to George Washington, "96, Good job Elliott!" Numerous charcoal, pastel, and watercolor artworks, each praised in red ink on a Post-It Note by Mrs. Pugh, the middle school art teacher. He would have had Mrs. Pugh in eighth grade this year for advanced art if he had not been so sick.

But he was on homebound now.

He was sick. He knew it, Mom knew it. So very, very sick.

Just like me, Ellie.

If you go to school today I might just be dead when you get home.

"Ellie? The set, I can't hear it and I can't get up. My back's doing it again."

Elliott went down the short dark hall to his mother's room. The door was open. Smells of stale cigarettes, medicated vaporizer, and illness hung around the doorway, a heavy, eye-stinging, invisible fog.

"Set, baby, fix it for me."

He stepped into the bedroom. The floor here was bare linoleum. It was not the pleasant coolness of the front stoop; it was clammy on the skin of his soles. But it was familiar. It was never a shock.

Mom was on her back in her bed, three pillows against the wobbly headboard, one set of white fingers curled around the bedspread at her chest, one set around a cigarette. In the blue light of the television set the skin on her thin face seemed to jump and crawl. When she smiled, Elliott could see her bad teeth. There were three of the cats on the bed with her. Next to the bed was the wheel chair the health department had given her.

"Can't hear it," Mom said. She drew on the cigarette. The smoke blew back out in the wind of a violent cough. She found her voice and said, "Just a little volume, honey."

Elliott stepped to the tiny black and white set on Mom's dresser, and poked at the volume button until Regis and Kathi Lee's voices were uncomfortably loud. Mom said, "That's just fine, Ellie."

"Anything else?" There was a cat turd on the bottom of Elliott's foot. He looked at the bottom of it but couldn't see except that it looked dark and it felt soft and warm. "You need anything else?"

"Teacher come yet?"

"No. Mrs. Anderson won't be here until two."

Mom sucked on the cigarette like it was the tube on an oxygen mask. She let the smoke out, then said, "I just can't rest good today. I'm hurting. My back, my heart is just hammering like it wants to come out. Lay with me 'til I'm asleep."

I thought you wanted to watch T.V., Elliott thought, but didn't say. He went to the bed and lay down beside his mother. The mattress was lumpy. When his mother turned to him, her breath was familiar and strong.

"I feel a little better, honey." One side of her mouth went up in what might have been a resigned smile. It looked as if even her face hurt her.

Mom always called Elliott honey. Never "Wee-wee Boy", or "Poop-Man" like the kids at J.E.B. Stewart Middle School did. Elliott's mother loved him, even as she was dying. And she had been dying since Elliott had been in fourth grade. Her heart was bad, she told him. She couldn't breathe very well because she was born with bad lungs. Her stomach made juices that were poison. Her muscles were giving in and her nerves had so many short-circuits the doctors couldn't even find them all. Month after month she begged him to stay with her and not go to school. Daddy had insisted, getting Elliott on the school bus when he could. But most of the time Daddy left for work before the school bus came, and three days out of five, Elliott would stay with his mother because if she died when he was at school, what would he do then?

Elliott awoke to the tune of *All My Children*. He had slept next to his mother for almost two hours. It was time to find something for them to eat for lunch. At two o'clock, the teacher, Mrs. Anderson, would come.

Mom didn't eat much of the bean with bacon soup Elliott fixed. She let Elliott wheel her to the bathroom but she would not eat with him in the living room. She insisted on a tray in bed, and then only sipped a couple of spoonfuls and ate the chips Elliott had put in a bowl for her. She didn't want the Dr. Pepper he'd poured for her. She wanted Sprite. There wasn't any Sprite, so Elliott told her he would made a list for Daddy when he came home. He could go into town and get Sprite for tomorrow. Mom settled down with another daytime show, and Elliott took the tray to the kitchen, ate his own soup and Dr. Pepper in the living room, and looked through the mail again.

He opened the bills and put them back on top of the console television in a pile for his father. He slid the paper cover off of one of the telephone books, and stopped.

The cover was not the normal photograph of the mountains or a rolling cattle farm, as the phone company was prone to use. It was, instead, a painting. A reproduction of a childish watercolor, splashed in its brilliant colors across the book's broad cover. The painting was of a bright blue-green ocean, and a sailboat with smiling people all lined up together on the deck. White sparks flashed in the water; the sky was pink and yellow. At the bottom of the painting was the title, "The Adventure on the Sea" by Mosby Paulson.

Elliott cleared his throat, feeling the raw pain of his own illness, his own poor blood and bad lungs and short-circuited nerves.

Inside the front cover was a description of the painting.

"Mosby Paulson is a sixth grade student at J.E.B. Stewart Middle School. She is in Mrs. Connie Pugh's art class this year, and entered the phone book competition along with over one hundred middle school students throughout the county. All the entries were judged by a panel of artists in the area, and Mosby's work 'The Adventure on the Sea', was selected as the winner for its 'lively depiction of movement, brave use of effective colors, and originality of shape.' "

Elliott looked back at the cover. Happy people smiling, going somewhere on a silly sailboat in a bright sea. Going places that Elliott would never know, places he would only see as return addresses on the mail that came daily to his dented mailbox.

He could have done better. If he'd been in Mrs. Pugh's art class this year, he would have entered the contest. And he could have won. He could have had his art somewhere besides on the door of the greasy refrigerator.

"Ellie?"

"What?"

"Can't find my lighter. It fell down under the bed, I think."

Elliott went into his mother's bedroom and dug under the bed while his mother coughed above him. In the shadows beneath the bed, one of the cats blinked at him. He found the lighter on top of a dust-softened sock, then crawled back out.

"Thank you, honey." Mom took the lighter, pulled a cigarette from the pack on the little table by the bed, flicked it three times before it would catch, then settled back into the pillow with a long, raspy draw.

Elliott watched his mother. Her eyes were closed, her cheeks sharp and skeletal. Her nose was runny and her hair was thin and short. The cigarette smoldered in her mouth, the tip glowing and dimming as she sucked on it and eased the smoke out through her lips without even taking the cigarette out.

"Mom?"

"Huh?" The cigarette did not come out; the word was muffled.

"The new phone books are in."

"So?"

"Thought you'd want to know."

The tip of the cigarette grew longer, glowing, smoldering. Then she said, "Our number ain't in it, is it? They put an unlisted number in there I'll sue 'em, I tell you that."

"No, we ain't in there."

The ash on the end of the cigarette trembled.

Elliott wondered how long until it fell to the bed covers.

"Good then. You go watch your T.V. until the teacher comes. I'm tired."

The ash wobbled. If it fell to the bed, it would catch the covers on fire. People who smoked in bed sometimes burned themselves to death, Elliott had heard.

"Go on now," said Mom.

Elliott went on.

Mrs. Anderson knocked on the door just after two o'clock. She was a young woman, hoping to get a permanent job with the county as a reading specialist. Now she was teaching two students on homebound, Elliott and a boy named Richard who lived on the other side of the county and who had polio real bad because his parents never got him his vaccination.

Elliott opened the door and Mrs. Anderson put on her happy-to-see-you smile. Sometimes, when Elliott heard her car out front, he would watch her get out of her car and come up the walk. She never wore that smile when she thought he wasn't watching.

"Elliott, how are you today?" Mrs. Anderson's eyebrows went up. They were funny eyebrows, drawn thin with a black pencil. Mrs. Anderson always smelled strongly of perfume, as if she didn't like the smells of Elliott's house.

"Okay."

Mrs. Anderson came into the living room, her huge, unbuttoned white spring coat billowing out when she moved.

She removed the coat and hung it on the door knob of the closet. She studied the sofa a moment, and then sat down with her briefcase in her lap. She said she liked cats but Elliott knew better.

Elliott sat on the lawn chair, the only other piece of furniture in the living room except the console television. His teeth found a loose piece of skin on his lower lip and began to chew.

"And your mother," said Mrs. Anderson. She opened her brief case and took out Elliott's lesson plan book. "How is she today?"

"Same," said Elliott.

"Mmm-hmmmm." Mrs. Anderson looked up at Elliott then. Her happy-to-see-you smile was getting heavy, folding back down into an expression of perfunctory purpose. "How are the exercises going?"

"Exercises?"

"We talked yesterday about your weight gain, Elliott. You've put on quite a bit of weight since you stopped attending school. Without a physical education program daily, you're doing your body a disservice."

"I didn't do any exercises yet. I tried one but my stomach hurt so much I stopped."

Mrs. Anderson sighed. Elliott had heard that sigh many times, from many of the adults at his old elementary school and at the middle school. On the days when Elliott had been put on the bus by his father, he would have severe stomachaches during homeroom. He would go to the guidance office but the counselors would try to talk him into staying. They would sigh that sigh and say, "Elliott, if you just stick it out through lunchtime you'll feel better."

Some of the days he would make it through art class, but then insist on calling his father to pick him up. Most days, however, he would wet his pants or have a bowel movement and the counselors had no choice but to send him home.

He was a sick boy. He was sick like his mother, and he needed to be home with her. If she died when he was at school, he would never forgive himself.

Elliott looked at Mrs. Anderson. Mrs. Anderson looked at Elliott. She said, "Are your parents treating you all right, Elliott? How are you getting along with them?"

"Fine."

"Anything you'd like to talk about?"

"No. We're getting along okay."

She rolled this around on her face a little, then let it go. "How about your math, did you finish the page of fractions?"

"I finished some of it."

"Why not all of it, Elliott?"

"I didn't feel good."

"And your civics?"

"I didn't have civics."

"Yes, you had a chapter to review. We were having a quiz today."

Elliott said, "Oh, yeah, I forgot."

"Get out your books," said Mrs. Anderson.

They spent the next two hours working through civics, pre-algebra, and English. Elliott wondered if a homebound student could have entered the phone book contest. He wished Mrs. Pugh could come at least one hour a week out of his required twenty and let him paint for her.

Mrs. Anderson left at four, and Elliott watched cartoons until six. He made supper of canned chili and chips and talked his mother into coming into the living room and eating on a T.V. tray next to him. She spilled half of her chili then went back to bed. Elliott rubbed most of the chili up with one of his father's dirty workshirts from the laundry basket.

He lay on the sofa and looked at the phone book. He could have painted one of his horse pictures. Mrs. Pugh had loved his horse pictures. She said they made her feel free just to look at them. He could have made a picture the judges would have loved. He could have had his work on all the phone books in the county.

Elliott fell asleep on the sofa. His father woke him when he got home from work at ten, and sent the boy to bed.

"Ellie, I can't get up. Bring me the bedpan."

Elliott was in the bathroom on the toilet, looking at the phone book. His teeth clamped together. He hated doing the bedpan. He pretended not to hear.

"Ellie, can you hear me? I need the pan 'fore I make a mess in here!"

Elliott squeezed his eyes shut. Behind his lids, he saw horses running, watercolor horses free and running across a yellow beach and into the water where a happy white sailboat drifted to places far away. When he opened his eyes, he saw his pants down around his ankles, and the penis his mother said the boys would make fun of when he had to dress out in p.e. class when he went to the middle school.

"The doctor made a mistake when they circumcised you, Elliott. You got a little penis with a nick in it and when the boys see you they'll laugh."

When his father had sent him to school anyway, Elliott would wet his pants before p.e. so he could go home to his mother. For a couple of days the assistant principal walked him to p.e. and made him dress out. Elliott had hid behind a locker door and cried while he pulled on the royal blue gym shorts. In the gym, he refused to participate, and sat against the wall with the back of his head pressed into the cinder block. After a half-year, Elliott was removed from p.e. and got to sit in the library and read a book during second period.

"Ellie!"

Elliott went to his mother's room. She was already wrestling with the hem of her nightgown, tugging it up. "Hurry, honey!"

Elliott took the pan from the floor and slid it under his mother's rear end, then turned away. He could hear the water run into the aluminum, could hear his mother's airy whistle of relief around the cigarette in her mouth.

"Done, honey."

Elliott took the pan into the bathroom and dumped the urine into the toilet. He glanced at the phone book on the bath mat. Mosby's painting lay face up, taunting. Elliott rinsed the pan and took it back to his mother.

She was already drifting to sleep.

"You want some breakfast?" he asked.

"My stomach hurts too much to eat. I don't got long, Ellie, I know that. This morning I'm in more pain then I been in for a long time. What you gonna do when I'm dead?"

Elliott did not know what to say. And so he said, "Do you know where my crayons are?"

"Your what?"

"Crayons."

"Crayons? Those things you had when you was little?"

"Yeah."

"Sure we throwed them away, Ellie. You ain't got time for crayons. I need you. You and me, wc need each other, we's so sick."

"I want to make a picture."

"Make yourself useful. Vacuum the living room so Mrs. Anderson won't turn us in for neglect."

I want to make a picture. I'm better than Mosby Paulson, so much better you wouldn't believe it.

"Get."

Elliott vacuumed the living room. The large cat turds he pushed under the lawn chair because the vacuum nozzle wouldn't pick them up. He put the vacuum back into the living room closet and went into the kitchen. The windows were still closed, and through the glass he could see the wild and green weeds of his side yard.

Horses eat wild, green weeds.

Beyond the weeds was the neighbor's house, a blue trailer with a homemade deck on the front. Elliott knew that the Campbells lived there. They were old people, and they used to have two children, but the children were taken away to live in foster homes because the Campbells beat them up a lot. For the first time in the four years since the Campbell children were gone, Elliott wondered where they were.

Maybe Pueblo, Colorado. Maybe Washington, D.C.

Maybe across the ocean on a white sailboat.

In a junk drawer, Elliott found several broken pencils and a knife. He sharpened the pencils with the knife and then drew a horse on a paper bag from under the sink. It wasn't as good a horse as one would have been had he had his crayons, but it was a fast horse. It ran with its mane and tail in the wind and its nostrils up to the air.

He hid the picture in his bedroom. Then he watched T.V. until Mrs. Anderson came at two with her concrete smile and bright white coat and her chastisements and her nose that couldn't stop twitching at the smell of cat pee.

Elliott's father woke him from his sleep on the sofa.

On the television, Jay Leno was well into his monologue.

"You snoring, boy," his father said.

Elliott wiped his eyes and tried to sit up. "Was not."

"Was too. You getting so goddamned fat you snoring like an old man. I wish to hell you was back at school where you belong."

Elliott blinked and rubbed his eyes.

"You can do jumping jacks, boy? Get up and show me a jumping jack."

"I'm tired."

"You's always tired. I work two goddamned jobs and you say you's tired. Show me a jumping jack!"

Elliott stood up and looked at his father. The man was short and dark and thin. His eyes were angry, dull chips in his skull. He worked at the turkey plant in the day and the Exxon station at night. Elliott remembered his father saying once that he wished Mom would go ahead and die.

It would be easier on us both, he had said.

Elliott had cried at that, and crapped his pants, and his father had never said anything like that again.

"Do it," said his father.

Elliott jumped up and down three times, slapping his hands together over his head as he did. When he stopped, his heart was hammering, and his breath was glass in his throat.

"I'm sick," he sputtered.

"Hell you are."

"I'm sick!" Elliott ran to his bedroom and cried and wet the bed. He didn't change the sheets until the next morning.

Elliott got the mail from the mailbox. He stood on the stoop and sifted through the stack. There wasn't much today, just a folded Little Caesar's Pizza advertisement and a bill from the oil company. He looked through the untrimmed hedge bordering his yard at the Campbell's trailer. He wondered how beat up the Campbell children were when they finally got taken away.

He went in and ate some Frosted Flakes from the box.

He then fixed a bowl of red and green colored special edition Cap'n Crunch left over from Christmas, stirred up some instant milk to wet it, and took it to his mother. She was awake, and clawing at the arm of her wheelchair.

Elliott put the cereal on the bedstand.

"Where you going, Mom?"

"Got a cramp, got to get up and get it out."

"Want help?"

"Course I do. I can't do without you."

Elliott watched for a moment. In his mind he saw his mother falling onto her face and breaking her nose. He saw the blood bleeding down into the cracks of the old linoleum where her food scraps and her cats' pee and her own existence seemed to be drawn.

"I know," he said. He helped his mother into the chair. "I got you breakfast."

"Mixed it up with that shitty milk I bet."

Elliott watched as his mother struck a match on the side of the wheelchair and touched it to the tip of the cigarette in her mouth. "Well, yeah."

"I don't like it."

"I'll give it to the cats."

Elliott's mother grunted and drove the heels of her hands against the wheels. The chair shuttered, then rumbled out of the bedroom.

Elliott followed her. She went into the living room and, after tugging weakly at the curtains until Elliott pushed them back himself, settled before the window and looked out at the yard and the cracked walkway and the untrimmed brush and the county road.

In the kitchen, Elliott picked up the phone book.

Already, Mosby's picture was scuffed and bent. Elliott's father had used the phone book already, treating the artwork like he treated everything else around him, as something made for a purpose, a single purpose, and nothing else. Daddy's purpose was to work and sweat and be the head of the household. Elliott's job was to go to school like all the other boys his age, like the boys who weren't sick and didn't have a ruined penis and boys whose mothers weren't dying. And Elliott's mother's job was to go on and die.

The grimy, strawberry-shaped clock over the stove read ten-thirty seven. Mrs. Anderson wouldn't be there for another three and a half hours.

Elliott went into his bedroom and sat on his cot. He pulled the paper bag out from under his pillow and looked at it. Even with the dull pencil lines, the horses were good. He was a good artist.

"Mom, you think I draw good?"

From the living room, "Huh?"

"You think I draw good?"

"Whatever."

Elliott put the horses back. He walked back through the living room into the kitchen, where, through the open door, he looked at the bony back of his mother's neck as she looked out the window.

He turned on the stove. He filled a pan with water and set it down to boil. He wondered how bad scald burns would look. He wondered how they would feel. He felt around in the junk drawer and took out the little knife he'd used to sharpen his pencil. He wondered how someone would have to push if neck skin were to part?

He went out to the living room and stood beside his mother. From outside, he could hear one of the cats picking on the door.

"Cat wants in," said his mother.

Elliott opened the door. The cat trotted in. Cats, Elliott thought, were like his father. Cats believed people had a single purpose— to serve them. Elliott shut the door and the cat ran into the kitchen in search of food.

Elliott said, "You want me to turn on the T.V.?"

"My head hurts too much. You gonna give me a massage on my head, Ellie?"

Ellie rubbed her head with one hand. In his other, he held the little knife.

He stopped then, because he could hear the water boiling in the kitchen. He left his mother and went to the stove.

Before lifting the pan, he went to the window, unlocked it, and pushed it open an inch. May air bled into the stuffy room. The crusty orange curtains trembled as if afraid of the breeze.

Elliott looked over at the Campbell's yard. He thought about their children, taken away.

He turned Mosby's wrinkled painting upside down.

The knife was put back into the drawer for next time, if the water wasn't enough.

Then, sucking air through his clamped teeth, he poured the boiling water over his forearms and hands. The skin erupted, bright and red. Angry, insulted blisters rose.

He caught his breath.

"Goin' back to bed, honey," said his mother. She rolled away from the living room window and out of sight.

He caught his breath. Pale cat hairs, floating in the kitchen, landed on the burns and beneath the pain he almost felt a tickle.

He dropped to the kitchen chair and lost his breath; he thought of horses running running running on sand toward the beach. He caught his breath again.

Elliott faced the living room and the front door and he waited for his smiling teacher with the white, billowing sailboat coat.

Damaged Goods

"You put your penis here," Darla said. Paul, sitting in the tall grass next to her, rolled his eyes in embarrassment.

"You hear me?" Darla repeated. She had her yellow cotton skirt up over her knees, and although she retained her pink panties, she poked her index finger with firm direction at the space between her thighs. "I'm the lamb, and it goes here. God, you're dumb."

Paul pulled out the nub of wild mint he had been chewing and turned on his butt, moving so Darla was no longer in his sight. He stared, instead, at the pasture in which they sat, and at the shallow river running nearby. He wasn't certain where the pasture was; he and

Darla had been rightfully blindfolded in the van until they were placed in the grass. The sun was behind the two of them, setting in the warm, late spring sky just over the woods to their backs. The men with the sunglasses were in those woods, hiding and silent.

Waiting.

"You're so fucking dumb," Darla continued. "Don't care about nothing except yourself."

Paul closed his eyes and tucked his head. She was right. He was afraid of responsibility. He wasn't good at it and he was afraid of it. Several years ago when he had been living at home, his mother had asked him to watch his baby brother. A simple request. "I got to get this down to the bank. Just let Timmy stay in the crib. I know you can do it. Just twenty minutes, you hear?"

Paul had heard. And Mom had left. But what a mistake she had made, giving him a chore. Silly old Mom. Paul loved Tim, and liked to play with the little boy. Paul had forgotten that his brother could not eat peanuts, that baby Tim had no teeth and couldn't chew, Paul thought a nut-eating contest would be fun. For each peanut Paul had eaten, he had put one in the baby's mouth. He sang as they played.

"Old MacDonald had a farm, ee-ii-ee-ii-oh. And on his farm he had a cow, ee-ii-ee-ii-oh."

Almost the whole can of Mr. Peanuts was gone after three verses. Paul got to giggling, and thought that Tim was giggling too, his face was all shiny and tight and he made funny noises in his throat. But, as Paul found out, the baby wasn't laughing. And Mom didn't laugh, either, when she came back from the bank to find the baby was dead.

But here was responsibility again. And Darla with her dress hiked up and her ass raised to the soft blue sky.

"I can't," Paul said without looking back.

"Hell you can't. All mens can do it. You got a dick, don't cha? It squirts, don't it?"

Paul cringed. Darla wasn't supposed to know about what men's things did. She wasn't yet eighteen. But she knew, alrighty. She had had a couple babies and a couple operations, too. She lived in the special church home where Paul lived. She did sex things with any man that could walk; residents, orderlies, old drunks from the street that she called to from her third floor window.

Paul, on the other hand, two full years older than Darla, had never done what she had done. He thought about it although he tried not to. He watched Darla during dinner or activity time, and he got a knot in his pants. Sometimes he even pretended his fingers were hers, late at night when the lights were low and the sheets were up over his head. Sometimes he sweated like a horse, he wanted it so bad. But this was daylight, and this was out in the open, and there were men with sunglasses in the trees. This was not pretend.

"Some lion you is," said Darla. She passed air through her lips in a noisy declaration of contempt, and Paul could hear rustling as she pulled her skirt down. He looked back. Her eyebrows were a thick, angry tangle.

Darla wasn't ugly, but she was scarred. Her nose was crooked where some man broke it one time, and the puckered remnants of a long knife wound cut across her throat. Black hair cupped the curve of her cheek in a thin cap. She squinted, because her eyes were bad but she wouldn't wear glasses. Paul wanted to do what had been asked of him, but he wasn't sure he knew how. He was nervous, even if it was for God.

In his nervousness, he began to sing. He couldn't help himself. He sang on key, soft and trembling. "With a baa baa here and a baa baa there, old McDonald had a lamb, ee-ii-ee-ii-oh."

Darla laughed at him, and he wasn't sure why.

"Old MacDonald had a farm, ee-ii-ee-ii-oh. And on his farm he had a lion, ee-ii-ee-ii-oh. With a . . ."

Then Darla grabbed Paul sharply by the shoulders. Her face squinted up like her eyes. "You might be stupid, but I ain't. I know what's going on here. And I ain't going to let you ruin it. It's for the world, goddam it, do you hear what I'm saying? We'll be famous, you fucker, not to mention going to heaven for sure. It ain't long to go, now, and you better be ready or I'll chew off your nose and send you to hell myself."

Paul watched her face. He felt tears pushing at his eyes but he worked them back down. She was right, and he knew it.

A new preacher had come to the church home last week.

He had walked around for a long time, and Paul had seen him go up and down the halls, all serious and stately in his black suit and white shirt, a big Bible with a tassley bookmark streaming from the middle pages. He had short brown hair and his ears were sunburned. Paul watched when he thought the preacher didn't know he was watching. But then the preacher had come right up to Paul as he sat looking at cartoons in the rec room. Without even asking, the man turned off the television set, took Paul out to the backyard, and read to him from the Bible.

"The lion shall lie down with the lamb," the preacher had begun, and Paul nodded because a preacher was a man of God and knew what he was talking about, even if it made no sense to Paul. "Do you know, son, that that line is the prophecy of the end of war and the beginning of true peace?"

Paul nodded again, and out of the corner of his eye watched a squirrel with a torn, bloodied back paw an acorn from the ground.

"I have had a sign, and I have shared it with others who understand. They sent me here, to find you."

Paul suddenly thought he was going to go to the electric chair for killing his baby brother, after all this time, and the preacher was to give him his last meal and pray with him. Paul started to cry.

"Weep not," said the preacher. "For blessed are the pure in heart. They shall see God."

Paul's lip twitched, and the tears continued.

"Blessed are the damaged ones, for they will bring perfection to our world."

The preacher told Paul of the Holy Plan, and kissed him before he left.

Now they were here. This was the day. It was secret, of course, because the masses, so the preacher said, would not understand the seriousness of what was going to take place. There was only one audience, and they were in the trees now, waiting patiently. Only One was missing, and He would arrive very soon.

Paul and Darla, the chosen ones, the damaged ones, were here to be the lion and the lamb. At their union, all the evils of the world would be bound and thrown to the pit of fire and onto Satan's head.

Paul reached under his shirt and scratched his chest nervously, leaving long fingernail lines. He looked past Darla's shoulder. Soon He would come. Then it would be time to act. Paul would either get over his embarrassment and do to Darla what he'd always wanted to do in the late night hours, or let the world continue to fight and kill and torture and tear itself into a million pieces.

Darla said, "Hey."

Paul blinked but said nothing.

Darla said, "Hey."

He looked at her. "What?"

"I'll rub you. It'll help."

Paul shuddered at the thought. But he became instantly hard.

"I'll rub you and it'll be easier. Big shit, you can think of somebody else if you want, I don't care. Damaged goods is what they wanted but you can think of someone else, okay?"

Paul said, "Okay."

Darla smiled then, the first time since the blindfolds had been removed. With the sun behind her head, she almost looked like an angel.

And then there was a shadowy sparkling from the trees, and Paul knew that He had arrived. The long car with its secret windows pulled up behind the outer edge of trees and stopped. Men in sunglasses became briefly visible as they shifted and stamped in silent respect.

"He's here," whispered Darla.

Paul reached under his shirt and scratched frantically.

Out of the woods came the preacher, and behind the preacher He came. Darla and Paul sat motionless. Paul felt his muscles kick into spastic idle; he shook uncontrollably.

The preacher wore his black suit and white shirt. He smiled a beautiful smile. The Man with him was tall and white-haired and wore a gray suit and sunglasses. He said nothing, but stood in command of them all.

The preacher said, "The lion will lie down with the lamb. In this will be the beginning of peace, and all nations will lose their love of war."

Darla's eyes were turned up in an expression of near-worship. Paul scratched his chest, making it burn.

"Thus it is said," continued the preacher. "When she who is the lamb and he who is the lion lie together, and become as one, the veil of hate will be rent."

The Man with the preacher crossed his arms. His hands were soft and strong, His fingernails trimmed and clean.

"Blessed be the lion and the lamb."

Darla whispered, "Amen."

"Please," said the preacher. "Make the prophecy come true." With that, the preacher fell silent.

Darla looked at Paul. "I'll rub you," she said.

Paul's fingers became still on his chest. He watched as Darla moved her hand to the snap on his pants and popped it open. The zipper was undone, exposing Paul's white briefs. Darla's touch and the cool spring air on the cotton stirred Paul's organ again. It tingled in anticipation, and pushed at the cloth. Paul wanted to cover himself. He wanted Darla to suck him and make him explode.

"Come on, lion," said Darla. "Lie with me."

Ee-ii-ee-ii-oh, thought Paul.

Darla slipped her hands beneath Paul's hips, and he instinctively rose up so she could pull his jeans down to his knees. Then she loosened his shoes and tossed them aside. His socks followed, and then the jeans, one leg at a time. Paul sat back on the prickly grass. He wondered if little Tim would have been proud of his big brother now, the new savior of the world.

The yellow skirt with its elasticized waist came up over Darla's head. Her pink panties appeared to be damp. Darla touched her thighs, her belly button, the damp pink panties.

Paul realized that she was not going to remove her own blouse, nor his shirt. Not that it mattered; the business ends were already exposed. He wanted to touch his penis, but was afraid. He would let Darla take charge. She knew what to do. Blessed be the lamb who sucks the dick of the lion.

Darla caught Paul's hand in her own. She moved it to the panties, and worked his fingers down inside. Paul gasped at the feel of coarse hair. "Oh," he moaned.

He thought he heard the Man echo, "Oh."

"Come on," Darla said, her breath hot on Paul's face. "I'll rub you and you rub me."

Paul's fingers began stroking the thick hair below the elastic. No longer could he feel the burning scratches on his chest; his own breath came in horrified, ecstatic jolts. Darla found his erection with the palm of her hand. Paul arched his back, pressing into her touch.

The Man with the preacher opened his own pants, and from the corner of his eye, Paul saw him reach in to stroke himself.

But Darla took his attention back with a firm squeeze.

"Lie with me." Her voice was barely audible. "Stop wars. Bring peace." She slipped her hand inside his briefs and brought his organ out into the sun. Passion, embarrassment, anticipation, and fear cut his heart. Paul groaned.

The Man and the preacher groaned, too.

Somewhere beyond the holy union, sunglasses, moving to the edge of the woods, winked in unison.

Darla tore the seams of her panties and tossed them out with Paul's socks. She ripped away Paul's briefs with sharp nails. She folded, and her mouth took Paul's penis in a wet caress.

"Ee-ii-ee-ii!" Paul shrieked. He felt the swelling pressure, the urgent demand as her tongue studied him. He wanted to stop for a moment, he was rushing ahead too fast, he could not think of what was happening and he wanted to, he wanted to have memories of this and think of it again and again but it was too fast. Too fast.

"Wait!" he screamed.

Darla dove backward, dragging Paul with her. She threw her legs apart, and shoved Paul into the wet place beneath the dark hair. Paul bucked instinctively, furiously. He was so swollen he knew he would rip her open but that was fine. That was good. The lion, tearing the lamb for the peace of the world.

And then, the divine, glorious explosion.

"Oh, my God!" shouted Paul.

"Oh, God!" shouted Darla.

"Oh, God," grunted the Man near them.

Paul fell, face into the sharp grass, arm crumpled up under him, folded against Darla's breast. His groin and stomach continued to shudder with aftershocks. He could hear Darla's pants. He could feel the sweat of her body. It was warm, like a beautiful, peaceful bath.

"Yes," said Darla in his ear. "We laid down together. Lion and the lamb. We done it." It sounded as if she were weeping with joy.

Paul began to laugh for the same reason. "We saved the world," he sang. "Ee-ii-ee-ii-oh, we saved the world from war!"

He heard the preacher laughing, too.

Then the preacher said, "Well, sir, that do the trick?"

Paul used his untrapped hand to wipe a gnat out of his eye. He squinted up at the men near them in the pasture.

The Man had his penis out of his pants, and it was erect. His mouth was a straight, tight line across his face. His eyes were still invisible behind the glasses. There were sweat droplets on his cheeks and hands.

For the first time, the Man spoke. "Not quite. Almost."

"Shit," said the preacher, and Paul flinched. Preachers didn't talk like that, not at the church home, anyway. "We got another go-round," the preacher went on. "If you'd like."

Paul worked himself up off of Darla. He sat and brushed dead grass from his legs. Darla lay still, basking in the glory of her success.

The Man wiped his mouth, gazed out past the river, then back to the preacher. He said, "Why couldn't I go for golfing?"

"Different strokes," said the preacher, and he laughed again, once.

Darla opened her eyes and looked at them all.

Then the preacher swung his foot and caught Paul in the ribs. "Get up, morons," he said. He kicked Paul again.

Darla sat up immediately. Her mouth hung open, bad teeth showing. "What the hell are you doing?" she said. "What is the matter with you?"

Paul began to shake. He stood, and looked over at his torn underwear in the weeds. He glanced down at his exposed penis. With a surge of supreme humiliation, he covered himself with his hands.

"Thanks for saving the world," chuckled the preacher.

Darla jumped to her feet. "What the fuck's going on?" she screamed. She raised her hand to strike the preacher, but he caught it and twisted it. Darla dropped to her knees.

"I've got State of the Union tomorrow," the Man said to the preacher. "Teddy got off on hunting, Ronald on his horses. Sports just don't cut it for me. I have to have my stress release or who knows what wrong decisions I might make?"

The preacher said, "You don't have to convince me. I'm just happy to be part of the smooth running of the government. 'Remembreth me as thou dwelleth in thy kingdom.'" He smiled a chilling smile.

"Another go-round," said the Man. "Please. That would be good."

The preacher pulled a small pistol from his black jacket. His smile was gone, but in its place was not anger, just emotionless duty. "To the river," he said.

Darla was crying. She stayed on her knees until the preacher put the pistol to her head. "To the river," he said. "We don't have time for this shit."

Darla stood up beside Paul. The preacher led them to the river's edge. He took white strips of cloth from his pocket. He tightly gagged Darla's mouth. Then he gagged Paul.

"Silence of the lamb," said the preacher. "And the lion." He laughed.

Paul began to choke against the dry cloth. He could not swallow. He felt his nose could not take in enough air. Had the wars stopped? Had the peace come?

"Hands back," said the preacher.

Darla shook her head violently. The preacher put the mouth of the gun against her teeth and she stopped. She put her hands behind her back, and the preacher tied them with cloth. Then he looked at Paul.

Paul put his hands back.

"Good little lion," said the preacher, and he secured Paul's wrists. "You won't be shot, though. Morons drown so much more naturally."

There was a rumbling from the woods, and Paul looked behind to see a van moving out into the pasture. The Man stepped back to give it room. It stopped, and the engine was cut.

Darla's eyes widened in hope. Paul tried to stumble forward. Rescue, oh God, yes, thank God, thank God! He uttered a choked whine of agonized appeal.

The driver of the van swung out and around, then opened the sliding door on the side. Two blindfolded people climbed slowly into the daylight.

A young blindfolded man. A young blindfolded woman.

"They're going to save the world, too," said the preacher.

Ee-ii-ee-ii-oh, thought Paul.

The preacher baptized Darla and Paul in the brisk, running water of the river.

No Solicitors,
Curious a Quarter

Across the kitchen table from Chloe sat Nannie, her right hand holding a melamine cup full of hot tea, her gnarled left hand trembling on the surface of the table, stirring grains of salt and sugar into miniature whirlwinds. Afternoon sunlight strained through the dusty window, and June bugs hummed a relentless tune in the woods beyond the side yard. Nannie lifted the cup to her lips, the nubs of the missing two fingers of her right hand beating the air. The bandage on her left elbow had begun to ooze again. Brown and red stains bubbled up beneath the gauze.

The rotary fan on top of the refrigerator rattled as it moved back and forth. Nannie's smell wafted back and forth with the moving air.

"Stony say it's gonna make tumors," Chloe said. She held a cup of tea as well, although her cup was a fine piece of blue china, inherited from her mother. The steam drew a pink glow from her face. Although only seventeen, her hair was bound like her grandmother's. A handmade ragdoll sat in Chloe's big lap, its face flopped over. "Stony say you gotta stop."

Nannie swallowed, then looked at Chloe. There was kindness in her eyes. There was even kindness in her reprimand. "You do the embroidery?" Nannie asked. Chloe shook her head. "You do the needlepoint, and the dolls? Honey, you'll just never understand this. We won't never be rich, but we don't care. We make enough from the people that come and see. You seem to be eating fine. You's getting to be such a big girl."

Chloe's fingers played across her pudgy face, and then dropped to her big stomach.

"You're my girl," Nannie went on. "We'll be all right. Enough of Stony."

There was a click beetle on the floor beside Chloe's foot, and Chloe stepped on it with her toe. She held the doll's head down for it to see. "Bad old bug," she said. Then she said,

"Nannie, Stony said you being bad."

"Child," said Nannie. She put her cup down and swiped her lips. Some of the drips were wiped away, many were left. A small string of spit followed the hand down to the table. "You's simple, but I love you. Trust me. Them boys'll never have the best of me long as I live. You'll always be my girl who needs me and I'll do right by you."

Chloe was silent. She watched her grandmother pull herself up from the table to put the cups away. There was no telling Nannie what to do. Stony, Chloe's older brother, was always trying. He would continue to come over once a week after a day at the turkey plant and try to scold some sense into the old woman. It did no good. Nannie would tell Stony to go home to his wife and son and take care of them because she would be all right. Then Nannie would take the knife to her side again.

At the sink, Nannie braced herself and rinsed out the cups. It was hard for her to walk. She hadn't gotten used to hopping on one foot yet. One cup clattered as it slipped from Nannie's grasp. Chloe flinched, and grabbed the straps of her sleeveless sundress, her forearms coming up over her breasts. She said, "Break, Nannie?"

"Nah," Nannie said. "It was my cup. Plastic don't break like glass, honey."

"Oh," said Chloe.

"Goin' to the porch?" asked Nannie.

Chloe nodded and helped her grandmother out of the kitchen and down the short hall to the barren living room at the front of the house. The doll went, too, crammed under Chloe's unshaved armpit. A breeze blew through the screened door, lifting the stench of Nannie's wounds and making Chloe rub her nose with her free hand. Out on the porch, the fresh air made sitting next to Nannie more tolerable. Nannie sat on her chair, the wood barely giving under her wasted body. Chloe's chair creaked mightily.

"Want me to read you the funnies?" Nannie asked after Chloe had retrieved the folded VIRGINIAN DISPATCH from the base of the porch step.

Chloe shook her head. She sat the doll on her lap and stroked the yarn hair.

Nannie fumbled the newspaper open with the three fingers of her good hand. "Fine then. Don't forget to fix that sign 'fore you go on your walk," said Nannie. Chloe nodded. "And you'll watch out for boys?"

Chloe said, "Uh huh. But you got to tell me what letters to put on the sign."

Nannie smiled at her granddaughter. It was Nannie's great pleasure to take care of Chloe. Chloe had been twelve and Stony sixteen when their mother died, the result of massive head injuries after being struck by a pickup truck on the road outside their home. Stony inherited the old family car and the gun that belonged to his long-since-run-away father. Almost an adult then, Stony had said he was ready to be on his own. He secured a cheap room with a friend and a job plucking turkeys at Plenko Poultry. Chloe, who received her mother's set of china, an old collection of perfumes and Avon decanters, and a little pocket change, moved in with Nannie. She grew up at her grandmother's house, quiet and obedient. Each year school classified her as mentally deficient, and her absence was subsequently ignored when Nannie took Chloe out of school in the seventh grade.

The old woman and girl sat on their porch chairs, watching the road as no one came by, squinting until the sun was gone behind the clot of maples at the road's shoulder. Nannie sighed, then shifted down as if to fall asleep.

Chloe got the paint cans and the brush from inside the house and walked down the short graveled driveway to the large sandwich board sign. The sign was gritty and as worn as the siding on Nannie's house. The bottom of the wood was frayed like an old hula skirt.

Nannie's old sign had been painted over and over many times in the past weeks. Originally, large once-red letters proclaimed that here was "Blue Ridge Country Crafts." Ever since Chloe had lived with Nannie, Nannie had been a maker of crafts. She designed marvelous corn husk dolls and warm, thick quilts. The entire front living room had been Nannie's show place. Travelers from the Skyline Drive, looking for another isolated route to wherever they were heading, came down the mountain in all seasons, driving the hairpin turns and cracked pavement to view the forest in its fall-splashed or snow-shrouded beauty. At the bottom of the mountain, the road passed Nannie's house. Nannie would sit on the screenless porch, sunning her arms, waving a gaily painted fan and wearing a homemade bonnet. The travelers, intrigued, would stop by to chat. And to buy.

Money from the vacationers' purchases as well as a little Social Security had kept Nannie and Chloe in food, craft material, and heating oil.

Chloe stooped down and pried the top from the paint can.

She flicked a few chunks of dried paint from the bristles of the brush. She called for Nannie to wake up, it was time for the spelling. Then she began to work on the correction.

Three months earlier, on a cool spring evening, some local boys had come riding by Nannie's house. They were loud and drunk, hooting over the roar of their trucks and throwing empty liquor bottles to smash on the driveway. Nannie had been awake at that late hour, embroidering a tea towel in the living room. Chloe had been awake as well, lying in bed and counting the allowance savings she kept in a paper bag.

The boys had crashed into the house, breaking the simple hook lock Nannie had on the front door. Hearing the screams and the laughter, Chloe stayed behind her bed on the floor. The assault was quick. The boys grunted and howled; Nannie's demands that they leave were reduced to muffled screams. Two minutes later, it was over. When Chloe heard the boys head outside to their trucks, she got up from the floor and looked out of her bedroom door. When the trucks roared out to the road, throwing rocks in their hasty departure, she crept into the living room.

Nannie was on the floor on her side, her legs drawn up and her arm spasming. She was bleeding from holes in the left side of her body. The craft shelves were overturned, and the crafts lay among the blood and wreckage, a carnival of carnage, a slaughterhouse of Nannie's dreams.

Chloe fell beside her grandmother. "Who done this?"

Nannie's head moved slightly. Her eyes seemed almost ready to shake loose in their sockets. One went wall-eyed, and Chloe thought the eye would pop out.

"Want the doctor?"

Nannie shook her head. Blood pooled in her mouth, and she pushed it out with her swollen tongue.

Chloe stared at Nannie, and was silent. She was certain Nannie would die. Nannie's right ear had been torn from her head. Large hanks of hair had been ripped out, and numerous knife scars traveled the length of her left arm and her torso. Her leg was mauled. But the old woman weakly demanded that Chloe leave it be. She said she would mend at home.

And so Chloe put Nannie to bed in the back room. Nannie only lost consciousness once, when she was stitching herself up. Most of the time she slept or stared out of the window. Sometimes she had Chloe bring in the newspaper and hold it up so she could read it a little. Chloe changed bandages and kept the sign on the front door flipped to "Closed".

Chloe went on her walks when Nannie was asleep.

It was five days from the attack that Nannie got back on her feet. She asked for tea, and drank most of it, then pulled herself up on her good leg and said, "Enough of this. I got work to do." She limped into the kitchen and tried to butter some toast. The severed nerves in her hand would not allow it, so Chloe tried to butter it herself. Then Nannie went out into the living room to see what was left of her craft shop.

She stopped in the middle of the room, put her good hand to her mouth. She said, "Oh, Chloe."

The room was nearly empty. The boys had broken most of the crafts, and Chloe had swept them up and tossed them out. The shattered shelf boards lay on the floor and against the wall where they had fallen. Only a few button-eyed chickens still sat on the floor beneath the window, and painted brick doorstops lined the back wall. The braided rug had been thrown out with the ruined crafts, having been stained with Nannie's blood.

Nannie sat down then, fell actually, onto the bare floor. She hid her face in her good fist.

Then she said, "Chloe, you cleaned up. What a good girl. But you could have hurt yourself with the bits of glass and all those splinters."

Chloe said nothing.

Nannie sobbed a few silent tears, then said, "What am I going to do?"

"Make a craft, Nannie," Chloe offered.

Nannie shuddered, then her back went rigid. She sat up as straight as her damaged body would allow.

"You're right, honey. Get me some material from my trunk, and find my sewing kit. Bring them to me."

Nannie spent the next hour trying to thread a needle with her dead hand.

Then she tried to unhusk a dried cob for a doll's body.

She tried to dab paint onto a brick from the pile out back, to make a flowered stop. The paint fell in large blue droplets to the wood floor. She looked at the drops and took a shuddering breath. She said, "Chloe, this is a good time for you to go on your walk. Take a stick in case you see any boys."

Chloe took a stick on her walk, but she left it in the woods just past the side yard.

When Chloe returned, Nannie had made it into the kitchen. There was water on the floor where she had tried to fix tea, and a burned biscuit in the oven. Nannie was sitting at the table, with a knife in her hand. Chloe stood and waited for Nannie to say something.

"No more crafts," Nannie said, finally looking at her granddaughter. "Boys took it away from me. Stole it from me. Criminals, all of them."

Chloe was silent.

Nannie brushed bread crumbs from the kitchen table with the blade of the knife, and said, "We ain't gonna make no more money with the shop."

Chloe said nothing.

"Your granddaddy was alive he'd go after them boys. But we's just two women." She laughed. "An old crippled woman and a woman with a baby mind. But never you bother. Maybe we can't get them boys, and maybe that's for God, anyway, but I got an idea."

Chloe sat down and picked her doll from the chair beside her. She held it close to her bosom. "What idea, Nannie?"

Nannie smiled, only one side of her lip going up the right way. "Fix dinner, honey. I'll tell you how to do the stove if you're real careful."

Stony came over at seven thirty that evening, thanking God that Nannie was up again, and not unduly surprised that she would not be making crafts again. He sat with them on the porch, holding his ball cap in his hands and alternating his gaze from Nannie's bandaged wounds to a patch of poison ivy by the porch step.

"There's state aid," Stony said. "And I got a little saved up. You got Chloe here to keep the house, 'though God knows she ain't half as dumb as she puts on. You ought to put her to work somewheres, least ways part time. Then she could keep house in the evenings."

Nannie shook her head. Her hair had not been brushed in days. "You don't know nothing 'bout your sister. She's a poor child God gave a body and no brains. She got a home with me long as I live and I'll take care of her. I'm making a plan. Leave us be. Go home."

"Damn it, Nannie, you can't work no more. I brought money, and I want you to take it." Stony shoved one hand deep into his overall pocket, and pulled out a wad of dollar bills. His hand was dirty and trembling, his face was sweaty and tense.

Chloe said nothing.

"Don't 'barrass me now by dying of starvation. You're family. Take the damn money," said Stony.

"You never tried to help before this. Just you and yourself. Then you get married and you never come over to show me your wife or your baby. That's family, Stony? That's how family acts? Go home."

"Nannie, you make me look like a fool. Everybody at work asks how you are. I have to look at 'em and say, 'She can't work no more but she won't take money from me, and now she's gonna eat dog food and roots and shoe leather'? Take the money."

"Go home."

He went home, and Nannie sat on the porch for a long time, while Chloe played with her doll and caught lightning bugs in her fists.

The next morning, Chloe found Nannie down the gravel driveway on her face, a paint brush in one hand and blue paint bleeding into the coarse gray rocks. Chloe pulled Nannie up with much effort, but the old woman's face, though stone-bruised, was smiling.

"What'cha happy about?" Chloe asked.

Nannie pointed at the old sandwich board sign by the road. Large, runny blue letters were painted in bold strokes over the faded "Blue Ridge Country Crafts." The new sign read, "Victim of Violent Crime. No Solicitors, Curious a Quarter."

Chloe shook her head. "What's that say?"

Nannie's smile did not fade. She tapped the bandages on her left arm, and on her hip beneath her cotton dress. "Crime gonna pay this

135

time, honey. It's gonna pay for us."

On the way back into the house for breakfast, Nannie flipped the "Closed" sign on the door back over to "Open."

At first nobody came. Nannie told Chloe the local folks were not ones to peek too soon, but after a few days there was a trickling of women and men and children, slipping up the driveway and coming hesitantly to the door. The first of the curious pretended to be on church work, bringing along homemade pies and fried chicken. They were anxious to see, but didn't want to appear anxious. The hands which held the pies and chickens were sweaty hands, and the pockets on those dresses and trousers were full of quarters.

Nannie sat on a stuffed chair in her living room where once her dolls and toys had sat. She wore a loose skirt and blouse. When the quarter was dropped into a can by the door, Chloe would pull up Nannie's blouse and the curious would ooh and ahh at the ragged, red scars of Nannie's violent crime. After an uneasy start, the flow became steady for more than a week. People came and paid, acting as though they were embarrassed to be there, making Nannie promise not to tell anyone about their visit, hurrying down to their cars as if they were afraid they would be seen and chastised. Everyone wanted to see; no one wanted anyone to know they wanted to see.

Chloe took the money on her walks. She would be gone a while, and would pick up groceries on her way home. Half of the time she bought what Nannie had asked her to buy, the other half she got an odd assortments of pretty shapes and brightly colored boxes and cans. She and Nannie ate well.

Then the money slowed and nearly stopped. Nannie's scars weren't so bad anymore. Kids even scowled and rolled their eyes after they saw what their school lunch quarters had bought them.

So Nannie gave the proof of her assault a little boost.

With a keen kitchen knife, she opened several of the healed wounds, making them a bit bigger than they originally were, and the curious came round again. Nannie upped the price to fifty cents, and displayed the red, draining cuts to those who would make crime pay.

Chloe watched the money clank into the can, and she helped Nannie undo her blouse and lift her skirt. In the late afternoons she took her walks. And after supper she sat and played with her doll while Nannie put on the nighttime dressings.

When Nannie took off her first finger, Stony was back in a rage. He would not come up on the porch, but stood at the bottom of the front stoop steps and shook a fist at the woman and the girl.

"You's crazy! No wonder Chloe ain't right upstairs, she got it from you."

"Go home, Stony," said Nannie.

"They are talking 'bout you at work now. You're the bathroom talk, Nannie. You're the lunch room talk! You can't do this to yourself. Take some money. I can't handle this shame."

Nannie licked her lips and patted Chloe's face with a four-fingered hand. "Go home, Stony. We don't need you."

"There's openings out at the turkey plant. Let Chloe come work there. She might be crazy but she ain't dumb like you think she is, Nannie. She's fooling you in a big way."

"She can't, Stony. Don't fool yourself. Go home."

"And why the hell's she getting so fat these days? She got bad glands or something? Won't take yourself to the doctor, won't take her, either, I guess."

"We's eating good," said Nannie. "Chloe's just a healthy girl. Go home."

"You pregnant, Chloe?"

Nannie's good hand shot out and cracked her grandson on the side of the face. "You speak trash on my porch?"

Stony almost exploded. "You ain't my family!"

"I always knew that. Go home."

Stony went home.

And so it went. Nannie cut herself in the daytime, while Chloe held a cloth to catch the blood and sometimes put a rag in Nannie's teeth so she wouldn't groan so loudly. At night, Nannie wrapped herself up so as not to bleed to death.

Stony didn't come back when Nannie took off another finger, nor did he show up when all the left toes came off. Nannie upped the price to seventy five cents. The locals knew it meant more gore, and coins filled the bucket again with new fervor.

"What's a 'r' look like, Nannie, I forgot," called Chloe from the sign.

Nannie made broad strokes in the air to show her granddaughter. "Take your time, now, you'll get it."

Chloe put the paint brush to the sign and formed a lopsided 'r'. Then she sat back and painted the length of her forearm with the paint. She held it up to show Nannie. "Pretty!" she shouted.

"Chloe, honey, now you got to wash that all off."

Chloe brought the can and paint brush to the stoop.

"All done," she said to the doll on the porch floor.

"That sign looks right nice all done over again," said Nannie, raising her one good hand and squinting out at the sandwich board. "Now with me asking a dollar, they'll know they got some real crime to look at."

Chloe sat on the stoop and rubbed the doll's face in the paint on her arm.

Nannie turned awkwardly in her chair. Severe shadows shadows cut down the side of her face. She stroked her throat and pulled at the wrinkles. She leaned over and pulled at the end of the sock on her left foot. The sock was orange with drainage. "Threads catching on them gone toes," Nannie said. "Ought to get me a prop-up chair."

"Nannie, Stony says I crazy like you."

"Stony don't know crazy," said Nannie. "You and me, we's just practical. Give me a hug."

Chloe leaned into the rancid dress and gave her Nannie a hug.

Nannie sat back. She said, "Stony tells me you can do more than I think you can. In a way, he's right."

Chloe put some of the yarn doll hair into her mouth to suck. She strummed the now-blue doll's face.

"I know you can do many things. You can help me move 'round the house. You help me do a little cooking in the kitchen. You paint the signs for me, don't think I don't love you for it. But there is something else . . ." Nannie's voice trailed. Chloe licked the palm of her hand, and watched her grandmother.

"Want you to do my eyes," said Nannie.

Chloe blinked, and rubbed her own.

"I can hold still I think. If I cry don't stop." Nannie scratched at a curly eyebrow hair. Then she took a butter knife from her skirt pocket. "Dull one'll do better."

Chloe flinched and she drew back from the knife offered in her direction.

"George Stewart lost a thumb in his thresher last Thursday," said Nannie, her voice thoughtful and sad. "Mrs. Stewart told me when she come 'round with her money. Ain't nothing to see gone fingers now."

Chloe squinched her nose and shook her head.

"Honey, crime got to pay. We got to eat."

"How I do it?" asked Chloe.

"Just a little twist, like scooping oleo margarine from the tub."

Chloe put her doll down. She gingerly took the knife.

"Like oleo?"

"Yes," said Nannie. She leaned over to Chloe and kissed her on the forehead. "I'm the tub, honey."

Chloe licked the knife once, for luck, she told Nannie.

Stony thundered into the living room, knocking over the can and spilling all the change. Coins rolled in a flurry through the dust bunnies on the floor. Chloe ran around behind Nannie's stuffed chair. She grabbed her stomach with one hand and the top of Nannie's head with the other.

Nannie, on her chair, buttons of her blouse almost all done back up but all done wrong, straightened and snorted.

"You!" Stony screeched, and stopped dead in his tracks when he saw the crusted holes where the eyes had been. "Oh, my God, you've really blinded yourself. I prayed the folks at the plant were lying to me, trying to get my goose for all this nonsense!"

"Weren't lying," said Nannie. "Chloe done it for me. Guess you was right, she can do some things."

Chloe looked around the back of the chair. Stony glared down at her. His face was red and his ears were sweating. He pointed his finger at Chloe. "You little bitch! How could you do this?"

"Don't talk like that in my house. She's my family. I asked her to do my eyes," said Nannie.

"And you're crazy!" shouted Stony. He spun on his heel and picked up the empty coin can. He shook it in Nannie's face, but her empty sockets could not see. "I ought to put you out of your misery. It would put me out of mine!"

"Go home, Stony," said Nannie.

"Home," said Chloe.

Stony hurled the empty coin can to the floor, and it bounced loudly. He clawed at his face. "How can I stand this? They didn't give me the promotion I was gonna get, since they said you is nuts. Said it must run in the family. It ain't fair. I gotta ruin my life for my crazy grandma!"

"Show Stony the door, Chloe," said Nannie.

Stony stood stock still, with nothing but his eyelids twitching. Then he reached into his jacket and took out out his pistol.

"I can't ruin my life for no crazy woman," he said. His eyes teared up, and he blinked the tears away.

"Chloe, honey, you hear what I said?" said Nannie.

"Show Stony the door."

Chloe stood up slowly. She and Stony stared at each other. Chloe held up her doll, and showed her brother. The doll's eyes were dug out.

"Christ Jesus," said Stony. He aimed the pistol at Nannie's head.

Chloe reached out for Nannie, and patted her arm. She did not look away from Stony. "I love my Nannie," said Chloe.

The pistol began to shake in Stony's grip.

Chloe leaned down and kissed her grandmother's mangled left hand.

"It's a sin!" Stony cried. "It's a sin! Goddam it, you witch, won't you stop this?" And he dropped the pistol. He turned, and holding his throat, stumbled through the door. The screen clapped behind him. He stopped on the stoop and put his face into his hands.

"Stony gone, honey?" asked Nannie.

"Yeah, Nannie," said Chloe. She picked up the pistol and held it to Nannie's temple. "He's all gone."

She bent to kiss the hand again, and then pulled the trigger.

Nannie's eyeless head jerked and fell forward. Blood spattered Chloe's hand, her face, the stuffed chair, and the doll tucked under Chloe's arm. The red was hot and thick, like paint on the sandwich board. The wound was round, like Nannie's empty eye sockets. Chloe licked the blood from her hand. She licked the barrel of the pistol.

"For luck," she said.

"Oh, Chloe," whimpered Stony from the stoop.

Chloe looked out the screen door. Her brother was pressed against the screen like a monkey caged in an outdoor zoo. His face was a mask of disbelief; his eyes white and huge.

"Chloe," he said again.

Chloe put the gun back on the floor. Then she crossed the bloody floor to the door and put her hand flat against the screen where Stony's face was pressed. "Nannie hated them boys," she said.

Stony closed his eyes.

"But I like boys. Like 'em for a long time. Since before Mama died. Mama didn't like me to see boys, but I did. Seen 'em on my walks a lot. Boys is pretty. They say pretty things."

"Chloe, you ain't dumb. You never was dumb."

"They give me pretty things, Stony. Things Mama never give me. Things Nannie never give me."

"Mama?"

"Boys do things for me if I give 'em my pussy. They call it that. Pussy! Like a cat!"

"Mama," whispered Stony. "Oh dear God."

145

"They didn't do just what they said, though. Not this time. Not like Mama. Nannie didn't die."

Stony looked at Chloe. Her lopsided smile was coated in blood.

"Bad Stony, you killed her."

"Chloe, you can't do that to me." Stony choked, and looked at the gun on the floor. "Chloe, I tried to help you!"

"And you give me a baby." Chloe rolled the palm of her hand around on her bulge. "Bad boy."

Stony said, "You wouldn't do that, Chloe."

Chloe chuckled. She tore the head off of her ragdoll and went over to Nannie's chair, where she dropped it onto her dead grandmother's lap. When she turned around, Stony could see her face clearly. She was silent.

And her smile was no longer lopsided.

The sale of Nannie's house made a nice profit for Chloe.

The money was put into a bank, and because of the trauma Chloe had survived, it was a flexible trust which allowed her to buy something nice when she wanted it. Stony was put away where the sun don't shine, promised a life sentence and lots of attention from muscular men who liked to do a little turkey plucking themselves. Stony's wife and child moved away.

Chloe was taken in by a charitable, elderly widow who had once brought canned peaches on pretense of seeing the marks of a violent crime. After all, it was not Chloe who was insane, it had been her grandmother, and her brother. Chloe was a poor child, with hardly a thought in her head. At her new home, Chloe played and ate and listened to the widow chat about church meetings and the neighbors. When the widow didn't know, Chloe handled the pretty glassware in the pie safe and played with the silver hidden in the cellar trunk.

When the baby came, Chloe gave it up to the state and didn't even cry.

"She's can't keep a baby," said the widow to the nurses.

"It's not that she's crazy, she's just slow as snail in the sun."

Chloe was quiet and obedient.

And in the early spring, she began taking long walks again.

Meat

'Though there were none there, the stench of animals in the basement was overpowering. Rodney Stewart stood at the bottom of the steps with one hand in his coat pocket, one hand holding his note pad. Beside him, Mrs. Brezeski clutched her elbows.

"What do you think, Mr. Stewart?" she asked. Her eyebrows, as fluffy and white as her slippers, went up and down over her eyes like caterpillars trying to escape.

"Don't know," said Rodney. And he didn't. Not only did he not know what the smell was, he didn't care what it was. This was not in his line of investigations. He was an adultery man. He thought his cards were clear enough for any fool to know that.

"I didn't call exterminators because they use chemicals, you know?" said Mrs. Brezeski. "Chemicals that can kill you. They poke around and spray and that stuff will kill you deader than a doornail. And so I called you. You're a private investigator. I don't think private investigators use chemicals, do they?"

"No, we don't."

Mrs. Brezeski scratched her elbows and shifted in her white slippers. Her wrinkled face twitched in the poor basement light. "I've only lived here a few months," she said. "This building was abandoned a couple of years then the owner fixed it up for us old people. Nice idea, yes, that was nice for him to do. I was hired as the building supervisor. But I live on the first floor as you know. And we got those old coal chutes. I started smelling something from out of that chute."

"This building used to house several businesses," said Rodney. He knew, because he'd actually been born in this building. He had been educated in local schools, and now lived down a block in a renovated boxcar apartment. Many of his family members had worked in the businesses in this building, for a number of generations past. Rodney's father, his grandfather, his great-grandfather, who had started his shoe shop on the second floor right after the building had been constructed. Rodney himself had played as a child in this very basement. As teenagers, he and his brother Joe had lost their virginity to schoolmates down here. There were a lot of memories in this musty place.

His little niece had accidentally been born in this building, too soon to make it to the hospital. And his own father had died here.

"Yes," said Mrs. Brezeski. "A fish market. A butcher shop." The building owner said the shops closed down last year. I'm new here. I'm still learning. Yes, there were businesses." Her face was intent, as if Rodney's comment would lead to a clue.

"But you won't call an exterminator?"

"I've got to be careful of toxins. Not just for me. But I'm the building supervisor. There are children that visit grandparents on the second floor, you know."

Rodney sighed. He put his note pad in his pocket.

"Probably dead rats," he said. "Stuck up in the walls. It'll go away with time. Unless you want to knock down the walls and get 'em out."

"Heavens, no! We'd cave in."

Rodney turned to go up the steps.

"Now don't you run off and leave me alone down here!" the old woman said. "You wait and walk up with me. I don't like being in the basement alone. There might be drug dealers."

"Drug dealers?"

"Hiding in the basement, waiting for me."

Rodney tried not to grin at that. "It's most likely rats," he said. "And there's nothing I can do."

"Hmmm," said Mrs. Brezeski. "Rats. I thought it might be . . ." She hesitated, pinching her nose. "Remember John Wayne Gacy? And Jeffrey Dahmer? The smell made me think that maybe . . ."

"Buried people?" Rodney laughed then, and walked up a few stairs. "I hardly think so."

"You're a man of the law, Mr. Stewart. You know about these things."

"I'm a private detective, Mrs. Brezeski. I specialize in surveillance. Just because I live down the street and therefore I'm handy doesn't mean I'm Colombo."

"Colombo?" Mrs. Brezeski fell in behind Rodney, and the two climbed to the top of the steps. Rodney shut the door.

"On T.V.," said Rodney. Don't old people watch reruns anymore? he thought.

Rodney walked the short hall to the foyer, then stepped out onto the stoop. Outside, the air was heavy with carbon monoxide and the screams of children and automobile engines. A cold fall breeze cut down the street, carrying with it some stray brown leaves from somewhere. Mrs. Brezeski held the door open behind Rodney, her sagging face peering out through the small crack. "How about meat?" she asked.

Rodney lit a cigarette; tossed the match to the wind.

"Meat?"

"Old meat, maybe left over from the butcher shop. Old meat in the basement somewhere?"

"Rats," he said. "Get an exterminator or you'll just have to wait until they decay to dust."

"Hmmm," said Mrs. Brezeski, but Rodney didn't wait long enough for her to finish her thought. He hit the sidewalk and drew on his cigarette, heading toward home and wondering how much of a bill Mrs. Brezeski would be willing to pay for his twenty minute visit.

Rodney dropped down onto his old plaid sofa and picked up the phone receiver. He punched the number of his sister-in-law, Annie. From a paper towel on the end table, he picked up the slice of soggy, microwaved pizza and took a big bite. He settled against the lumpy sofa back and waited for the phone to begin ringing.

Being a private investigator was a major step above Rodney's last occupation. He had been a security man at the U-Store-It warehouses. Late night. Rain and snow and all the same shit a mail carrier went through, but for a lot less bucks. Rodney had tried investigating tentatively at first; he'd run an ad in the local newspaper. "Private Investigator will help locate missing persons or locate information pertinent to personal relationships." He'd had Annie, who had been a teacher for ten years, help him come up with the word "pertinent."

He kept the security job, but actually had several calls on cases. These had been easy; mostly chasing around cheating husbands and wives and then dropping photos and lists of addresses into the hands of the one who had employed him. Then, a wealthy woman from the east side of town had paid Rodney to find out recent filth on a city politician. That, too, had not been all that hard. She had been thrilled with the dirt, and had rewarded Rodney with several thousand more than he had expected.

So Rodney quit the U-Store-It. After all, Rodney was a proud Stewart. Stewarts had always been independent people. Sooner or later, they took care of their problems with no help from anyone else, thank you very much.

He was feeling good. He was feeling young and sharp.

He started needing a good woman.

Annie's husband Joe, Rodney's younger brother, had left Annie for another woman not a month earlier. Annie hadn't been particularly concerned; after all, Joe Stewart was one violent son of a bitch. For a week, Rodney was afraid Annie was going to ask him to do some private snooping to bring him back, but she didn't. She sighed heavily, lit a candle in church to appear concerned, and then tossed out her husband's clothes and bought some new furniture for the bedroom.

Annie answered on the fifth ring.

"Annie, Rodney." Rodney swallowed the bite of pizza.

"Got plans for tonight?"

Annie giggled lightly on the other end of the line.

Rodney could see her, her small body draped in a sheer negligee. Even at fifty-two, she had a body he would kill for. She lived in the building he had just left, the building with

Mrs. Brezeski-The-Wonderful Supervisor. But Rodney never dropped in unannounced; he didn't want to seem overly attentive or interested. So, the gentleman detective that he was, he called first.

"No, not really," said Annie. "I had a Stouffer's in the oven. I was going to watch *Millionaire* on T.V."

"I see."

"Do you have a case tonight?"

Rodney grinned. He still liked the sound of that. A case. Just like Dick Tracy. James Bond. A Man From U.N.C.L.E. "Not tonight. Got a night off for once."

"That's nice."

"Would you like to go out for dessert? It's too cold for ice cream, but I was thinking a nice warm cider and some muffins from the Pratt's Bakery would be good."

"Hmmm," said Annie. "Well, I suppose that would be very nice. Let me dress. When should I expect you?"

"Half hour?"

"That should do it. Oh, jimminy."

"What's that?"

"Mrs. Brezeski downstairs. She's screaming at someone. A child, I think. She has a voice that will strip wall paper."

"I met her," said Rodney. He suddenly wondered if Annie would be peeved that he had come by the building and not dropped in. "She called me on a case. Hah, not a case. She thinks Jeffrey Dahmer hid chopped-up people in the basement. I think it's dead rats."

"Rats," said Annie. "There is a stench; I smell it coming up through the holes around my radiator. So you think it's rats, do you?"

Rodney shrugged, then felt stupid as Annie could not see the gesture. "What else?"

"She's a funny woman, Mrs. Brezeski. From up north. She doesn't fit in well here."

"No," said Rodney. "Half hour, then?"

"I'll be ready."

Rodney hung up the phone. He took the rest of the wilting pizza with both hands and licked dripping tomato paste from his wrists.

Two days later, Annie called Rodney. He was his on the way out the door, coat over his arm, beer in hand. He grunted and caught the receiver.

"I'm on my way out the door, what do you want?"

The voice on the line was strained, and Rodney was instantly embarrassed. "Rodney, this is Annie."

"Oh, sorry," Rodney said. Beer caught in his windpipe. He spit what he could out onto the floor. "What's up? Delayed poison symptoms from Pratt's?"

"What?" said Annie, then, catching the weak stab at humor, said, "Oh. Ha. No, nothing like that. It's Mrs. Brezeski. She has been worse than usual the past couple of days. She stays at her door, grabbing everyone she can to take them into her room to sniff at her coal chute. Even the mailman. She asks them what they think the smell is. I tell you, I hate coming and going now. I've been in her apartment three times to sniff her chute. What does she want me to do? I think she's lost it. She should go back to wherever up north she came from. I'm not the only tenant who feels this way. But nobody will go down and check for her. They don't like her. They think she has too much power as supervisor as it is."

"Uh-huh," said Rodney. He put the beer can down on the doorside table and took a deep breath. "I'm just a detective. What do you want me to do?"

"I don't know. Well, yes I do. Why don't you come over and pretend to find out what the matter is. Bring in something that smells, a dead cat or dog, something really ripe. Hide it in the basement. Then find it and clear it out. At least that would satisfy her for a short while. Maybe that would give the real smell time to fade away. Smells do fade away, don't they?"

"I don't know. I used to work with a guy named Simon. He smelled all the time. His smell never faded away."

"I don't mean living things," said Annie. "Horses always smell, I suppose. I mean decaying things. They can't smell forever, can they?"

Rodney didn't know. He wasn't a scientist. In the right conditions, maybe smells could stay forever. He said, "I don't think so."

"Well, then, find a dead dog. There have to be dead ones lying around in an alley somewhere. Bring it over and then find it. Okay?"

Rodney picked up his beer can and took a long swig.

"Sure," he said.

"Mrs. Brezeski," called Rodney from the basement of the apartment building. "Could you come down here?"

Annie stood with Rodney on the cold concrete floor near the back wall. The light was poor, and the shadows cast on the walls huge and distorted. Spiders pattered in corners. Annie and Rodney waited. Again, Rodney called, "Mrs. Brezeski, please come down here into the basement."

Mrs. Brezeski obviously heard the second call, and in a moment her footsteps hit the old cellar stairs. Rodney looked at Annie and winked. Annie tried not to laugh at him.

"Who is it," Mrs. Brezeski said, staring into the shadows at the back of the basement. "Mr. Stewart, is that you?"

"Yes," said Rodney. "I decided to do a little detective work, after all. I've heard you've been quite concerned. Please come over."

Mrs. Brezeski stopped four steps away from the base of the stairs, blinking in the yellow light. Her eyebrows twitched.

"Mr. Stewart?"

Rodney said, "Yes, it's me, not a drug dealer. I've found your problem."

Annie stuck a knuckle into Rodney's ribs, trying not to laugh. Rodney found it surprisingly titillating.

"Come see," he said.

"There are cracks," Mrs. Brezeski said. She sniffed.

"I'll twist my ankle."

"It's safe," said Rodney. "Annie's here, too. We both are fine."

Mrs. Brezeski took a step closer. The light flowed down over her shoulders and back, ending in a pool on the floor. Her face was in darkness. "Annie?"

"Annie Stewart. Second floor. Apartment above yours," said Annie.

"Oh," said Mrs. Brezeski. "All right then. Have you got a flashlight?"

"No. Straight ahead," said Rodney.

Mrs. Brezeski nodded. Tapping her feet before her like a tight rope walker, she moved toward Annie and Rodney at the back wall.

When she was within touching distance, her foot went down and her mouth flew open, making a wide, dark hole in the dark, stinking basement.

"Watch it there," said Rodney. "It's a pretty foul mess."

Mrs. Brezeski's mouth hung open, then snapped shut.

When it opened again, a guttural squawk came out.

"It was behind the crates here," said Annie. "Not far from the coal chute. It's sad, actually."

"Oh," came a strangled cough. The old woman moved back a step, slowly, as though a string of gum were caught on her shoe. But it was not gum. "Oh!" she screamed. The dog entrails, tacky with days-old blood and decay, looked in the shadows to be an old jump rope, coiled and frayed, left unloved in a subterranean store room.

"It was meat," Rodney said. "After all."

"Obviously not from the old butcher shop upstairs," added Annie.

Mrs. Brezeski reeled backward, jumping out of her shoe and spinning on a dime. She retched and heaved as she clamored up the stairs, one shoe clapping, one stocking-foot slapping.

Rodney laughed and crossed his arms. Annie smiled and wrinkled her nose at the maggoty dog.

"Best get that out now," she said. "It really is rank."

Rodney used a coal shovel to scoop the dog remains back into the trash bag he had dumped it from. He hauled the bag to the bottom of the steps.

"Rodney," said Annie from the blackness by the back wall.

Rodney went back and Annie caught him in a tight embrace. She kissed his lips fully, moving her mouth against his in slow, sensual circles.

Lifting his head to catch his breath, he said, "This is the kind of payment a detective prefers."

"Maybe she'll lay off the worrying now," said Annie.

Rodney put his face next to Annie and sniffed the perfumed shampoo of her hair. Then his nose wrinkled.

"But there still is a bad smell down here," he said.

"Hmm?" Annie nuzzled her forehead on his chest.

"It still smells down here, from over here. It isn't the dog."

Annie said, "Let's go to my apartment."

Rodney moved in with Annie. Not officially; most of his clothes and valuables, such as they were, remained in his other apartment down the street. But he began to spend nights at Annie's. He ate meals with her. The ease surrounding this change surprised him; never had a woman been more accommodating or so accepting.

He was falling in love.

Five days after the dog trick, and four days after he began staying with Annie, Mrs. Brezeski was at it again.

"Come in and smell down that hole," she fired at anyone who entered the threshold of the building. "There's a smell, you wouldn't believe."

Annie was furious.

"People used to ride other people out of town on a rail when they caused trouble," she said at supper, across the small wooden table from Rodney. "Tar and feather her, something. What do you think?"

"I don't know," said Rodney. "She's harmless. Everyone ignores her, as they should."

"I don't think so. Lucas next door said she's going to hire a private building inspector and let him chip around down there."

"I'm surprised she didn't do that in the first place."

"You want her to?"

"Should I care?"

Annie was quiet for a moment. She put her head down on her arms and sighed, heavily. Then she said, "Joe's down there."

Rodney dropped the chicken from his fork. "Joe?"

Annie lifted her head. Her eyes were pinched. She stared at the curtains over the kitchen window. "He's poisoned. He's down in the cellar. I sealed him up. But not so good now, I think."

Rodney sat, mouth wide.

"It's so wet. I think he's festering. It's not sanitary, like a good grave. Rodney?"

Rodney felt his cheeks hitch as a grin pulled at the corners of his mouth.

"Rodney, why are you smiling?"

"Truly a Stewart," Rodney said.

"What?" Annie's eyes were tight, like she wanted to be angry.

Rodney said, "Come to the basement with me."

*   *   *

He took a flashlight this time. He stuck it in his back pocket where it poked out like a bold tumor. He and Annie snuck down to the first floor, Rodney holding his hand up so they would not catch the attention of Mrs. Brezeski. It was just after seven. The sounds of *INSIDE EDITION* came, muffled, from under Mrs. Brezeski's closed door.

Rodney and Annie went down the basement steps. Once down, Rodney clicked on the flashlight and said, "I love you, you know."

Annie, looking unsure, was silent. The two went to the rear wall.

"Why are we here?" Annie asked. "I can't undo what I've done."

"I don't ask you to," said Rodney. "I want to show you something, that's all."

Rodney shown the light along the stretch of concrete wall. There were many cracks in the foundation, connecting and spiraling outward from each other like spider webs. Rodney walked carefully, watching. Then he stopped, and shown the light down on the concrete floor.

"Here," he said.

Annie looked down. There was some graffiti in the concrete, something a child would have down when the place was still setting. A simple, smiling face, drawn with a finger. A hand print.

"Look different from most concrete floors?"

"Well . . ." said Annie. She looked closer, moving the flashlight. The hard surface did not really match the floor out near the steps. In its dirtiness, it still was whiter.

"It looks newer here," said Annie.

Rodney nodded. He stooped down and pulled a pocket knife out of his shirt. He flicked open the blade and began picking at the palm print in the concrete. Flakes of flooring came up.

"Plaster of Paris," Rodney said.

After a minute, something straight and thin began to show.

Like a careful archeologist, Rodney chipped at the concrete. The white thing elongated. Annie recognized a dull, white finger bone.

"My dad," said Rodney. "He was a violent bastard. The old flooring comes out in easy chunks with a hammer. A quick hole in the dirt beneath and in went dad. Plaster of Paris sealed it off."

"You killed him?"

"Joe and me."

Annie stared at the finger bone.

Rodney snapped the knife shut, then shone the flashlight along the base of the wall. There were patches in the floor, now obvious to Annie.

"My grandfather is in one of these. My Aunt Marcie, a bitch, in another. Grandma Arnold got her with a poker, so I was told. There's a crooked policeman down here somewhere, from 1934. Stewarts are independent. We take care of our own problems."

Annie said, "Oh, I see."

"Joe near the chute?"

"In a wooden box. I covered it with old dry wall sheets."

"No good, it'll leak for sure. I'll help you redo if you'd like."

Annie nodded. Rodney caught her around the waist and pulled her close. "I want you, now," he whispered into her neck. Colombo, Kojak, Hunter, Magnum, eat your hearts out.

"Who's down here?" called Mrs. Brezeski from midway down the basement steps. Rodney and Annie jumped apart and stared in her direction.

"Who's down here? I'll have the cops, I swear I will."

Annie looked down at the chipped plaster and the small white finger bone. She looked up at Rodney.

"You do Joe," she said softly. "Show me how." She reached for Rodney's pocket knife. "Show me how, Rodney. I'll watch."

Rodney whispered, "I love you."

Annie said, "Then I'll be a Stewart. I'll take care of this other problem by myself."

Rodney let her pull the knife from his grasp. Annie flicked the blade open. It threw blackened sparks against the back wall.

M is for the Many Things

Mother was dying. Her forehead was splotched and red, and her hair was brittle and dry on the pillow. She sweated without relief, her body like a huge hot cloud on a summer's day, raining steadily, the water collecting in the creases of her flesh and dripping to the folds of the sheet beneath her. The sweat smelled of Vick's Vap-O-Rub, and the soiled linens, piled in the corner of Mother's room, added a scent of urine and diarrhea. It was Barbara's job to do the linens, but they were dirtied so quickly now that she had a hard time keeping up.

Grace, feeling ill herself, dabbed Mother's body with the edge of a towel. Mother's

Join the Leisure Horror Book Club and

GET 2 FREE BOOKS NOW—
An $11.98 value!

— Yes! I want to subscribe to —
the Leisure Horror Book Club.

Please send me my **2 FREE BOOKS**. I have enclosed $2.00 for shipping/handling. Each month I'll receive the two newest Leisure Horror selections to preview for 10 days. If I decide to keep them, I will pay the Special Members Only discounted price of just $4.25 each, a total of $8.50, plus $2.00 shipping/handling. This is a **SAVINGS OF AT LEAST $3.48** off the bookstore price. There is no minimum number of books I must buy and I may cancel the program at any time. In any case, the **2 FREE BOOKS** are mine to keep.

— *Not available in Canada.* —

NAME: _____
ADDRESS: _____
CITY: _____ STATE: _____
COUNTRY: _____ ZIP: _____
TELEPHONE: _____
E-MAIL: _____
SIGNATURE: _____

breathing had been labored for two days. She was dying. The sense of impending loss and despair roiled in Grace's bowels. Emotions of which she could make no sense were tangled in her chest, causing her lungs to hurt. She shuddered, and wiped the length of Mother's collarbone.

Greg, Grace's brother, came into the room. He stepped lightly on his bare feet, and sat beside Grace on a low chair. Grace gave him the towel. He dabbed Mother's arm. He said nothing. Grace knew he was waiting for her to decide if she could talk about this, or wanted to leave it in silence.

Pain squeezed Grace's vocal cords, and she said, "How can I bear this?"

Greg didn't look at Grace, nor touch her. None of the brothers and sisters knew how to comfort each other. That was Mother's duty. He lifted Mother's massive hand and gently dabbed the moist places between each finger. Then he said, "Stay strong if you can. I've been through this before, and I know what I'm saying. Stay strong."

Grace swallowed, and it hurt.

"Why don't you go to dinner?" Greg said. He put Mother's hand down, then wiped her breast. "I'll take my turn. Mary has made a nice stew. She's upset that no one was on time to the dining hall tonight."

Grace closed her eyes. Several heavy tears joined the sweat on the bed. Then she rose and left the room.

Outside the door, Grace slipped on her clothes and stepped into her shoes. She walked along the hall to the top of the staircase, passing the two open doors of the girls' rooms, and the closed door of the nursery. A soft squeak emanated from behind the nursery door, and Grace let her hand touch the wood briefly as she went by. It was Grace's job to do the hourly feeding, but it was only six thirty. From below was the bland aroma of Mary's cooking, and the sound of Eldon buffing the living room floor.

At the top of the stairs, Grace's kitten lay in a weak ball. Grace picked it up and squeezed it tightly. It was a shame; this kitty was no good. It had been a nice, healthy animal when Grace had found it in the back yard, but now it was thin and weak and its fur was coming out. Just like all the other kittens Grace had tried to keep as pets. They had been playful and cute and full of energy. Then they each got sick and died. Grace had loved them greatly. And they all died.

Suddenly, Grace was flushed with the need to go back to Mother. She dropped the kitten and grabbed the top of the banister, her jaws clenching. Then the sensation passed. Greg was with Mother, it was his turn. And Grace did need to eat. It was almost twenty minutes past dinner time.

Downstairs, Mary stood in the dining hall, arms crossed, bushy eyebrows a furious dragon across the top of her face. She was the oldest of the children, nearly thirty nine. She was usually the cook, and always the assigner of chores. She was the rememberer of the rules and the doler of punishments. Mary was the only one of the children to have a room to herself. No one argued with Mary; they complained about her under their breaths at work or in the darkness on their cots at night.

"You're last," Mary told Grace. "You'll have dish duty, then."

Grace said, "That's all right." She slumped to her assigned seat at the long wooden table, poured herself a glass of milk from the carton, and picked up her spoon.

Mary took up a rumpled cotton napkin and looked at it steadily, then sat down across from Grace. "How is Mother?"

"The same."

Mary sighed. "Maybe I'll help you with the dishes," she said. "It will keep me from thinking."

Grace ate a piece of carrot. It caught in her throat.

171

"I wish I'd had time in the infirmary, Mary. Don't you? Maybe then we would know what to do."

Mary shook her head. "Nobody worked in the infirmary, and you don't wish you had. It was bad in there, a lot of sickness we could have caught. Don't you remember Celia Duncan? She died in the infirmary, Grace. Some awful disease. They were right not to let us in there unless we were sick ourselves."

Grace nodded and chewed a bit of cubed beef. Mary cooked just as good as Mrs. Griffith used to. But tonight the food seemed to have no taste.

"You've only been with us a year," said Mary. She paused, then scratched her graying hair. The sound of the buffer stopped, and there was the bumping and scraping as Eldon put the machine back into the front hall closet. "You'll be all right."

Grace wiped her mouth on the cloth napkin and put it back into her lap. "You don't have to help me with dishes."

"Suit yourself."

"Who has devotions tonight?"

"Paul."

"I don't think I can eat all this."

"You don't eat it you get no snack."

Grace sighed and brought another spoonful of stew to her lips. Eldon came into the dining hall. He was just three years Mary's junior, but appeared much older. He was skinny and ugly, with ears that pointed forward like fleshy megaphones and white hair shaved close to his bony head.

"Whole downstairs is done," he announced. There was a pride in his voice. "Could skate on it. Could see your own face if you looked close enough. But I won't be doing upstairs . . ." He trailed, then blinked and looked away from Mary and Grace. "Could I at least buff the nursery?" he asked softly.

"No," said Mary.

Eldon's shoulders went up, then down.

Mary said, "Shake the rugs?"

Eldon said, "Yes. All done."

"Barbara and Al and Paul will be in soon from their after dinner chores. We'll have devotions. A special one for Mother. Why don't you wait in the living room for us, and find a nice verse for Mother in the Bible?"

"But Paul has devotions tonight, don't he?"

Mary frowned, and Eldon became immediately submissive.

"Okay," he said. He pulled at one huge ear. "A long verse or a short one?"

"Long," said Grace. Her stew bowl was empty. She held it up and Mary said, "Better."

Grace took her dishes into the small kitchen at the back of the house, and washed the pile that waited there for her. They were nearly all dried and put away when Paul and Al came in the front door. Grace carried the bowl she was drying to the kitchen door and leaned against the frame.

Paul shed his windbreaker and hung it in the closet between the dining hall and living room. He was thirty three, with short black hair and brown skin hardened to parchment by the outdoor work he and Al did to earn money for the others. Al stood beside Paul with his hands in his jeans pockets. Al never wore a coat, even in the coldest weather. He kept the sleeves of his tee-shirts cut off, and he sported a constant sunburn.

"Mother?" asked Al.

"The same, I think," said Mary. "Greg is with her."

Grace ran the dry rag around and around in the bowl.

Paul set his jaw and his eyes hitched. "Devotions in a few minutes," he said. He turned and went into the living room.

"Barbara out back?" asked Al.

Mary nodded. "Hanging out sheets," she said. "Lots of sheets this past week."

"Want me to get her?"

"That's fine, Al. Tell her its devotion time, the sheets'll wait."

Al walked past Grace into the kitchen. Grace took the bowl to the cabinet and put it in with the others. Al opened the door leading to the back yard, causing the blinds on the door's window to clap noisily against the glass. He stepped out to the stoop and called for Barbara to come inside.

Grace hurried upstairs for a quick seven o'clock feeding, then came back down to the living room. It was a long, narrow room with a single window facing the street. There were pots of plants that Barbara tried to keep, but most of them were dead or nearly so. The room was kept shaded, because Mary did not like the view of the street. She did not like seeing all the people going about their busy business in their frantic ways; she did not like the bustle of the independents, nor the stiflingly close vicinity of the neighbors. Grace knew Mary kept the shade down so she could imagine she was still at the Home. Mary liked to dust the empty bookshelves and sew up sock holes and think about the Home she had been forced to leave when she was eighteen, twenty years ago.

"Greg going to come down?" asked Paul. He was seated on the flowered sofa beneath the mantle. The Bible was in his lap. Beside him, Eldon pulled at his ear.

175

"Greg!" called Mary from the base of the steps. "Devotions. Come on, now."

Al sat down beside Eldon. Grace took the floor beside the broken recliner. Barbara, her thin brown ponytail blown askew by the backyard wind, sat on the straight-backed wooden chair by the door, across from the sofa. Mary sat on the recliner.

They all waited in silence, Eldon holding onto his ear, Barbara twisting the end of her ponytail, Paul strumming the pages of the Bible, Grace picking lint from the rug. They did not look at each other.

Greg came downstairs, buttoning his shirt. He entered the living room. "Mother moved a little," he offered, but said no more. He sat on the floor beneath the window.

Paul cleared his voice. "Verses first," he said, and he began. "Ye shall find the babe wrapped in swaddling clothes, lying in a manger."

Eldon said, "Jesus wept."

Al said, "A bone of his shall not be broken."

"They came round about me daily like water," said Greg.

"Jesus wept," said Grace.

Paul said, "Nope, already used."

Grace crossed her arms, frustrated. She could barely think. Then she said, "I will open my mouth in a parable."

176

"And he was with them coming in and going out at Jerusalem," said Mary from her chair.

"How much then is a man better than a sheep," said Barbara. This was one of the few verses that Grace liked, and that she understood. When she heard it she thought of pictures in her Sunday school class long ago, little baby sheep suckling Mother sheep, with Jesus standing by.

Verses done, they all looked at Paul. He opened the Bible to a little torn scrap of paper marking a place. "I found something to read in honor of Mother," he said. He sighed heavily. Nobody liked to be in charge of devotions. But Mary was stern; each took his or her turn. Paul's voice was awkward with the words, and embarrassed. "Therefore we are buried with him by baptism into death: that like as Christ was raised up from the dead by the glory of the Father, even so we also should walk in newness of life."

Grace listened as intently as she could, hoping this time she might find something that would make sense.

"For if we have been planted together in the likeness of his death, we shall be also in the likeness of his resurrection."

Paul read on another five minutes. Grace sat and heard the scriptures, and it was as it had always been, a jumble of old words, a ritual of ancient babble. She did not need to ask the others to know it was the same for them as well. But they were trained to sit and read and quote and listen. In that repetition was the only small sense of calm.

Grace let her gaze wander to the photos and certificates on the mantle over the sofa. There was a picture of Mary back at the Baptist Home, no more than fifteen, wearing an apron and a wan smile, in the huge, smoky kitchen with Mrs. Griffith standing behind her. There was another picture of Al and Paul, twelve and thirteen, just old enough to be allowed to do grounds work, Al sitting on the seat of the Home's tractor, Paul standing on the grass. Behind Paul and Al were George Brennen and Ricky Altis, both fourteen at the time. Both George and Ricky had gone on from the Home, gotten jobs, and had married. They had become independents. They had been able to. Most of the children who had grown up in the Home had been able to. To the right of Al and Paul's snapshot was a photo which had been posed for inclusion in the Home's annual fund drive brochure. In it, a ten-year-old Barbara and an eight-year-old Grace were holding hands and running across the lawn in front of the Administration Building. There were no photos of Eldon. He hated to have his picture taken, and always hid when the Baptist Home board of trustees came out on excursions with their cameras.

"Amen," said Paul.

"Amen," repeated the others.

"Tonight, we'll each have a shorter time with Mother," said Mary. "No more than three minutes each, you hear me? Now, who was first last night?"

Eldon wiggled his hand.

"Then it's you, Barbara," said Mary. "Let's go upstairs."

The seven filed up the steps.

Barbara took off her clothes, and went into Mother's room, closing the door behind her. Time with Mother was private, and respected. The others sat on the floor in the hallway. This was the most favored time of the day, yet Mother's illness had given it an urgent touch, and Grace sat quietly, trying to prepare herself. Usually Grace told Mother about her day as she snuggled and sucked on the great white breasts. Tonight, however, Grace thought that she, like Mother, would be without a voice.

They sat and waited. Mary went into the nursery for a minute, then came out and sat down again. The kitten rose from its spot at the top of the stairs and stumbled toward the gathering, then fell several feet short, panting and mewling. Grace didn't want the cat now, she wanted Mother, and so she let the cat lie.

Paul went in after Barbara. Grace had wondered what the boys did in the room alone with Mother, but would never ask. Before Grace had come to live with her brothers and sisters, she had tried to be an independent. She had lived with a man, and he had made her do awful things, like suckle him. She had tried to please him but could not do it, and he beat her. When she tried to kill him, the state put her into a home. Not a good place like the Home, but an ugly place where she had no chores and no devotions and they wanted to talk about her feelings. Grace wondered if Paul and Al and Eldon wanted Mother to suckle them as Grace's man had wanted.

Mary took her turn, and when she came out, her face was ashen. "Not long," she whispered as she zippered her skirt and sat beside Barbara. "She won't eat." Barbara put her head down on her arms. Mary stared at her fingers.

Grace went into Mother's room. As required, she went to the nightstand and chose a nice piece of candy for Mother. She mashed it in her fingers to make it easy for Mother to take, then leaned over the huge, naked body and pressed the candy to the sick lips. Mother did not take the candy, nor acknowledge that it was there. Her eyes did not open. Grace blinked and waited, hoping Mother would awaken and take the offering. But she did not. Grace dropped the candy to the floor, and crawled onto the mattress with Mother. The cold dampness of Mother's sweat on the sheet made Grace's skin tighten and crawl.

"Today I began a picture of a cat," Grace said, pulling herself more tightly into the body. "It will be a nice one, a picture for you, and you can hang it up in your room." Grace looked up at the wall above Mother's head. On it were sketches that she had done with pencils and crayons crumbs. Pictures of sheep and their babies and Jesus and children doing chores and reading Bible verses and mowing lawns and saying prayers at cot-side and eating meals in the dining hall.

"It is a picture of the kitty I have now. She was a nice kitty, but not so nice anymore. But the picture is what she looked like when I first got her. Gray and white. You'll like it, I think."

Mother said nothing.

Grace closed her eyes and continued with her tale of the day.

"Mary made stew, and it was good. Sometimes I wish we could have candy, but candy is sweet for sweet Mothers. Maybe one day

I'll be a Mother and will have nothing to eat but sweet things, like you."

Mother did not move, but Grace could feel a pulse in her huge arm. Grace straddled Mother, and took a breast into her mouth. For a few minutes, she suckled in silence. Peace settled on her and she lost awareness of the smell and the sweat and the fact that Mother was dying. Grace's body calmed. This was Mother. This was what they all had wanted. The others had banded together after they left the Home, forming a Home again in this house. They lived as they had learned, doing as they had been taught. But Greg had decided a Mother was the missing element. They had all needed a Mother for so long. After Grace's release from the hospital, she had called the Home and got Mary's new address. She was accepted into the home of her long-ago brothers and sisters, and into a family that had at last, thanks be to Greg, a Mother.

Grace let go of the nipple, then rolled off the bed. As a parting gesture, she offered another piece of candy, and again, Mother did not take it. Grace stroked Mother's arm and thigh.

Suddenly, Mother arched her back and her eyes flew open.

"Mother?"

Mother did not seem to recognize Grace, nor focus on anything.

She trembled violently and her throat rumbled. The soft but strong terry towel restraints which were tied about her ankles and neck and shoulders drew taut and caused the bedposts to groan. Mother's mouth dropped open, and she grunted. The massive woman fought the cords. Her eyes spasmed.

She is dying certainly,' Grace thought.

Then Mother slumped down again to the bed, and her eyes closed. She was silent, and the shuddering breathing resumed.

Grace went out into the hall. She put on her clothes.

Al took his turn with Mother, closing the door behind him.

When the turns were done, Mary directed Eldon to take first watch with Mother during the night while the others slept. She did not believe Mother would last until morning, and it would be wrong for her to be alone when she died.

Mary told the others to brush their teeth and say their prayers and be off to bed. Grace washed her hands for the eight o'clock feeding.

Mary joined Grace at the nursery door. She said, "Why don't I help you this time?"

Grace shrugged. "You don't have to."

183

"I know I don't. But we'll do it together to-night."

Grace said, "All right."

Grace opened the door and the two went quietly inside.

There was a bed in the center of the nursery, a bedside table, and the rest of the room was bare. No one stayed in this room long enough to need a chair. This room was strictly business. It was a room for tending and cleaning and monitoring. It was dark and quiet and busy, like a little chamber in a honey bee comb.

Mary and Grace moved to the bed. Grace opened the box of candy on the bedside table. She smashed the chocolate between her fingers and held it out.

The figure on the bed strained and caught the candy.

Then the mouth opened for more. Grace smiled slightly, then looked at Mary for approval.

"This is good," said Mary. "She's healthy and she eats."

Grace held out more mashed candy, and it was gobbled up.

Even Grace's fingers were mouthed clean when she held them close enough.

Grace wiped her hand on her hip, then looked down at the woman on the bed. The woman was filling out nicely. With hourly feedings of good, sweet candy and soft drinks, she was beginning to look like a Mother, with soft, fleshy side rolls and arms like foam pillows. Soon she would be big enough to cuddle, large enough to hide in, soft enough to suckle. This woman, like Mother, was secured to her bed. This woman, also like Mother, had no voice. This was Greg's idea. He was the one to find the women and bring them home; and he was the one who said it was best to remove the tongues. This way, each in turn would be a good Mother. A good Mother who would listen and not scold.

Grace touched the woman's arm. The woman looked at Grace. Her eyes were alive and sparkling, as if mad tears swirled in them. She grunted and pulled at her restraints. Mary smacked her soundly.

"She'll learn," said Mary.

Grace picked another piece of candy from the box and looked at it. Candy tasted good, but Mother's breasts were sweeter. Mother's love was peace.

Grace crushed the candy. She offered it to the woman on the bed, who took it even as her eyes spilled and then brimmed over again.

At two the next morning, Mother died.

White Hair, We Adore

The Carmen Brothers were a staple clown act with Terry McCarvey's Traveling Circus. The identical triplets had been purchased by Terry from the children's mother for fifty dollars apiece when the mother came begging and shouting at the entrance tent when the circus had been playing in Danville.

"They's good boys," she had said after Terry had been summoned by the security man. "And they's freaks, don't you think, what that they all three look exactly alike and they's all three retarded as table legs? Look, I'll go down from a hundred each to fifty. It's as legal as we want it 'cause I'll swear you's a relative if anybody asks me."

Terry had shifted from one black-booted foot to the other, glancing over his shoulder as if hoping someone would come and tell him what he should do. But he was the circus owner, and although the thought of buying children ran his blood in a cold path through his veins, he agreed. The mother looked like she needed the cash, and the three boys were certainly something of an attraction.

The deal was made, the triplets' mother never came back, and Terry went about the task of teaching three simple-minded eight-year-old triplets some simple tumbling and dancing. The little black-haired, blue-eyed boys were happy and obedient, and they became a toast of the show.

The Carmen Brothers' Clown Show was a morality play, scripted by Terry. It was a three-skit tale kept brief and easy. Three virtues were extolled, three values demonstrated. Don't steal. Don't lie. Respect one's elders.

Between the acts of the trampolinist and the lion tamer, Randy, Ronnie, and Ricky rolled and skipped into the tent, then began their performance. In the first skit, Randy pretended to steal a bag of candy from Ricky. Ronnie, the judge, chastised, "Steal a penny, steal a treasure. The difference of it can't be measured!" He then put Randy into a red-striped jail until he apologized to Ricky.

The second skit had Ronnie lie that he hadn't seen a lost poodle dog, just moments after the same poodle had jumped up and hid inside Ronnie's blousy clown shirt. Caught in the lie, Judge Ricky stood Ronnie up against a tent pole while Randy unfurled a lion tamer's whip. "A lie's lash does cut the soul," Ricky quoted. "Back up, then, beside this pole!" Ronnie hastily begged forgiveness and all was forgiven.

In the last skit, Ronnie donned a white wig and limped about as an old man. Ricky knocked him down, and ran around in the stands, laughing. Caught by Judge Randy, and dragged back to the grassy floor of the tent, Ronnie produced a silver gun and brandished it at Ricky. "White hair, we adore," said the judge. "Our elders teach what life is for." Ricky adamantly repented as Ronnie pulled the trigger, and the silver gun exploded with a bang and a white flag with red lettering, "POP", sprang from the barrel.

Then the brothers would all hold hands and bow to the crowds, shouting "Always together!"

The skits were popular with children and as well with their parents. Morals were easier to grasp when presented with the fun and frolic of little child clowns. Outside the tent after the performances, the triplets shyly shook hands with admirers, yet said little, because speaking much beyond the well-rehearsed lines confused them and made them anxious. At night, the triplets were treated to sugar-coned ice cream and pancakes by George, the chef in the dining tent. After many months, the circus folks still couldn't tell one from the other, and Terry had to keep the boys in different color carnations to keep them straight.

But if anyone had truly taken the time to look, if anyone had leaned over and peered into the faces when the boys ate their pancakes or practiced their tumbling for the next day's show or chatted in their trailer, they would have seen the one difference in the three.

There glowed in Randy's eyes a brighter light than that in his brothers'. There strained on Randy's brow a tight line of intelligence, and on the corners of his gaily-painted clown lips, there pulled a twitch of frustration and despair.

Laurie the Horse Geek joined the circus the spring that the Carmen brothers turned nineteen. She was a flamboyant, skinny thing with red hair and long legs, joining the troupe just outside of a dying town on the southern border of West Virginia. She brought her own ratty chestnut mare with her. She was desperate, she said, to get away from home and make a life on her own.

She played her stint to Terry and other more curious members of the circus community. Terry had shooed away the Carmen triplets, because "You boys got chores to do. You got to get your boots polished before tomorrow." But Randy had come back after his two brothers had willingly returned to the trailer to polish boots, and he watched the audition from the shadow of a nearby tree.

"Ladies and gentlemen!" she cooed, bowing deeply and whirling the ends of a red feather boa as if it were indeed a living snake. "I present to you an act of life and death! An act of skill and danger!" She hoisted herself up onto the back of her horse and worked the mare into a circled canter about a small wooden crate Laurie had placed on the ground. "As quick as an eagle, as fast as a hawk! Don't blink or you'll miss the fun!" The horse's hoofs pounded the ground in a slow, rhythmic lope. Laurie, letting go of the reins with both hands, braced her knees against the mare's sides, and lowered herself until she was sideways on the horse and parallel to the ground.

The horse's circle became smaller, closing in around the crate. And then, so quickly it could barely be seen, Laurie's hand flicked out and knocked the lid to the crate back. A startled chicken rose up in fear. It squawked and flapped its stubby wings. Laurie stretched out her neck and caught the chicken between her teeth. The chicken's body dropped, the head, draining blood, stayed between Laurie's teeth. She pulled herself up, slowed down the mare, and bowed.

The circus folk applauded hesitantly. Terry licked his lips and said, "You have skill, without a doubt. Let's talk."

Laurie slid to the ground and surveyed the audience with a triumphant grin. Randy pulled farther back into the shadows.

Terry hired Laurie, modifying the act. Laurie would ride her horse and do tricks that any five-year-old could enjoy without tossing his caramel corn. The geek act was to be relegated to the specialty tent at night, where a viewer had to be sixteen to get in.

Her riding act was put between the clowns and the lion tamer, yet she avoided the three clown brothers as much as possible. Randy could see her obvious disgust when she was near them. Her nose wrinkled if they tumbled into her at her entrance, and she would move away if the triplets sat at her table in the dining tent.

Randy and Ricky and Ronnie, tall now and muscular, had new suits with spangles and sequins. But their skits were the same as they had been when the boys were eight. Randy still stole candy, Ronnie still let a poodle jump into the folds of his shirt to the pleased shrieks of the children in the audience, and Ricky continued to knocked down an old man and laughed at his mischief.

And in spite of it all, Randy fell in love with the horse girl.

He watched her from behind the infirmary tent as she exercised her horse in the early morning. He let his eyes catch brief glimpses of her when she came out of the trailer she shared with the nurse. He dreamed of her at night, feeling the red boa drift about his naked shoulders, tasting the curve of her pink-tinted mouth, caressing the smooth skin of her legs and belly. He would awake to the snoring of his brothers, who lay in their beds clutching a variety of sawdust-stuffed animals. And Randy would cry.

One evening in October, Randy sneaked from the dining tent and hastily picked flowers from the weeds behind the Big Top. Then he hid behind the hay bales next to the horse's portable pipe stall. He held his breath as Laurie brought the horse in from the evening cool-down. And before he could stop himself, he stood up.

Laurie gasped and spun about, holding the curry comb before her like a sword.

"Get the fuck out of here moron, or I'll kill you!" Randy began to tremble. Then he began to laugh. "I'm not what you think," he managed.

Laurie's eyes tightened. "I know what you are, retard."

"No, really," said Randy.

"Really!" Laurie shouted. "This circus shit is bad enough without me having to put up with a sloppy, pea-brained clown!"

"No," said Randy. His laughing quieted, but the pounding in his chest did not. "No," he said again. "I'm really not what you think. I'm not what anybody thinks." He pulled out a bouquet of chicory and Queen Ann's lace from behind the hay bale and offered it to Laurie. The laughing subsided. "It's not me, it's my brothers. I'm not what you think. Please listen to me."

Laurie lowered the curry comb. She stared at the black-haired clown, her teeth raking her lower lip. Then she said, "Tell me what you're talking about."

They sat in the corner of the pipe stall as the mare chomped her oats. Randy told her about himself. Laurie listened intently, moving closer to him as the story progressed.

Within the week, they were lovers.

"Randy, Randy, turn 'round now," said Ronnie. Beneath the huge red smile, Ronnie's mouth was a straight line of worry. "You get in line."

The triplets were at the tent flap, listening for the closing chords of the trampoline tune. Ronnie, Ricky, and Randy wore the matching gold suits; the props of the skits- wig, gun, and whip- were stashed inside the folds of material to be pulled out at the right times. Randy was the last of the three, and it was all he could do to keep his cheeks slack in retarded clown style. His gaze continued to flick in the direction of the row of Port-a-Johns, where Laurie was tightening the girth on the mare's saddle.

"Randy, you ready?" asked Ricky. He took Randy's hand in his own and gave it a tentative squeeze.

Randy didn't look back, but stared at Laurie as she bent and tugged. Hint of muscle rippled beneath the skin of her long legs. "Yep," he mumbled. "I'm ready. Don't worry. Always together." His penis ached with desire. He was glad the costume material was loose.

"Always together!" crowed Ronnie, pleased.

"Always together," repeated Ricky as he leaned over and gave his brother a kiss on the white-painted face.

The trampoline music faded, and the three clowns ran into the tent to the cheers of the crowd, and played the stories of the wrongs of mankind.

"So you gonna be ready in two days?" asked Laurie. "We passing back through my hometown then and I tell you, if you ain't ready I'm going without you. I know you been doing this since you was a baby and this damned circus don't make you wanna barf like it makes me, but if you's lying to me then I want you to tell me now and I'll make my move all by myself."

Randy lay beside Laurie, watching as the smoke from her cigarette curled in a thin string toward the ceiling of the infirmary tent. The nurse was out gambling with the lion tamer, and Ricky and Ronnie were playing checkers with Terry in their trailer. Time alone was hard to catch; Randy had been pretending for the past nights that he had flu, and needed to sit in a Port-a-John until the waves passed. Ronnie, deeply concerned, had offered to sit outside in the grass and talk to

Randy until he was feeling better, but Randy declined. The fifth night, Ronnie stopped offering.

"I ain't lying to you," said Randy. "I'm going to be ready. I want to leave, just like you. I want to meet your mama, I want to get a real job at the mine like you said I could get. I just . . ." Randy stopped talking. Laurie put her cigarette between Randy's lips and he took a long draw. Laurie's hand went to his crotch, and pressed gently.

"You just what?"

Randy's hips rose slightly, moving into the touch. He didn't want to tell her that the thought of leaving his brothers and taking off on his own scared the living shit out of him. He didn't want to tell Laurie that he was torn between what she had offered him and what he knew as his life and his living. He felt he would be betraying Terry McCarvey. He knew he would miss his brothers dreadfully.

"I just haven't got enough money yet," he decided to say. "I did what you said, and I've saved every penny of my pay for weeks now. It's just not much. They don't give us much. Terry thinks we clowns just need food and a bed and toys to fill in the blank spaces."

Laurie began to rub. "Now, Randy. You got a hundred dollars by now, don't you? And I got over that. Sold my mare to Terry, telling him if I ever got killed falling off or if I ever swallow poison chicken blood he could at least get another girl to ride. He give me two hundred for her. Not bad, huh?"

Randy nodded. He watched a granddaddy longlegs climb the angle of the tent roof and held his breath at Laurie's caress.

"And your brothers each got at least that," Laurie said. "And what do they do with their cash? Buy balloons and cotton candy? Take the money. They won't miss it. And if they do, they'll think they lost it."

Randy sucked on the cigarette, blew smoke through clamped teeth, and gave it back to Laurie. He closed his eyes and rode the pleasure current in his groin. "Stealing is wrong. Didn't you ever see our skits?"

Laurie chuckled and kissed Randy's cheek. "It's a children's story, Randy. Jesus."

Randy felt his head nod up and down on the thin pillow of the infirmary cot, and then felt the ecstasy of buildup as Laurie loosened the zipper on his jeans and lowered her kiss to the place of his urgency.

"I love you Laurie," Randy said.

Laurie said nothing, but her touch and her kisses sang a song sweeter than any calliope Randy had ever heard.

* * *

Terry McCarvey's Traveling Circus caravan rode through Tickton, West Virginia, making a bizarre and colorful sight on the main street of the small town. It was early November and the trees which sprouted at irregular places along the road had shed most of their orange leaves into piles untouched by the business folk. A few cars were parked on curbside, but many of the stores were dead. There were no visible shoppers on the walks.

Randy watched the town from the window of the trailer. Terry was in the truck at the wheel; Randy, Ronnie, and Ricky rode in the back. Randy was perched on a stool, looking out. Ronnie sat on the floor playing with a deck of cards, making a lopsided house. Ricky lay on one of the small beds, eating from a bag of popcorn he'd bought the night before.

"Randy, look!" called Ronnie. Randy looked. Ronnie waved his hand at his card house.

"Nice," said Randy.

"Really?" said Ronnie. "Really nice, Randy?"

"Yep," said Randy. "Really really nice."

Ronnie beamed.

Randy looked back out the window. The town was cold, and it seemed as if it had recently rained. Black spots of damp on the street and walks reflected the lights of the circus caravan. This was Laurie's hometown, and tonight was the night they would run away from the circus and start a new life. The town did not look inviting. Randy shivered. It was strange that Laurie was running back to where she had come from in the first place. But she said she'd been gone long enough now, that circles came back around, and that with a good man, she'd be ready to settle down.

Ricky, on the cot, snorted in sleep and turned over. Randy wrapped his arms about himself, trying to catch and hold the sense of safety he had here. If only he could take his brothers with him. But that would be wrong. They would never understand this kind of love, the kind of love that was adult to adult, woman to man. He wrapped his arms more tightly, and sighed deeply.

The caravan found its way to an abandoned drive-in lot just outside Tickton. The trailers and trucks parked temporarily; Tickton was not to be the recipient of a show because the last time through six months ago, attendance had been slim. Instead, the circus folk made their way on foot and scooter to the nearby grocery for fresh supplies of foods and toiletries. The triplets took the spare time to practice their tumbling on the dusty gravel of the drive-in lot.

Randy tumbled with fresh fervor; his heart thundered in knowledge that this would be his last day with his brothers. His head ached with love for them. When the practice was over, he took the white wig from Ronnie, buried his face into and inhaled the scents of family and familiarity. He then put the wig on his head and his brothers giggled.

"Randy's a old man!"

"White hair we adore! Randy Randy we adore!"

Randy tossed the wig back to Ronnie. "Always together," Randy whispered, thickening his tongue and playing the part of the simple clown, the truthful brother one last time. He collected Ronnie and Ricky in an tight embrace. Then he strode to a Port-a-John where he sat for a long time, counting the money he'd saved and the dollars he'd stolen from his brothers. Six hundred and twenty three dollars all together. Laurie had been thrilled with the count the night before. That was enough, she said, to rent an apartment for a whole month and still have some left to buy a television and VCR.

"Laurie, I love you," he said softly to the fistful of dollars.

When his heart had slowed and his mind had regained focus, he left the toilet and joined Terry and the other circus folks in stocking the supply truck and letting the hoofed animals have a leg-stretch before picking up and moving again.

It began to rain in Tickton. Laurie had a cloak, a long blue velvet one that she wore when performed on her chestnut mare. Randy, though, did not have a coat. He'd forgotten it back in Terry's trailer. When the two had gotten as far as Main Street, the afternoon sky had ripped and the torrent fell. Laurie had taken Randy's hand and said, "You ain't sugar. You won't melt."

Then they paused beneath a green awning and waited until the heaviest of the downpour was past.

Laurie had never looked so beautiful. The heavy blue velvet was matted against her body and the wet curves of the hood framed her small face. Randy wondered if his brother would ever know the magic of love and the fierce glory of passion. With simplicity came limits.

But with complexity came painful choices.

"I called my mom," said Laurie. She watched out at the rain on the street. A few stray cars whisked by. "She said we could stay with her tonight. She's cooked us up a great dinner, you just wait." Laurie looked back at Randy. Shadows cut her features. "Beans and muffins and pork and scrambled eggs. Pie, too, three different kinds. We have to be there by five thirty, though, or she'll be madder'en hops. She'll toss the food out to the pigs, she said."

"Kiss me, Laurie," said Randy. His heart hurt.

"Silly, you'll get all the kissing you need real soon," said Laurie. "Now the rain is gone down. And it's near to five thirty. We best get on."

"Sure."

They stepped out to the walk and moved along the street. Laurie's gait quickened. Randy kept up. Laurie began to hum "Turkey in the Straw." Randy tried to hum along, but didn't quite know the tune.

At the end of a block, Laurie turned and went into a narrow alley. Twenty feet in, Laurie spun about to face Randy.

"Give me the money, Randy," she said.

Randy stopped and blinked.

Laurie pulled the hood off her face and put her hands on her hips. "Give me the money, Randy. I don't mind biting heads off chickens, but I don't really want to bite the head off you."

A raindrop coursed Randy's nose and held to the tip like a dark jewel. "What did you say?"

Laurie shook her head and grunted. "You may be smarter than the other two, but not a whole hell of a lot. Give me the damn money or you'll wish you had."

Randy took a step backward.

"Laurie?"

Laurie laughed. "What, Randy?"

"I don't understand."

"Of course you don't, you clown. At least you'll never understand how you could be so easily tricked. But you better understand that I want the money."

From the trash barrels at the side of the alley, a large man stepped out and joined Laurie. He was thick and burly and held a baseball bat.

"Joe," said Laurie. "I didn't want to hurt him, like I told you on the phone. But if he don't give me the cash in ten seconds, beat the shit out of him and I'm gonna eat his ears."

Randy said, "Laurie, you said you loved me."

"Liar," said Laurie. "I never said that, only you did. Stupid, forgetful clown!"

"I'm going to get a job at the mine. We're going to have an apartment, I'm going to meet your mama . . ."

Elizabeth Massie

"You gonna stay here and live or stay here and die. The circus already gone off to the next town. You told your brothers you was gonna ride in the truck with the lion tamer and talk about cats. Your brothers ain't gonna know you're gone 'til they're long gone, themselves."

"Laurie . . . !"

"Get him, Joe."

The large man lunged forward. Randy tumbled out of his way, then rolled back upward and dashed from the alleyway. He heard Laurie's gasp, and a whoosh as something was hurled in his direction. Then with a crack, his vision shattered and he dropped face down onto the pavement.

Circus colors and discordant sounds spun in his brain. He lifted on hand to his skull and found a slick coating of blood. Then, to one side, he could hear shuffling of feet. Fingers roughly dug through his pockets and then pulled away.

"Got the cash," said a man's voice.

"Retarded, hard-headed clown," said a woman's voice. And then there was breath close to his head. A tongue stroked the wounded flesh, then moved away.

"Don't taste too different from chicken blood," Laurie said. "Sorry, Randy. It could've been so much easier if you'd just handed it over."

The feet moved away. Randy's head rocked with pain. His lungs cried with tears too crushed to come out.

The rain softened even more. It became a mist that seemed to melt on Randy's neck and on the hot blood on his head, its caress taunting and tickling. Randy licked a piece of sharp gravel from a cut in his lip.

And then there were more feet beside his head, feet stepping tentatively, many feet, some in soft shoes, a pair, it sounded like, in boots. Randy could not move his hands well enough to cover his head for any further blows. But a pair of hands reached down to him, and gently turned him face up.

In the blur of a distant street light and haze of mist, Randy saw the face of himself, twice over. He saw the face of Terry McCarvey, staring down in compassion and relief.

"Thank God," said Randy. Three pairs of hands gathered him and lifted him to his feet. He felt the world going away, but that was all right. He would awake where he belonged, either in heaven, or in Terry's warm little trailer with his two brothers.

It wasn't heaven, and it wasn't the trailer. Randy's eyes opened and at first all he could see was a small rectangle of light that made his head throb dreadfully. He shut his eyes, then opened them again. He leaned slowly toward the light, and saw then that he was inside something which was inside the supply trailer.

"Ronnie?" he whispered.

He put his face to the rectangle. It was a window, a small window in a wooden box. Yes, he knew now. He was inside the red-striped jail the Carmen Brothers used in their skit. He was propped against the side of the box. His arm was asleep. He wondered how long he had been in the jail. He wondered why he was in the jail.

"Ricky?"

The supply trailer was dark, lighted only by a single lantern sitting on a stool. But Randy knew it well. He and his brothers had for years been helpers at loading and unloading all the equipment that made the circus a circus. Balls and tubs and whips and carts, giant plastic flowers and flags and sets of Big Top lights. A happy piece of the circus, where he and Ricky and Ronnie had played carefully many times when Terry had given them permission.

"Ronnie?"

A face appeared suddenly at the window. It was Ricky, and he was dressed in his clown's suit. Makeup was applied to his face, carelessly, as though Ricky had done the job himself.

"Ricky, my head hurts. Please get me out of here."

Ricky frowned. He said, "Steal a penny, steal a treasure. The difference of it can't be measured."

Randy's gut clenched. He stretched his arms out through the window, reaching for his brother. He said, "Ricky, get me out please. I'm so tired. I need to go to bed."

Ricky said, "We found you in town. You forgot to take your coat to the lion tamer's truck and so I took it for you. You weren't there. We thought you was lost, Randy."

Ronnie's face appeared beside Ricky's. His, too, was covered with streaks of makeup. The circle of rouge under one eye made it look bigger than the other. His lids appeared to be trembling. "Lost," said Ronnie. "Terry and us came to look for you. It was raining. It was so cold."

"Ronnie, I'm hurt. Please get me out."

Ronnie said, "A lie's lash does cut the soul." He moved back, and picked up the lion tamer's whip. "Back up then beside this pole!" He flicked the whip's handle, and the braided leather cut Randy's knuckles. Randy jerked his hands inside the jail.

"Randy! Ronnie! What are you doing?"

"You stole money," said Ronnie. "You stole money from us."

"How do you . . . no, I didn't steal, Ronnie."

Ronnie wiped a tear from his eye, streaking his smudged makeup even more. He dropped the whip to the trailer's floor. "You stole, I seen you. I thought it was a game, but it wasn't."

Randy's mind whirled. He could get out of this. He could explain it so they would accept it, would forgive it.

He said, "Ronnie, I have to tell you why. I made a terrible mistake."

Ricky said, "It wasn't a game. You lied to us. You said, 'always together.' But you went away with Laurie."

Randy reached out of the window again, clutching frantically for the costumes of his brothers. "No, listen. I didn't mean to steal. I didn't mean to lie."

"White hair, we adore," said Ronnie. "Our elders teach what life is for."

"Yes, yes," said Randy. "Now let me out."

Ronnie put the white wig on his head. He said, "Terry is an old man. He teaches us what life is for. You ran away. You scared him. You were so very, very bad to him. You musn't make old men scared."

"I'm sorry. But our skits, Ronnie, are make-believe. They aren't real. Let me out, please, now! I'll go tell Terry how sorry I am for scaring him."

Ricky held up something silver, something which flashed in the light of the lantern. It was a gun. Not the play gun from the skit, but the sharp-shooters gun from the wild west act. Ricky pointed the mouth of the gun at Randy.

"You think we're dumber than you. You think we don't know pretend. The play is pretend. The bad we do is pretend. But the bad you did is real."

"The bad you did," said Ronnie. "Is real." His voice broke, and spiraled upward.

"Is real," echoed Ricky.

"Is real," repeated Ronnie.

"Randy, Randy, we adore." Ricky caught Randy's flailing hand and gave it a brotherly kiss. "Randy, now, will be no more." Then he squinted down the barrel.

Randy thought the "O" of his mouth must have been as round and big as the hoop the circus poodles jumped through, but even as a clown, that thought didn't make him laugh.

Honey Girls On Line

It was a myth. There was no such thing as a female orgasm. Men created the myth to make women think there was something in sex for them, something that if they just worked hard enough for, they'd get. "Relax, baby. Suck me a little harder and let me stick a couple fingers up you. And if you're a good girl, you'll have an orgasm. Just like me."

Patty's lovin' husband was one of the myth's greatest fans.

Liars.

"Do what I say, do what I like, do it do it do it and you'll come. You'll come!"

Liars, liars, pants on fire.

Patty dropped the magazine onto the floor, pulled her underwear back up over her hips, and sat down on her bed. This would have been a good time to cry, if she was the crying kind. But crying was a waste of time. It didn't do anything but make your face puff up and your eyes get squinchy and your throat hurt like you had the strep.

Hate was a dry emotion. Cold, hard, and dry.

Pulling her feet up to rest on the bedframe, Patty looked out the window at the rolling fields behind the house. If she'd looked out the side windows of the bedroom, or the window in the kitchen in the front of the house, she would be seeing the same thing. Fields, tree-shadowed fence lines, black spots indicating distant cattle. No neighbors in view, the kind of landscape where city people would expect to find scorched imprints of flying saucers and strange overhead lights in a midnight sky. There was a single gravel road that passed Patty's house out front, heading off to somewhere better than this no-man's land. Few cars traveled this gravel road on any given day, usually just the mailman and the truck that delivered heating oil every couple months and Henry, coming to and from his job at a neighboring cattle farm in the wee morning and the late night hours.

Elizabeth Massie

Patty and her husband, Henry, had lived in this little white box-house for over three years now. They rented it. "Be ass-stupid to buy something like this," Henry had said the month after they married and the day they moved in. "We'll save our money and get us something real nice some day. You just bet we will."

But three years later, Patty's bet was they wouldn't. Henry worked every day, and worked long hours, too. But he didn't seem to understand the concept of saving money. He had a piggy bank in the kitchen that he pointed to with pride, a bank he'd slam-dunk a couple quarters into every now and then, but the bulk of his paycheck, after the rent and oil and phone bill were taken care of, went to his hobby.

His porn.

His subscriptions to Playboy and Penthouse and Hustler and Jolly Geriatrics and even a couple months' worth of Man's Man. His video collection, a massive stacking of tapes including *The Mighty Fucks, War and Piece*, and *Assie, Come Home*.

Henry didn't know Patty knew about his hobby. The magazines came in the mail and Henry picked up the mail when he came home, so as far as he knew, she'd never seen them. Of course, there were times when, out

212

of boredom, Patty walked down the dusty driveway and peeked into the mailbox to see if there was anything for her (there never was) and had spied the brown paper-covered periodicals. And the video tapes, bought God-knew-where, probably in the backroom of the video section at the Happy Mart at the inter-section of Routes 245 and 486 seven miles to the north, were kept in a green draw-string garbage bag behind the washing machine in the basement. Patty had found it by accident when a sock once did a high kick off and landed behind the machine.

How much Henry had plugged into this hobby, Patty couldn't fathom. Tapes had to be at least thirty dollars apiece, and he had scads. The magazines were, what, twenty dollars a subscription? No matter. They weren't saving up to buy a house, this she knew. Henry seemed content with the way things were—working, eating, and trying out new sex tricks with Patty in bed, enjoying himself immensely, insisting that Patty tell him that she'd come and come hard; leaving Patty sore, confused, and increasingly furious.

One morning, after the dishes were washed and the beans from the garden were snapped, Patty pulled a video from the trashbag in the basement and put it into the player.

She had sat down on the sofa, feet tucked beneath her, waiting for the magic. Her heart raced.

The music had come on, a rinky-dink tune that sounded like it belonged in a traveling carnival. She giggled nervously. Actors and actresses came on, read their lines from cards somewhere off-screen, then got down to business.

Patty stopped laughing. She watched, she waited, her teeth clamped down on each other, a glass of Big K Cola with melting ice sitting on the end table by the sofa.

The men "oohed" and "yeah-babied". The women licked their lips and fingered themselves and stuck their high-heeled feet up in the air as if they were trying to impale the ceiling.

Patty rubbed herself through the thin fabric of her underwear, ran her fist back and forth across her nipple, wishing the stupid carnival music would stop so she could concentrate and find the magic. Henry liked this, Henry got off big time on this stuff. But the music didn't stop, and the men, slick-haired and slick-voiced and blue-veined, came all over the breasts of the panting, high-heeled women and Patty thought, Is that all? Where's my orgasm?

She put the video back into the trash bag and tried to forget about sex. She busied herself with the garden and the dishes and the talk shows in the afternoon.

But maybe, she thought days later after Henry had given her a morning quickie and hurried off to work in his truck. Maybe the magazines are better than the tapes. Without the music, they have to be better.

Patty knew where the magazines were. Henry had a couple shoe boxes on the shelf in his closet behind some old ball gloves and caps. She'd searched for them after she'd discovered they'd been coming into the house, but had never looked much beyond the front cover and the table of contents. She wasn't sure if that had been because of disinterest or anxiety. For a while, it hadn't really mattered.

Now, though, with the video viewing a failure, she thought, Maybe my orgasm is in here.

She didn't sweep the porch that morning, nor did she do much more than give her mother a cursory "I'm fine, Henry's fine" when the older woman made her weekly phone call. Patty climbed into bed, fluffed up the pillows, and snuggled down with two boxes full of magazines. She looked through them page after page, gazing at the beautiful naked women and the pen-drawn one-frame sex cartoons. She had read letters to the editors, and had stared at the hard bodies and sweat-shiny organs of the lusty guys of Man's Man.

Nothing.

Patty climbed from under the covers and ran to the kitchen for something to help out. The carrot was cold and once inside, too rough and sharp. The soft cloth icing bag, squeezed slowly, filled her so much she felt she had to go to the bathroom. And as she sat there on the pot, she was suddenly afraid that all the icing wouldn't come out before Henry got back home.

And there was no orgasm.

Fucking liars. It was a myth. A story to keep women in bed, or one to make them hop back in. A goddamn carrot on a stick. Or icing bag on a stick. Whatever.

It was then she realized how much she hated Henry. Hated her old boyfriend Jack who had been much like Henry. Hated all the lying, selfish bastards.

Patty looked back at the magazine on the floor. This one was a copy of Little Girl Lost. These magazines focused on women in their late teens and early twenties dressed up like school girls, sans skirts or bras. As Patty stared at these women, she knew she hated them, too. She hated them because they promoted the female orgasm lie. "Dress like us, Patty. Pretend you're a ten-year-old in need of a good spanking from the headmaster. Maybe you'll come."

Picking up the magazine, Patty made room for it in the shoe box with the others. If she had the nerve, she'd burn them all. "Damn you!" she said through clenched jaws.

The magazine dropped from her hand to the bed, and Little Girl Lost flopped open to the back section. The classifieds.

Classifieds. Not your normal missing puppies or car parts for sale.

"No kidding," Patty said, but as she lifted the magazine again, she saw an ad she had missed in her earlier perusal. It was a small two-column deal, bold print. No illustrations.

"HONEY GIRLS ON LINE. A women-to-women phone line. Share your secret frustrations and desires. We understand. We can give you what you've been wanting. Call. We understand. We understand. We understand."

Patty frowned, closed the magazine, and put it into the shoe box. Peculiar ad to have in a men's magazine, where women were not likely to see it.

You're seeing it, Patty.

Unless, of course, those looking were women just like her, trying to unearth the thrill in all this sticky mess.

She took the magazine back out, and opened again to the classifieds.

"We can give you what you've been wanting. Call."

"I don't think you can," Patty said. "You probably dress in bobby socks and saddle shoes."

"We understand. We understand. We understand. You're just playing another mind game. A man's mind game." Outside in the distance, a lone cow mooed. The cow didn't understand. Henry didn't understand. The house didn't, the television didn't. No one understood.

"We understand."

Patty reached for the phone on the nightstand. Her fingers were cold.

It only took two rings before there was an answer. The voice on the line was smooth and womanly and friendly.

"Honey Girls on Line. Hello, Patty."

"I . . . ," Patty began. How the hell? Did they have caller I.D.? But if they did, they would only know the number, right?

"Patty," said the voice on the other side. "I'm so glad you called. We've been in business here for about two years, and I knew you'd get in touch with us soon."

"I . . . ," said Patty. "You know me? Who is this? Do I know you?"

The laughter on the line was gentle and kind and soothing. A laughter of camaraderie. "Tell you what, Patty. We'll trade secrets, all right? First, tell me why you called."

Patty swallowed. She looked out the window at the fields and tree-lines and sky. There was no one around for miles. There was no reason she couldn't tell this woman what she was thinking.

"Orgasms," Patty said. "I don't think they're real. I think men made them up and it pisses me off. It more than pisses me off. We're lead along like stupid little calves, hopping up and down, being good and doing what the big ole farmer man wants, spreading our cute little holes for him in hopes that one day the magic will come to us. But I think it's all a lie. It's a lie, isn't it?"

A pause. Then, "No, Patty. It's true."

Patty looked down at the receiver. The coldness in her fingers shot down to her hands. Not this woman, too. Damn it all.

"I don't believe you," Patty said.

"May I try something, Patty?"

Patty hesitated, then nodded, then realizing a nod couldn't be seen, said, "Okay."

"I want you to listen to me. When I'm through talking, if you still believe women's orgasms aren't real, I'll make it up to you."

"How will you make it up to me?"

"Will you listen?"

Patty nodded again, but said nothing.

The voice sighed, long and low. It was a sound like the wind in a wheat field, like the sound of a cool, trickling stream. Patty shut her eyes. Her grip tightened on the receiver.

"Patty," said the voice. Patty listened, waited for the voice to give her proof.

"Patty," said the voice. "Patty, Patty, Patty, Patty." What the hell is this? Patty thought. It's a recording, it's screwed up.

"Patty, Patty, Patty, Patty. . . ."

But then the sound of her name began to blur, to become a flow of meaningless sound. The sound was sensuous, tingling, and when Patty was first aware that the sound was not just entering her ear but moving into her blood and coursing her body, she flinched.

Although she didn't hear the actual words, she felt the instructions.

"Relax, Patty. We understand you."

Patty took a breath and eased it out through her teeth. Then she saw the beach. The vision flowed against her inner lids as easily as the sound through her mind, her muscles, the tactile-rich nerves just inside her skin.

She was on a white stretch of sand, warm and naked, listening to the hiss of the waves as they licked the sparkling grains. The sky, a light pink, was streaked with blood red ribbons and golden winking sparks that reminded Patty of glitter she used to use to make pictures in grade school.

Where? she thought, but the peace that moved within her blood made her realize she didn't care where.

There was a brightness behind her, somewhere beyond the rise of the beach to her back. A sun, its rays playing with her arms and back and thighs like an affectionate cat nuzzling and rubbing for attention.

And then, she came up from the water.

She was beautiful.

Patty felt her back straighten. She brushed her hair from her face. Her heart kicked, and picked up speed.

The woman was tall and curved and nude. Her long black hair curled around her shoulders and fell to her waist. Her breasts were small, her pubic area a thick thatch hiding what was within.

An old rhyme, told in the elementary school yard, flashed in Patty's mind:

"Went downtown to see Aunt Molly,
Paid two cents to see her wooly.
Hair so black I couldn't see the crack,
Made her give me my two cents back."

Patty felt a laugh crawl up her throat, but the flowing energy twisted the laugh and forced it, almost painfully, back where it came.

"Patty," she thought she could hear, the voice mildly scolding, softly tsking. "Patty, Patty, Patty, Patty."

The woman waded through the shallows, her arms lifting and then reaching out, greeting, welcoming. She stepped from the water onto the sand. Patty wanted to move forward toward the woman but could not. Her legs, which were stretched out before her, opened on their own accord.

Smiling, the woman came closer. Patty could see the pale down of body hair on her stomach and hips. Just above the tiny navel was a white line that traveled along the skin to the left breast.

A scar?

The woman, without moving her lips, said, "Do you remember me, Patty?"

The scar.

"Remember me? You always loved me."

Jenna?

"Yes," said the woman. "Jenna."

Oh, God, Jenna! Suddenly, Patty was able to move her arms. She lifted them for Jenna. Jenna knelt down and the two women folded together, Jenna's body melting in the space between Patty's legs, Patty burying her face in the warm hair on her friend's head, then putting one hand down to the warm hair on the woman's mound.

Jenna and Patty had been friends in elementary school. Hand in hand they had played and laughed. And even then, Patty knew she loved Jenna.

One day, when the two girls were talking under the jungle gym, Patty had leaned over and kissed her friend on the cheek. Jenna, whose mouth had turned up in a surprised but genuine smile, never had the chance to kiss Patty back. There had been a roar from the world beyond the jungle gym. Jenna's father had come to pick her up early from school, and had seen the kiss. Patty couldn't remember his words, only that they were enraged and ugly and wrong.

Jenna had missed the next three days of school. And when she had come back, she showed Patty the scar from the belt.

"Kiss me again, Patty," said Jenna.

Patty kissed her friend. Her love from so long ago. Her only love, even today. She wrapped her legs across Jenna's back and dipped her mouth to the small breasts. The nipples rose, hard and loving. The sand beneath rolled gently, like waves of water, pressing the two bodies together.

"I have something for you," whispered Jenna. She eased Patty back on the ground, then lowered her face to Patty's cunt. She

223

parted the lips with her fingers, then, looking up to smile one quick smile, put her mouth to Patty's clit.

The magic, Patty thought. Oh, God, the magic! Henry, you bastard, you have no idea!

Jenna slowly moved her tongue around the sensitive inner flesh, pressing and sucking the little pearl, her hands clutching the bulge of Patty's thighs, holding her in place on the sand.

The magic!

Jenna licked, her tongue stroking Patty like a caring, caressing hand. The energy that had flowed from the telephone into Patty's body raced now to Patty's clit, and grew there, swelling, pulsing, demanding. Patty lifted her hips, pushing into the force.

Magic, Jenna, Magic!

Jenna freed one hand from Patty's thigh and poised it at Patty's wet slit. "I have something for you," she said.

Magic!

"Give it to me, Jenna!" Patty cried.

And Jenna shoved her hand into Patty's cunt, deep into the hole, up into Patty's very bowels, and Patty's clit screamed in joy and her whole body was ripped with convulsions of release. Something flowed into her depths, into her womb, rippling and coiling in a firm, pleasant caress.

"Magic!" screamed Patty. Her eyes had

closed, but she could feel Jenna's panting breath just over her stomach. "Oh, Jenna, it's not a myth."

"Now," whispered Jenna. "All you have to do is kill him."

What?

Patty opened her eyes. One hand flew to her throat, the other out before her for protection.

It was not Jenna leaning over her.

"Patty, Patty, Patty, Patty," came the voice in her head. Tsk, tsk, tsk.

The creature smiled. It stood and tipped its head. "It's all right, Patty," it said kindly. "Don't worry. We understand you."

"What?" Patty managed.

"We know the cruelty and selfishness of man. We know the craving and the unhappiness of women. It was the same here, on our own world, before we females learned we could rule and reproduce without the other gender."

The creature's smile was wide, and Patty could see, genuine. She lowered her hand and pressed it against the sand.

"It isn't a myth, is it?" the creature asked. "The beauty of release?"

"No," said Patty.

"We can have peace and passion without the torment and the abuse. We can have it all by ourselves."

225

Patty said, "Where am I?"

"In your mind, honey girl. At home, in your mind. We've reached you on line. But this connection is real. You are pregnant now, with a beautiful female child. And in time, with more calls to us and more women understanding what needs to be done, we will eventually clear the Earth of its scourge. It has been going well. And we are patient."

"Kill him?"

"Men have killed for less."

The creature's eyes sparkled with love.

And then, there was a phone in her hand and she was alone in the bedroom on the bed with a shoe box full of girlie magazines beside her. A puddle of sunlight sat on the floor by the window.

Outside, several cattle called to each other.

Out of the road, a lone car, probably lost, rumbled past.

She put the phone receiver back into the cradle slowly. She put her hand to her belly, and wondered what wonderful, peaceful female child was now growing there.

Henry got home, as usual, around eleven p.m., with a hot, hard, wet thing ready to give Patty a stick.

And in her hand behind her back, Patty had a cold, hard, dry thing with which to reciprocate.

Crow, Cat, Cow, Child

It took almost ten minutes to catch both the beetle and the centipede, but Hannah Livick's paper cup finally had the captives securely inside, and she walked them down to the grassy stretch behind the dumpster and let them go. Better to be out in the wild than in her apartment, where they might get stepped on or caught by one of Hannah's cats. It was more time consuming now to keep up with her promises. With the onset of fall, more insects sought warmth inside, and she spent more time chasing them and putting them out. But promises she had made, and promises she would keep.

She went back inside and dropped down on a kitchen chair. On the table before her was an opened letter from her father. The bastard. She flipped her hand and the letter fluttered to the floor. The two stray kittens she'd rescued from the college parking lot blinked at her from the hallway.

Timothy jumped onto the table. Hannah kicked off her shoes and tucked her hair back behind her ears. She waited as her breathing eased and her heart slowed. She needed to let things like this go. She was thirty-two, for heaven's sake, no teenaged flower child. She should no longer be thrown for a loop when others didn't understand. In fact, their lack of understanding only clarified her own. It clarified that of Karla Casey and little Ben and Joe and the other student members of Voices for the Voiceless, people who had true commitment to great causes.

"Great causes," she said to Timothy. She gave him a kiss.

Last night had been a glorious moment for a great cause. Another round won for the animals. Hannah and her friend Karla had led Voices for the Voiceless in a midnight raid on the county animal pound. The pound was clean enough, and part of their purpose, that of placing unwanted animals for adoption, was humane enough, but Joe had said the holding cell of unclaimed animals was now full and an execution was pending. Joe Farrish, a psychology major at the college and one of Hannah's brightest students who worked part-time at the pound, had stolen a key and the break-in was not a break-in at all but a calm open-the-door-and-help-yourself-in.

Dressed in a denim skirt and black sweatshirt which read "A crow is a cat is a cow is a child", Hannah had hacked the padlock from the holding cell, then stepped back as Karla's nine-year-old son, Ben, was allowed the first rescue.

"Go in, sweetie," Karla said, giving the little boy an encouraging push. "Those kitties and puppies are going to be poisoned to death if we don't set them free. They will cough and shake and vomit and suffer. Go get the first one out."

Ben, in his tiny red "Peace Now" ball cap, had gone into the dingy cell among the condemned, cats in a cage on the right of the cell and dogs in a cage on the left. The condemned watched him with hesitant wags of tails and blinks of eyes. He pulled the pin to the cat cage and lifted out a scraggly calico. As he turned to face the other rescuers, Joe snapped a Polaroid photo.

Grinning child and living cat. The crow is the cat is the cow is the child. Bless the beasts and the children. Equality beyond specieism.

The photo was now displayed on her refrigerator along with photos of other events in Hannah's activist life; protests, marches, passing home-computer generated pamphlets out on the street in front of the college and the nearby grocery stores.

Commitment and courage. Promises kept.

As little Ben would say when asked if he would always look out for the weaker creatures, "Cross my heart and hope to die."

Hannah stared at the photos, letting pride in what she was doing squeeze out the irritation at her father's selfishness. It took a little while, but it worked.

Joe wore a red plaid flannel shirt, not quite grunge but amazingly attractive in its carelessness, faded jeans, and boots. He sat, as he always did, in the middle of the classroom, leg crossed casually, pen top in teeth, scribbling notes faster than Hannah spoke. Interpretations, she assumed. His own additions to her lessons, questions, comments, insights.

As humans went, he was beautiful. Young and dark. Committed and courageous. And agonizingly sensual.

Hannah spoke today on the contrasting beliefs within the fundamentalist denominations in early twentieth century America. As was true in any class period, some students leaned forward with interest, some slumped back in boredom. Timothy, brought to class each day in his airy cat-tote, lay in his window sill overlooking the campus green. Every so often he would stretch, arch his back and scoot down a bit to catch the movement of the afternoon sunlight.

Class ended with the usual assignment, Hannah's challenge to younger minds. "Study those around you. See what we are. Observe and remember. Until tomorrow." And the students were gone then as quickly as water from a draining tub.

Joe sat unmoving at his desk, leg crossed, pen tapping his closed notebook. Hannah collected her books, scooted her podium over to the wall so the janitors could better clean, and took a last sip of the coffee from her Love Your Mother mug. Joe did not move. Hannah patted her hair and smoothed the tight bridge of her nose, then looked at him directly. He was smiling his beautiful smile. Her heart clenched at the beauty.

"Did you have a question?" she asked.

"I wanted to thank you for letting me be part of the rescue last weekend, Miss Livick,"

Joe said. His pen continued to tap.

"We couldn't have done it without you," Hannah said.

"Yes, you could have. It'd have been a little more dramatic, but you could have."

"It was your idea."

"And you agreed to take me up on it."

"So we both should be congratulated."

"Congratulations to us. And to those we saved."

Hannah sat on the top of a front desk and crossed her arms. There was more to come here, she just had to wait.

"We should celebrate." Joe stopped tapping the pencil. He uncrossed his legs. "How should we celebrate our success?"

"I don't have balloons or confetti."

Joe shook his head. His dark hair rippled. "I was thinking more in line of a dinner. Do you have plans tonight? We could have dinner and toast our beliefs."

Yes, I have plans, damn, she thought. But I'll work around them. No problem.

"Do you want to invite some of the others?" she asked. "Susan and Thomas and Barbara helped us set those animals free."

Joe stood up and put his notebook into his satchel.

The pen he slid through the thick hair to rest on his ear.

"I thought just us."

"Just us," said Hannah. Oh, God, yes. "Timothy!"

The cat turned his head and blinked. He was clearly too comfortable to move.

"Timothy, we've got to get. Come on, boy."

Timothy shut his eyes and rolled over, exposing his stomach to the warmth of the light.

"Jerk," said Hannah. She went to the window and picked up the cat. He drooped in her grasp, a furry soft-sculpture with twitching whiskers. "Into the case with you." Then she looked at Joe. "He'd get up under the gas pedal if I didn't contain him. They may have the same rights as humans, but I don't think they're quite as smart."

"Oh."

"That was supposed to be a joke."

"Oh. Ha." Joe walked over to Hannah and the cat carrier, stuck a finger through the slat and scratched the cat. He brushed Hannah's retreating hand as he did. "So, you can make it tonight?"

"Sure. And there is a wonderful restaurant, the Garden Gourmet, out on Booker Street. What do you think?"

"Actually, I have a lot of food at my place. Would you mind eating there? It's not a bad apartment. I'll actually run the vacuum for you. My roommate is gone for a few days, and I don't often have a chance to cook for someone else."

"That's fine."

"Seven?"

"Could we make it eight? I have to meet Karla at six and then I need some time to get ready, feed the cats, all that," said Hannah.

"Eight's good. You won't change your mind, now? You won't call and say you've come down with something?" He smiled, one eyebrow going up.

"I don't break promises."

"I knew that. After we eat we can take Timothy to the park. So bring him."

Hannah bit the inside of her cheek to keep the insipid grin she felt building from showing on her face. "Sure," she said.

Joe gave her a wink and strode from the classroom.

Hannah hugged the cat tote to her chest, listened to Timothy's purring, and waited until the thumping between her thighs eased.

Karla was late getting home from work. Hannah sat in her car in front of Karla's house, drumming her fingers on the steering wheel as Timothy whined in irritation from his cat tote.

"I'm sorry," she said. "We'll be home soon. Be patient."

On the back seat of Hannah's Bug was a boxload of Voices for the Voiceless brochures that she had run off at Kinko's just an hour earlier. Karla was attending a state senator's re-election campaign rally this weekend, and planned on getting a copy of the Voices mandate into every flesh-pressing palm. No doubt it would either catch the attention of the press or security, giving Karla the brief limelight she sought.

Tonight, Karla was going to work on her presentation and make a couple of conference calls with folks across the state. And Hannah had agreed to babysit Ben.

"Come on come on come on," Hannah said. "Damn it."

Karla's blue two-door pulled up behind Hannah's car and stopped. Karla climbed from the driver's seat, looking weary. Ben hopped from the passenger's seat and bounded around to Hannah's window. Hannah rolled the window down.

"Hey, sweetie!"

"Hey, Hannah!" said the boy. "I got an A on a science test today! It was all about earthworms. Do you know an earthworm swallows dirt and then poots it out the other side?"

"Uh, yes, I think I remember something like that," said Hannah. She smiled at the child's enthusiasm. Whenever she imagined herself as a mother, she envisioned her child beautiful and innocent, like Ben.

Karla came up and draped her arm around Ben's shoulder. "Hi, sorry I'm late. It's been a day and a half, I can't even get into it."

"Don't worry about it," said Hannah. "Do you have Ben's things ready for tonight?"

"Yep," said Karla. "Ben, here's the key. Go get the overnight bag out of the front hall."

Ben raced up the sidewalk, unlocked the front door, and disappeared.

"You're a saint for agreeing to keep Ben," said Karla. "It's not that he gets underfoot, really, but sometimes I just need to be alone to keep my thoughts straight. This campaign is so important, Hannah."

"I know. You don't need to convince me," said Hannah. "Come on, Ben, hurry up."

"Give me a call if you need anything," said Karla.

"We'll be fine," said Hannah.

Ben bounded out of the house and hopped into the passenger's seat of the Bug. Karla gave him a quick kiss through the open window, then went to the house.

Hannah smiled at Ben and said, "You know, there's a really good movie on down at the Tripoli."

* * *

She'd given Ben a quick meal at her apartment; homemade macaroni and cheese, some carrot sticks, and orange juice. Then, at 7:20, she'd driven him to the Tripoli Theater, which had a 7:30 Disney double-feature. They'd parked, and Hannah had walked Ben to the box office.

"My mom never lets me go to movies on school nights," Ben had said in the car, his eyebrows drawn up, as though he was afraid the confession might make Hannah change her mind.

"And you can't spend the night at friends' houses on school nights, either," Hannah had answered. "But tonight is different. It's special."

She'd bought the boy a ticket, had glanced around to quell the nagging sense that it might not be a good idea to send a child to a theater alone, had seen nothing in the movie-going crowd but parents and children, and so, relieved, had kissed the boy on the head, pressed six dollars into his hand for snacks, and said, "Be watching for me at nine-thirty, sharp. I'll pull up to the curb right here in front. And don't talk to strangers."

Ben giggled. It was clear he'd heard this many times before. "I won't, Hannah." And he'd stood on the sidewalk, waving, until she was out of sight.

I have an hour and a half for dinner, Hannah thought as she drove back to her apartment to take one last look at herself in the mirror and to collect Timothy. An hour and a half isn't bad. Dinner, some conversation, maybe time to work up another get-together.

She turned on the radio and hummed along, even though she didn't know the song.

Joe's apartment was pure college-man. Hannah walked in, holding Timothy in his tote in one hand and some daisies she'd picked up at the grocery store on the way over. Nostalgia washed over her; memories of her own shared flat when she'd been an undergraduate, a place she'd shared with buddy and fellow history major Charlotte Reeder. The furniture was salvage, the music loud and fast and current. Even the smells were familiar— that of spoiled food cleaned up but not completely, trash taken out just moments earlier, cigarettes and incense, sweat and air freshener, youth and vigor.

"Great place," Hannah said, standing on the living room mat just inside the door. In his tote, Timothy whined.

Joe laughed. "Oh, well, thanks. It's not quite what I'd call great, but I like it. It's home. I vacuumed."

"Thanks." Hannah glanced at Joe. His gaze was steady and a bit disconcerting. It made her heart kick in expectation.

"Dinner is still brewing," said Joe. He reached for the tote and popped open the lid. Timothy's furry face appeared at the top. "Hey, guy, how you doing in there?"

Timothy whined again and caught the edge of the tote to pull himself out.

"Is it all right if I let him roam around?" asked Hannah.

"Sure," said Joe. "As long as we can keep an eye on him. There are a lot of little nooks and crannies in which a cat could get stuck."

Timothy gratefully stretched when his paws hit the worn carpet, and he began to sniff the perimeter of the room. His whiskers stiffened and twitched.

"Sit, please," Joe offered. Hannah sat on the faded plaid sofa, Joe sat beside her. "Now, do tell how you got interested in teaching. It has to be one of the hardest jobs of all." He put his hand on the back of the sofa, near Hannah's hair. She wished he would touch it.

"I'm from a long line of educators," Hannah said.

"My mother, who died when I was seven, was a high school principal. And my father . . ." Hannah took a deep breath. Her father. Shit on it all.

239

"What about him?"

"He's an elementary school teacher. Third graders."

"Why did you make a face when you mentioned him?"

"Ever the psychology major, aren't you Joe?"

Joe grinned. "I suppose. So tell me."

"Oh, we don't exactly see eye-to-eye on some matters."

"Such as?"

"Such as animal rights. In fact, I think he hates me for my views."

Joe tilted his head. He put his foot up on the Afghan-covered trunk that served as a coffee table. "Really?"

Hannah glanced at her watch. It was only 8:12. She wished the meal was ready. Regardless, she had to be out of here by 9:20 to get to the theater on time. "Yes, really. He had a favorite student last year, a little boy with cancer who had gone into treatment at the children's center west town. Well, the same day the boy was admitted, there was the freeing of the animals at APD and then the bombing of the APD lab, remember?"

"Yes, I do."

"There was no connection. I mean, the hospital is on one side of town, the lab on the other. But the boy died after a month, and my father suddenly blamed all animal activists. He said it was our fault because we don't want cancer cured. I tried to talk with him, to tell him I'd love for cancer to be cured but not at the peril of other living things. But he went on a rampage. My mother dying was my fault then, because of her emphysema. My grandfather and his heart attack. It all fell on my head."

"Were you in on the bombing?"

"No," said Hannah. "I do my work in a peaceful way. I mean, what if all the animals hadn't been released? They would have died in the bomb." Joe's fingers found the top of Hannah's head and began to stroke. For a second, Hannah couldn't find her breath, but then she said, "My father writes me every so often, with all sorts of information he gets from an organization called 'Putting People First.' I just throw it away."

"Good for you," said Joe. "Want a drink?"

Hannah thought she should say yes, but doing so would take his hand from her hair.

"Well," Hannah began.

"No?"

She looked him in the eye. "Maybe in a minute," she said. And she knew the breathiness of her voice told him what she was thinking, what she was hoping.

And then Joe's lips were on her own.

Her body instictively pressed into his.

And the lust was as wonderful as she'd dreamed it would be.

She might have imagined it, but sometime during the love-making, Joe had laughed and called her a cheetah. Indeed, she felt she was one. Her blood raced like red-hot ice, her heart hammered like a native drum. She thought she heard the sound of distant chains rattling as he probed her cunt with his lips, and Joe growled with delight as he mounted her and caught her breasts in talon-fingers.

God!

"God!" Joe had cried. And then he had crumpled onto her, spent and panting. Hannah held still, then bucked in the throes of her own orgasm. Moaning, then, she curled her face into him and licked the sweat from his neck.

Finally, Joe's face lifted from hers. His eyes were wide and bright and as cunning as a cat's. Hannah grit her teeth to pull her soul back into her body. Never had such sensations invaded her; never had she felt so like an animal in her passion.

And then Joe stood abruptly from the sofa, his limp cock dangling, and smiled. "Now the question," he said.

"What question?" Hannah liked the sound of her voice. It was gritty with sex.

"A crow is a cat is a cow is a child."

"That's not a question," Hannah said. She sat up slowly, and saw then that Joe had indeed chained one ankle to the leg of the sofa. She laughed gently, and touched the chain. "You beast," she said. "What's this? We're through now. Unhook me."

Joe narrowed his eyes and make a tsking sound. "I thought you'd figure with a psychology student there'd be a test before the night was over. Come on now, surely you knew."

Hannah reached beneath her and tried to straighten the crumpled skirt. She scooted to the sofa's edge and planted the free foot on the floor. "Psychology or not, Joe, now, this is uncomfortable." She looked at her watch. It was 9:00. "And I don't think I'm going to have time to eat. I have to pick someone up at 9:30. Sorry."

"Scoot closer to the chain and you'll be all right. I really don't mean the test to take very long."

He stared at her. There was no smile there. She stared back, and the buzz of passion froze and crumbled in her chest like sharp fragments of ice.

"Joe," she said, her teacher voice pulling into place.

"Hannah," he responded, and the voice contained humor although the face did not.

"Joe, I have to go. Unlock this damned chain now."

"No, Hannah. We're not done." He went out of the living room and brought back two jars. Inside one jar was a spider. In the other, a mouse.

"It's a study, Hannah, now you can appreciate that. You're of an academic family." Joe sat on the trunk in front of her, holding the jars.

"What study?"

"A crow is a cat."

"So?"

"So, really? I want you to choose which of these will live and which will die."

Hannah tossed her head. She pulled against the chain on her ankle. "Don't be ridiculous."

"Which?"

"I won't choose. Life is life."

"Then I'll kill them both."

Hannah stretched her neck. This man, this beautiful man, was insane. She would not show her fear. She would not play his game. Her jaw chattered. "Your hand is not mine, Joe."

"Choose?" he asked.

"No."

Joe unscrewed the lid on the spider jar. He tapped the arachnid onto the floor and squashed it with his foot.

Hannah turned her face away.

"Your hands aren't mine," said Joe. "But your will is my command, like the old genie story. Therefore, what I do is your responsibility." Joe smashed the mouse jar on the edge of the trunk, sending glass fragments into Hannah's lap.

"Shit," mumbled Joe. "He isn't quite gone." She heard his heel drive down onto the floor. Hannah's stomach squeezed and turned over. She knocked the glass from her skirt. Joe laughed.

"What's your point here?" Hannah asked.

"A study of convictions, of promises."

"Asshole."

"Let's try again."

Hannah looked around as Joe left the living room again. She could not bear to look at the floor. Joe came back with two more jars. In one was a mouse. In the other, paws folded and eyes popping, was a baby guinea pig. Joe sat on the trunk. "Now," he said. "Mouse, or guinea pig? Whose life is more valuable? If you can't decide, then both lives are gone."

"Bastard."

"Regardless."

"I won't choose."

"Hannah."

"I believe what I believe."

"Fine." Joe lifted both jars and at the same time, brought them down against the edge of the trunk. The guinea pig squealed as his back was broken and he dropped with the bloody, shattered glass to the floor. The mouse was only dazed, and again, Joe finished it with his boot.

Hannah fought the cuff. She clawed at the sofa leg and shook it to break it. She then drove her free foot onto the glass on the floor and dove at Joe, but he jumped back beyond her reach. Hannah's trapped ankle tripped her and she fell on her face onto the trunk. Glass fragments on the wood splintered her palms. "Stop this now!" she screamed.

"Not until the test is over, I told you. Then you may go. Now get back on the sofa, you look very uncomfortable." He caught her under her arms and put her back on the seat. "Now, again." He left the room and returned with a large birdcage. Inside, two parakeets fluttered, working to keep themselves on the wooden perch. He sat the cage on the trunk, then took an extension cord from the top of the television and held it up. On one end was the plug; the other end was raw and frayed.

He plugged it into the wall and drew the raw end over to the trunk.

"Which one, Hannah? The green parakeet or the blue? I don't mean to sway you, but I'm partial to green."

Hannah held her fists up. They shook madly. "You fucker!"

"And you are a good test case, I have to tell you, Hannah. You're holding out better than I thought you would. Now, green or blue?"

"I can't!"

"All right," said Joe. He stuck the cord's end into the cage. The blue bird clenched its claws and dropped to the gravel at the bottom. Then the green bird joined it. A little tendril of smoke curled from it's wings.

Hannah put her fist to her eyes. If she had the courage to dig them out so she wouldn't have to see this anymore, she would.

God, help the animals.

Then she heard Joe calling, "Timothy, come here, boy. Timothy, kitty, kitty, kitty."

Hannah's head jerked up. "Don't touch him!"

Timothy trotted up to the man and wrapped around his legs. Joe laughed and lifted the cat, then found the abandoned tote by the front door. "Here you go, my friend," Joe said. "We'll tuck you right in here."

"Joe, don't do this. Listen to me, are you listening, Joe?"

Joe eased the cat inside and shut the top. He came back to the trunk. "Nice boy, nice kitty," he said.

Hannah reached down and tried to lift the sofa leg. It came up an inch, but the chain would not slide over the round sofa foot. "Goddamn you!" She yanked; the chain bit into her ankle, drawing a thin line of blood. "Goddamn you, stop, please!"

"Sit down, Hannah, this is the last test. Get a grip, Christ." He pushed her back. She fell against the sofa cushions with a grunt.

"Now," said Joe, standing by the trunk. "We have one animal here, but we need a second. Where should we find another one?" He stroked his chin. "Let me think."

I can't let him kill Timothy. I can't.

"I don't know if I have any more. You've killed them all so far, Hannah."

"I haven't killed a thing!"

Don't kill Timothy!

Joe put the tote on the floor by his foot and said, "You killed that little boy in your father's third grade class."

"What?"

"As sure as you put a bomb in the school, you killed him." Joe's jaw was tight. His voice hissed. "You and all your bleeding heart, idiot, moronic friends."

"Joe, you make no sense."

Joe reached over and slapped Hannah soundly on the cheek. Her head snapped back, reeling.

"He was my little brother, Hannah. You didn't even know his name, did you? Your murder victim. His name was Denny Farrish. The sweetest little boy you could ever know. Never to grow up. You bitch."

"I . . . didn't . . . kill. . . ."

"Oh, shut up and let's get the test finished. One more and you'll be free to go. Now, we have a cat. And," Joe looked down at the trunk. "Yes, we have another animal in the trunk, I remember now." He pushed the afghan off to the floor. "An animal in there. You choose, Hannah. The cat in the hand, or what's behind trunk number one."

"I didn't kill your brother."

"Oops, forgot," said Joe. He went to the television stand and pulled a pistol out from the single drawer. He came back, and a smile had returned. "Now, then, which animal shall live, my dear teacher?"

I can't let Timothy die. Whatever dog or cat or groundhog is in that trunk isn't as precious as Timothy. I can't let him shoot my cat!

"Don't make me wait," said Joe. "Your father told me you were always such a slow-poke."

"Father?"

"We know each other. I visited my brother's class occasionally. I even went on the field trip to McDonald's with all those little kids. Your dad asked if I could bring you to your senses somehow. I said I didn't know. I was a psychology major, but not a shrink yet. I need a few more years on me for that. But that's an aside. Now, pick, Hannah."

"You can't kill Timothy," Hannah growled.

"Fine, then, this shouldn't take long." Joe flipped back the lid on the trunk. He raised the pistol and aimed it inside. Hannah didn't look. It no longer mattered. She had broken her promise to herself. A crow might be a cow but a cat was of more importance to her. She wanted to vomit.

"Oh, before I do this," said Joe. "Maybe I should just loosen this little gag here."

There was a pause, then the sound of crying.

Sobbing.

A child.

There was a child in the trunk.

"Oh, my God," said Hannah.

"Hannah!" shrieked the child.

Ben.

"I followed you all afternoon," said Joe. "To Karla's, to your apartment. To the theater. Ben doesn't talk to strangers, but we saved puppies together, didn't we, Ben? You know me."

"Hannah!" cried Ben.

"I told him we were going to surprise you, that we had a party here at my apartment for you and the other animal rescuers. He thought it was a fine idea," said Joe.

"Shoot the fucking cat!" screamed Hannah.

"Fine idea," said Joe. He pointed the gun at the tote and emptied four bullets into it. Hannah felt each one, cutting through her mind, searing her brain, tearing up her sanity and spitting it out like a catnip toy.

Joe stepped to the sofa and leaned in to Hannah, his mouth on her ear. "Now, you see there is a difference, don't you, Hannah?"

She said nothing.

Joe shook his head and stroked her hair. "Hannah, there is a difference. Admit it."

"Yes."

Joe straightened, sighed, and nodded. "Thank you. Now." He put the gun down and wiped his hands. "That's about it. I'll get little Ben out of this thing and you two are free to go. Good psychology test, don't you think? Too bad I won't be able to use it as part of my deviant class research. No control subject.

Careless, I know. If my damn head weren't screwed on!" He chuckled.

A crow is a cat is a cow.

Hannah began to cry.

"No, don't," said Joe as he put pliers to the chain on her ankle. "I know I lied about dinner. But believe me, it's not worth a single tear."

A child is a child is a child is a child.

A promise is a lie is a promise is a lie.

"I can't cook very well." The chain fell away. "You didn't miss much."

Shadow of the Valley

One, two, three, four, five, six, turn, one, two, three, four, five, six, seven, eight, turn, one, two, three, four.

He stopped, scratched his ear and his neck. Several drops fell from the ceiling and he put his fingers to the wet, then brought the wet to his mouth and sucked at it. Then, he picked up where he left off.

Five, six, turn, one, two, three, four, five, six, seven, eight, turn, one, two.

And then he remembered, and he remembered hard, and he dropped to the damp concrete, his bare knees, so accustomed to this move after two years, cushioning the fall with thick, bulbous layers of scar tissue. His butchered hands went together, his blood vessels picked up a rhythm of familiar, sweat-driving dread, and he prayed his impotent prayer.

"Lord is my shepherd. Shadow of the valley of death. Do unto others all the days of my life. I pray the Lord my soul to take. Little hands be careful."

He repeated it until the words lost their meaning and he was freed again from the knowledge of his past, his present, and his inevitable and horrific future. Standing, he felt his way in the darkness to the corner and began again.

One, two, three, four, five, six, turn, one, two, three, four, five, six, seven, eight, turn, one, two, three, four, five, six, turn.

His name was Marcus. He knew that. He knew he was thin; he could feel the rib bones and hip bones beneath his naked skin. He knew there were people beyond the darkness, and these people were his jailers. He knew he was fed once a day, and he knew that sometimes, the water he was given through the slot in his door was fouled with urine. But he drank it, anyway.

He knew these things, but he didn't think about them.

Thinking made him remember, it opened the door of his mind and the truth came in and if he couldn't pray it away, he would spend the next hours screaming and crying in a corner. And so, he walked. He counted. He prayed. And when weariness came mercifully, he slept, curled against the door in the single tiny sliver of silver light that came through the food slot, his arms wrapped around his knees, his penis tucked between his legs to keep it safe from the centipedes and spiders that shared his cell with him.

Marcus stopped walking and looked at the sliver of light. For a moment, he saw his father's grim mouth, set hard in soft, fat flesh. Then the vision shifted and he saw the stern countenance of God.

"Shadow of the valley," he whispered. He went to the wall by the door. His hands suddenly dove forward as if they'd forgotten that the wall, as was the floor, was damp, solid, cold. Immovable.

Like God in his judgment.

His hands banged on the wall, and he counted. "One, two, three, four, five, six, seven, eight." He could count no farther because there was nothing past eight. The cell was six feet wide, eight feet long. The door is six feet tall, three feet wide. The ceiling, which he could touch with upstretched arms, was seven feet high. He had eight fingers, four on each hand since he had his thumbs removed for an infraction he couldn't remember. He had eight toes, for the same reason.

A shiver caught his bare spine and shook him like a mouse in a dog's mouth.

Dropping his hands from the wall, he turned. He walked.

One, two, three, four, five, six, seven, eight, turn.

In a tiny nick in the long wall, six feet from the floor, was a spoon. Marcus had kept the spoon from one of his daily meals. In truth, he hadn't kept it on purpose. It was only a plastic spoon and though made of sturdy material, could not have been much of a tool for burrowing a hole in the concrete. That was, if Marcus had considered trying to burrow from his cell of eternal night. And he hadn't. Even if the spoon were a chisel, it wouldn't matter. He was in a center cell. He knew this; he remembered being brought down here from the main population on the ground floor so many months ago, and remembered the guards stripping him of his clothes, hosing him down to get rid of fleas and lice he didn't have, then throwing him in and locking the door, shutting off all sounds, nearly all light.

His cell was in the middle of the prison cellar. If he dug through a wall it would only be to find himself in another solitary cell. And then another and another and another. This was not the movies. There was no air vent system to hasten him to the outside world, no sewer system to slide through, no rivers in which to float unseen to a safe haven.

And even if there were, there was no safe haven. Safe from what? His torment in the cell? The random tortures by the sergeant guard? Perhaps. But not from eternity.

Nothing could save him from eternity.

Five, six, seven, eight, turn, one, two, three, four, five, six, turn, one, two.

"Little hands be careful. Shadow of the valley of death." He hit the floor on his knees, his clutching fingers finding each other in the dark like brittle insects driven to copulation, his mind, his heart, his soul tearing at each other, clawing each other to shreds in certainty of his eternity.

He'd been told by the minister of his fate.

"God will not forgive you," the man had whispered after sentencing had been pronounced. "You are beyond the grace of God and no prayer, no supplication, no pleading will deliver you from the eternal damnation in the lake of fire."

To Marcus, who had been sitting in the jail cell awaiting delivery to the state prison, the minister's words hadn't registered. He'd been angry, furious beyond reason that he'd been sentenced to life for a murder his brother had committed. He'd been there, certainly, he'd even taken the Twizzlers they'd found in his grimy pockets. But he hadn't killed the shop owner. Brad had done that with a blow to the skull with a tire iron. Marcus had stopped in his tracks in the shop's candy aisle and had stared as the owner dropped to the floor like a sack of potatoes. Brad had screamed for Marcus to come on come on come on let's get the fuck out of here when a shopper came in, the little door chime tinkling. The man had been carrying a concealed weapon, newly legal in their fine state, and had shot Brad with a single blast directed at the forehead.

The tire iron had been in Brad's fist, but the shopper didn't feel there was enough dramatic justice to have a dead murderer to present to the police. You can't discipline a dead murderer before the public. And so he'd claimed that Marcus had wielded the iron, and as Marcus had used the iron many times in the jack when helping Brad change blown retreads on his truck, his prints were on it. He was convicted.

The shopper had been praised for attempting to stop the robbery and save the already-dead owner's life. Marcus, fifteen at the time, though tried as an adult had not been given the death penalty as most citizens had screamed for, but life in prison. Two times over.

Five, six, seven, eight, turn, one, two, three.

He was sorry now. He knew he shouldn't have listened to Brad. Brad was his brother and Marcus loved him but Brad didn't know shit about right and wrong. God have pity, fuck it all, where was Brad now? In the never-ending lake of torment? Of course he was.

Forever and ever and ever and ever and ever and ever and ever one, two, three, four, five, six, seven, eight, turn, one, two, three, four, five, six, turn, one, two, three, four, five, six, seven, eight, turn, one, two, three, four. . . .

"Your tongue's ticklin' my ear!" whined Tonya as she pulled away from Jimbo. "You feel like a old wet worm."

Jimbo pinched Tonya's cheek and pulled back and tugged the sweat-crusted brim of the guard's hat down, covering Tonya's eyes. "A wet, willin' worm, honey," he said. He grinned and lit a cigarette. He was good-looking, and Tonya knew she was lucky to have him like her. He was twenty-three, muscular, and covered with knock-out tattoos. She'd first seen him in the 7-Eleven in his guard uniform, buying a pack of smokes before he went to work. She worked behind the counter. When she'd slid the pack across the countertop to him, he'd put his hand on top of hers and said, "Want to light one for me?"

Tonya, at nineteen, was ecstatic. She'd never had a boyfriend before Jimbo, had never even been touched in that way by a boy before. Her height, six-one, had scared off most boys, and besides, she was skinny and flat as a train track and her bottom teeth poked out a little. So, with a trembling match she'd lit a cigarette for Jimbo, and the next morning when he got off work and came back by the store, she'd gone out with him and lit more than that.

Dating hadn't exactly been what she'd thought it would be, and she didn't have any girlfriends to compare notes with, just what they did on movies and on the T.V. But Jimbo kept coming back for more, so she figured it was going okay.

They'd been a couple for four months now. At first, Jimbo had made love to her easy, in her bed or his, once out by the pond and once in the back of his pickup on the overlook at Raven's Roost. Then, it began to change. It wasn't making love anymore. It was screwing, fucking, humping. And she had the bruises to prove it. But he was her boyfriend.

Most of the time now he scared her. But he was her boyfriend.

My boyfriend, she thought. She had no idea exactly what he wanted today, a fuck in the prison basement? Probably. Just so he didn't try to put ants down her blouse like he did one time in the woods so she'd buck harder when he came.

They stood alone at the end of a narrow hallway in the far reaches of the prison. Jimbo had a tangle of keys hanging from his belt. It made him look very sexy.

"Now don't be making any noise, you hear me?" Jimbo warned Tonya. "My friends aren't going to say anything but Captain Harner will have me out of here on my ear if he finds I got you in here. He'll probably fine me or even have me arrested. Fuck. You want me locked up in here with these stinking criminals?"

" 'Course not." The gum she'd had resting in the side of her mouth made its way back to her teeth. She stretched it, blew a bubble, and it popped. "Now, what are we gonna do, Jimbo?"

"That's for me to know and you to find out. And you be a good little girl and keep your fucking mouth shut. You hear me?"

Tonya nodded.

"It's gonna be underground." His brown eyes sparkled, his square jaw cracked in a smile. He unlocked the steel door to the cellar stairs, tugged the door open, and grabbed Tonya's hand.

Tonya had come into the prison easily, under pretense of visiting a prisoner, Eddie Stratford, who had twenty-five years for armed robbery. Eddie had no desire to see Tonya; she reminded him of his fucked-up old girlfriend that he tried to kill one time, but he was willing to play the game in exchange for the cash and cigarettes Jimbo was able to provide. "Hi, Tonya, good to see you how's the baby how's the job?" During the visiting hours, Jimbo had sneaked Tonya away from Eddie and hid her in the male guard's restroom. There she'd donned an old uniform and put on Jimbo's cap. Her heart had beat irregularly with dreadful hope.

Jimbo's guard friends had let them slip deeper and deeper into the prison confines, through the gates and down the passageways, Tonya bending low beneath the bulk of her costume so the prisoners wouldn't notice her; so Captain Harner, who strode these corridors with regularity, according to Jimbo, wouldn't notice her. After many twists and turns, they came to the stairs leading down to the solitary confinement cells.

"Ain't supposed to use the cells down there no more," Jimbo explained in a hushed voice as he'd opened the panel to the light box and flicked a switch, throwing yellow glow down the steps. "Warden don't even know we use 'em. Ain't humane. Fuckin' ACLU. Pussy-lickin' cry-babies. It's their damn fault. What do they think punishment is, a tea party and a birthday cake? I say screw 'em. Hang the thieves, the drug-addicts, the dealers, the murderers. Hang the goddamned white-collar crooks and those women who don't get off welfare in a year. Torture 'em first, then string 'em up where the public can watch and take pictures. Put the pictures in the post of-fice."

"There's guys down here in cells?"

"That's what I'm saying. Keep up with me and keep your goddamn thoughts to your-self."

Tonya nodded.

"I know what I'm doing, okay?"

"Okay," said Tonya. She didn't know any-thing about criminal justice, but Jimbo sure did. He knew about everything, cars, politics, religion. He would make a hell of a president, she thought. Straighten everything out. She followed Jimbo down to the cold concrete floor of the cellar, keeping one hand in his, the other on the crusty, crumbling wall. The smell, wafting up from the cellar, was strong, a blending of wet and mildew and cold sweat.

"Only got two down here now," said Jimbo. "Both murderers. Since neither of them made it to death row, some of us guards decided we would give 'em a little treat down here for a while.

"Captain Harner approved it, and the warden won't never hear of it 'cause he doesn't take much stock in the day-to-day. One's an old fart, been a con for, shit, over thirty years now. We put him down here for throwing food in the cafeteria. Now he can throw it all he wants, nobody knows or cares. That's him there."

Jimbo pointed. Tonya looked.

The cell was directly in front of them. It looked like a steel closet, with a slot in the door like a mail slot. There was no door knob, only a keyhole. Tonya guessed you tugged the door open with the key. Above their heads, the long, bare fluorescent lights pulsed and hummed.

"Is it dark in that cell?"

"Guess so."

"No lights at all?"

"Don't think so."

"How do they see in there?"

"They don't, idiot."

Tonya took a deep breath that stung her nose. She shifted one foot to the other. "How long's that guy been in solitary?"

Jimbo shrugged. "I don't know. Couple, four months. He don't make a sound, but he's alive 'cause he eats what we stick in the slot. He's got a mattress, too, so he can't complain. Homeless people ain't got mattresses, so this asshole should send us a thank you note, don't you think?"

Tonya said, "Guess so."

Jimbo put one arm around Tonya's waist, glanced around, then put one hand on Tonya's right breast. "Shit, it makes me hot, being one of the good guys."

"Where's the other con?"

"Cell down this way," said Jimbo. He gave Tonya's breast a healthy, painful squeeze, then ushered her down the hall thirty feet, past other steel doors and knobless keyholes. Centipedes scurried into drains; brown, fat-bodied spiders clutched draglines in the shadowed corners. God, don't let him want to put spiders down my blouse, Tonya thought.

Half-way to the second con's cell, Jimbo spun around, put his hands down the front of Tonya's guard pants and kissed her neck. "Can't stop, baby," he hissed, and Tonya tried to think of what he was doing to keep her mind off whatever the hell he might be asking her to do in a few minutes.

* * *

He took up the spoon and felt it and put it into his mouth, pretending there was food on there and that it tasted good. He sucked the good food, it was mashed potatoes with pepper this time, then licked the spoon eight times until it was clean. He licked his lips and put the spoon back in the nick. Then he paced.

One, two, three, four, five, six, turn, one, two, three, four, five, six, seven.

He remembered again. The sledgehammer of memory slammed him in the back of the head and he stumbled.

God pity me have mercy why why why don't please don't I don't want to die I want to live forever so I won't go into the lake of burning torment God no! Marcus fell to his knees, then stretched prostrate, his cheek losing skin on the concrete.

"Lord is my shepherd," he said to the floor. "I pray the Lord my soul to keep. Shadow of the valley, all the days of my life." He burst into sobs. His tears were thick with salt. If he could have killed himself at that moment, he would have. But that would only bring him into hell more quickly. He'd thought of death many times, and of how to some it was relief, it was ecstasy in the arms of God.

But not for him. There was nothing ahead of him but life's agony. And then death's agony.

When the crying eased, he touched the tears on the floor and brought the wet to his lips. Then he stood, found the wall, and walked.

Jimbo pulled his fingers out from Tonya's bush, sucked them, then shoved his hands into his pockets.

"Can't push that too far," he said. "I want something raring to go when my time comes. I'm a steel rod, baby." He winked. "You like steel rods?"

Tonya said, "What do you mean, when your time comes?"

"It's gonna be something special today," said Jimbo.

"What is it?"

Jimbo said, "I mean this." He walked another ten feet, then planted his hand on a steel door. "There's a lover boy in here, ready and waiting."

Tonya came over and touched the door, too. She peeked in through the food slot and couldn't see a thing but tar-blackness. She had promised herself to do anything for Jimbo. He was her man. He bought her stuff. He liked her ass. He didn't hit her. Anything, she had told him. But her stomach turned with uncertainty.

There were many things she'd done to keep Jimbo happy. She'd let him pee all over her in the bathtub once. She'd screwed him in a gravelly parking lot where a gang of construction men could look down on them. She'd gone without panties into a hardware store, then bent over to show the clerk what kind of nails she wanted to buy while Jimbo watched through the store window.

But she'd never fucked somebody else.

Especially not no damned con in solitary confinement.

"I'm gonna fuck him?" she asked.

"He's probably too weak to hurt you, baby," said Jimbo. He touched her cheek and tweaked her nose.

"You mean he'd want to hurt me but he's too weak?"

Jimbo frowned. Tonya didn't like his frown. "I don't know, Tonya. Don't press me. He's been there a while. He ain't gonna hurt you."

"How long he's been there?"

"Two years. Longer than I been here. But, like I said, what the warden don't know won't piss him off. This con's got no family, no lawyer checking on him. He could stay here his whole life for all I care."

Tonya's head began to pound. "Ever see him?"

"No. But I been down here for feeding. He eats, so he's alive, just like the other one. Hear Captain Harner took off a couple the guy's digits one time."

Tonya shivered.

"Harner hates rule breakers and human trash," Jimbo continued. "He even put a buddy guard of mine down here in a cell for a couple weeks for smart-mouthing off." Jimbo laughed. "Harner's right on."

"Why don't you just go on and let the cons here die? I mean, if the warden don't know and all. You think they ought to die, right?"

This seemed to make Jimbo think. His lip drew up and one eye squinted. Then he smiled. "Guess it's more fun like this. Kind of like a secret club. You like secret clubs?"

Tonya's nose wrinkled. She hoped it looked cute. But in truth, it was a spasm of fear. "Yeah. But what if he's a queer and don't like me? He might hurt me then, Jimbo."

"I'll be watching, so if he starts to hurt you I'll kick his ass, how about that?"

"Well. . . ."

Jimbo took Tonya's arm, and it hurt. "Well, what? You gonna do this, aren't you?"

"Sure. 'Course I am."

Jimbo nodded, then put a key into the hole in the door. "Thought so," he said.

*　　*　　*

He knew every corner of his room, every crack, every lump, every chink. His fingers were his eyes and they were rough but clear. Sometimes, though, his mind became his eyes and it showed him the cell from above, a clear picture with him in it, twenty years old, naked, shivering, and doomed.

"I'm sorry," he said to himself. Five, six, turn, one, two, three, four, five, six, seven, eight, turn, one, two. "Sorry, sorry, sorry, sorry, sorry, three, four, five, six, turn, one, two, three."

His hand rode again over the nick with the spoon. He took it out and carried it with him, dragging it along the wall's surface so he could hear something besides his own voice and his own breathing.

There was rattling at the food slot, and he ran to the corner and crouched, covering his head with his hands and the spoon and screaming "I'm sorry!" The phantom toes and fingers flamed into agony, recalling their disciplinary amputation, wondering if the fingers and toes beside the scarred spaces might be next.

"He's screaming!" said Tonya.

"Shut the fuck up and get in there," said Jimbo. He pulled the door open, and the dim light spilled into the bare-floored cell.

*   *   *

He saw the silhouette in the middle of the blinding light, a tall, thin human form with long hair. It wasn't a guard. It was a devil.

Death was here, and it was time to step into the lake of eternal fire and damnation for his unending punishment.

"I'm sorry!" His knees pulled up to his chin and his eyes blurred. "Not now, please!"

The devil stopped in the doorway, said something he couldn't hear, then took a few more steps. The minister had said to Marcus, "When you die, you'll wish you could kill your spirit, too, because it's going to suffer for ever and ever and ever, you murdering bastard!"

Marcus' throat twisted, and he sputtered in a strangled hiss, "No, please."

The devil, in a surprisingly high-pitched voice, said, "Be quiet."

And so he was.

"Be quiet," Tonya said to the man in the corner. He was hard to see, hard to imagine. Jimbo had said the man was weak and couldn't hurt her.

He better not, she thought. Or I'll kick him in the nuts.

"Don't just stand there, seduce him," whispered Jimbo. "Bring him out where I can see and take off your clothes. Spread your things and get him going. Damn, this is going to be something!"

Tonya said, "Come out here, let me see you." She clenched her fists on the ready. "Slide over here into the light."

"Slide over here into the light," the devil said. On his butt, dragging against the rough of the floor, Marcus went. He kept his head down, his knees up. He didn't want to see the face of death.

"Lay down."

Marcus lay on his back. He wondered if, in the moment of death, there would be at least a second of peace. He closed his eyes. The devil said, "Open your eyes." He did.

The devil knelt beside him. It was a she-devil. Her face wasn't clear, but her hair was golden. She had on guard's clothes. Like the wolf in sheep's clothing, the devil came in disguise. A thief in the night. She would strike him now, and claw out his open eyes before she sucked his life away and then spit his worthless spirit into damnation.

A hand reached out and touched him on the face. It was warm, not icy cold or fire-brand hot. Marcus waited. She took her hand away, stood, and stepped out of the clothes. There was no tail, no scales. Only smooth, silky skin.

Marcus' heart picked up a new rhythm, one he'd not felt before. "What?" he asked.

"They did cut off your fingers, didn't they?"

"Yes."

"And your toes."

"Yes. Captain took them. And now you're going to take the rest." Marcus heard the doom in his own words. The devil would chop him up and then put him back together so he could burn alive forever.

"That's pretty shitty," said the devil.

Marcus blinked. What had she said?

How can I do this? Tonya thought. He's fucked up big time. He's ugly and he ain't got all his fingers and toes. Shit.

She could feel Jimbo's steady, horny gaze on her back. She could feel her own insides recoiling at the idea of this con's naked flesh against her own. Slowly, she knelt again and put his hand on her breast. He was so cold and thin it was as if she was trying to fuck a dead man. Touching him was the worst thing so far Jimbo had made her do.

"Seduce him," growled Jimbo.

Her voice was pine cone dry as she said, "Hey, honey, I'm going to take you to heaven."

* * *

She'd said heaven.

Before he could think more she was touching him, pulling his hand up from his chest and placing it on her breast. His breath caught and the hairs on his arms went erect. His penis, which he had covered with the spoon, did likewise.

God help me!

He jerked his hand away and sat up, thrusting the spoon in her direction to keep her from touching him again. It sounded as if she swore quietly, then she reached out again. "Don't you want to go to heaven with me?"

"The minister said I was going to hell!" Marcus screamed.

She sighed and rubbed her face. She said, "Let me touch you." Her hand went to Marcus' crotch and she caught his penis with warm fingers. She began to rub and tug gently. "Come on, honey. I'm your angel today."

Marcus didn't resist. He watched her as she aroused him. Her eyes were visible this close, and they were beautiful eyes.

She had said angel. She had said heaven.

Heaven.

Oh, God.

He dropped the spoon onto the floor.

Oh my God. Am I forgiven?

* * *

His smell was the worst. But she told herself not to think about it. Get it done, get it over and get out of this place.

She let go of the penis and folded herself around the thin, stinking convict, her lips rolled in so she wouldn't inadvertently try to kiss his fouled mouth and rotting teeth. Her hands, less critical than eye or nose, explored the ravaged territory of his body. He was indeed young, no older than she was. On his chin was a growth of prickly hair; on his head filthy, limp hair that came at least to his shoulders. His cheekbones were prominent, and his shoulders narrow. There was no hair on his chest, and his heartbeat could be felt through the skin.

"I'm your angel," she said. "Let's go to heaven." She rolled onto her back, pulling the thin man with her. He tried to resist, but he was light, like a featherless bird. He said something she couldn't understand, and she said, "Yeah, honey, that's right." Her legs opened and she found the penis once more, now hard as a stick, and guided it into her slit. She felt his face come down on her right, and he said, clearly, "Am I forgiven?"

"What?" she asked.

The man was crying now, even as his hips began to pump. "Am I forgiven?"

She opened her eyes. Over the man's head she saw Jimbo, hands on hips, clearly disappointed with this pathetic show of lust. Then she looked at the man, whose face was turned to the floor, his bony hand beneath his nose. A drop was on his nose and it was shaking.

She, in turn, began to tremble. "Sure. Sure you are."

He sighed, a sound soft and gentle and full of rapture.

The angel said he was forgiven.

God had sent her, and he was forgiven. The minister was wrong. Marcus was not damned to eternal fire. The love of God came to even the lowest animal such as he. Oh, God, he thought.

He held the angel, he loved her and praised her. It was over. It was done. He was no longer despised. He was no longer hated.

She loved him in return, touching him with her unearthly warmth, healing him with her divine breath.

He came inside her, humbled and grateful.

"Bless you, angel," he said. "Thank you. Thank you for saving me."

There was a long pause. Then she said, "You're welcome." Then she stood up, looked at him a moment longer, and left the cell. The door shut, and it was dark again.

* * *

"That sure wasn't much," said Jimbo as he locked the door and turned on Tonya. "What the fuck was that, anyway? A game of patty-cake? That was as sexy as a junior high school dance."

"Fuck you, asshole," said Tonya, her words stammered, caught on her tongue but spit out before they could change their mind.

Jimbo's eyes widened. One hand went up as if to strike her. "What did you say?"

Tonya said, "I said fuck you. I'm through with your games."

Jimbo shoved her with his fists, and she landed on her butt on the hall floor. But she didn't take her gaze from him, and she said, "You ain't gonna treat me like shit no more."

"I treat you like I want, bitch!"

"I'm not a bitch."

Jimbo laughed. "You're a bitch of the worst kind. You're a mindless, stupid, buck-tooth bitch."

"No." Tonya took a hissing breath through her teeth. She said, "I'm an angel."

Jimbo eyes rolled up and his head followed, angling back on his neck, his mouth dropping open. A howl of glee came out. "Angel? What the fuck are you talking about? I ought to crush your skull for talking trash like that! Goddamn, did that guy fuck with your head or something?" Suddenly, he grabbed her by the throat and hauled her up. She clawed at his fingers.

"Did he fuck with your head!?"

Tonya let herself go limp. She gasped, "No. It ain't nothing. I'm kidding, just spoutin' off. Sorry."

Jimbo glared at her then loosened his hand. "What'd you say?"

"I said I'm kidding. You kid with me. I thought it'd be funny. It wasn't. Sorry. Let's get out of this place. I'm cold."

"You best be sorry. I ought to beat the devil out of you when I get you back to my place. I just might, you slut. What was that shit?"

"Nothing."

Jimbo grabbed her arm, gave it a painful tweak, then let go. The two moved down the hall and climbed the steps to the main floor, leaving the dark solitary cells behind.

Tonya thought, I'm an angel.

"Bitch," muttered Jimbo.

I'm good, she thought. I don't deserve Jimbo's shit.

Jimbo pushed Tonya through the door at the top of the steps and locked it. The keys jingled haughtily. "Put the damn hat back on," he said. "Pull it low like before, you whore."

She did.

As they walked through the corridors, Jimbo dragging her, pissed off more than she'd ever seen him, Tonya watched for the best moment to shout and yell that she was being kidnapped. Wouldn't old Jimbo be shocked at that, and wouldn't his smart mouth be silenced when Captain Harner came to help her, an innocent female in the hands of an ego-crazed guard? Wouldn't Jimbo be surprised to find himself handcuffed and taken away? Maybe to have a digit off by the trash-hater? Maybe to have a little time down in a solitary cell himself?

Wouldn't the pussy-licking ACLU look pretty good to him by then?

Marcus found the spoon, and found a corner. He wedged himself deep into it and said his prayers. Then dragged the sharp plastic spoon handle across both wrists and waited as the blood and warmth and life drained away, safe in the knowledge now that God was waiting for him with open arms.

Learning to Give

The mockingbird was singing, and it was morning. The bird was alone, but close by in a shrub, and its song was forceful and clear. From somewhere beyond the roof of the tool-shed, the baleful medley crossed the yard. It drifted in the stifling summer air and entered the tiny attic window where the flies and the gnats and the smoke came in.

Anna knew the song belonged to a mock-ingbird. Very long ago, her mother had told her of a bird that knew how to sing many dif-ferent tunes. A bird that could change its mel-ody in a heartbeat. This was a survival skill for the bird, and it flourished. Anna remem-bered her mother's story clearly, although she could no longer remember her mother's face.

As the bird sang to the sun, Anna and all Greta's other friends sat in the sooty dust in a circle on the attic floor. They wore dirty, sleeveless summer tops and matching short pants, but they sweated just the same. Greta's mother had sewn the clothes for the friends, a large set for Joseph, who was fifteen and the tallest, a small set for Margarette, who was nine, and sizes in between for the others. Anna was twelve, William ten, and Susanne eleven. No one in the circle spoke because they didn't have permission to speak. It was time for class.

Greta sat on a short-legged chair. She had her fingers linked about her knees, causing the hem of her pink dress to hike up around her ankles, revealing pink embroidered socks. Her blond hair was curled about her chin. She smiled at her friends as she looked them over. She had an elegant smile. No living soul, regardless of race or class, could have seen that smile and not said it was elegant. The dimples on the smooth cheeks, the gentle parting of lips over perfect teeth. Greta gave the smile to the friends frequently, and it made their blood run cold.

"Good morning, children," Greta said.

In unison, the friends said, "Good morning."

Greta tilted her head and licked her upper lip with a slow motion of her tongue. Anna thought Greta must have had a teacher once who had used that very gesture. Greta was enamored of the adults in her life—her relatives, her parents' acquaintances. Sometimes she talked to the friends at great length about the adults she knew: her father's coworkers, her mother's dressmaker, her grandmother and her uncle Geoff. Greta's eyes danced, and her hands were dramatic understudies to her lively voice. When Greta talked this way, Anna would nod as if she were listening while throwing all her concentration on the sounds of the birds outside the window. She knew the other friends did what they could so they would not have to listen either. To hear of family, to think of family was to open wounds that would never heal.

"Joseph," Greta said.

Anna felt her own body draw up in unison with Joseph's.

"I see that your hair's grown long. How could you come to class like that? You look such the ruffian, like a boy from the ghetto."

Greta smiled a horrible and elegant smile.

Joseph, tall for fifteen and as lean as a willow branch, turned his good eye toward Greta and shrugged.

"What is that? What is that shrug?"

Joseph, now having permission to speak, mumbled, "I don't know."

"Hmmmm," said Greta. Like Anna, she was twelve, but she already had gained the matter-of-fact conversational style of her father, Erik Brummer, the adult she admired the most. "How can we conduct class with a ruffian here on the floor? We should cut it, then, shouldn't we?"

Joseph said, "Yes. We should."

There was, of course, no other possible answer.

"Good," said Greta, and she smiled her smile at them all.

She went to the small chest near the open window and lifted the top. From inside she brought her sewing set and from the set, a small pair of scissors. She stood and turned to face the friends in their circle on the floor. She smiled.

"I should like to be a beautician someday, like my Auntie Kate. She is a wonderful woman. She plays the piano as well as she can fix hair and polish fingernails."

Little Margarette raised her hand.

"What do you want, little one?" asked Greta.

"Would you need help for the cutting? I could catch the curls." Margarette sat still. Her tiny smile was not as elegant as Greta's, but it was a true smile. Margarette was the treasure in the attic; she was the friend of the friends, and Anna knew if she would ever allow herself to use the word love, it would be for Margarette.

Greta, who because of Margarette's youth was usually more patient with the girl, said, "No, you stay in the circle and see how it's done. See the scissors, how sharp they are? Dull ones tear the hair. And see how they are short? Long scissors can snag and make a mess."

All the friends were silent. They had learned the importance of paying attention.

"Tip your head my way," said Greta. She sat back down on her stool, and Joseph slid around on his bottom until his back was almost touching Greta's knees. He stared straight ahead, and the other friends averted their eyes from his. It was best not to look and see the fear that had flared there. Joseph would have to handle the haircut as best he could. Whatever the haircut would entail.

"Head back," said Greta.

Joseph put his head back. Anna could see, from the corner of her vision as she looked at the barren bookshelf beyond the soft tousle of Joseph's hair, the thin fifteen-year-old put his head back. She could see his blind white eye, but not the good one. She was glad because the blind eye was dead to emotion. Emotion was a dangerous commodity.

Greta slid the scissors' tips into the mass of black curls. They came together. A curl dropped to Greta's lap, and she brushed it off with the brusque movement of someone slapping a fly away. In a matter of minutes the haircut was done. Anna let herself look at Joseph then. The haircut was poor, but no other harm had been done.

"Now, isn't that much better?" Greta said. No one moved except for Margarette, who nodded slightly.

"Isn't that much better?" Greta's voice held a sudden, sharp edge.

Everyone on the floor nodded vigorously.

"Good, then," said Greta. "And I hope you watched carefully and listened to the lesson because I will ask someone to cut hair very soon, and it best be done the right way."

No one moved.

"Joseph," said Greta.

Joseph glanced over his shoulder. "Yes?"

"You may go back to the circle."

Greta stood and shook the remaining hair from her lap. As soon as she was gone down to her family for lunch or for piano lessons or for whatever else she did when she was not in the attic with her friends, Anna and the others would scoop up every strand and throw them from the open attic window. Listening was a lesson they had learned well, and so was cleanliness. Not so much cleanliness of themselves; Greta did not see much use in giving soap and water to the friends in the attic. Greta believed as her father had taught her; children such as these were used to being dirty. They liked being dirty.

"Now," said Greta. She walked to the open window, fanned herself with delicate motions of her hand, and moved back to the chair. "I'd like to hear a story. William, you tell the class a story. A story about a day at the beach because it's so hot in here. A cool day by the lake where the children go swimming and the parents sit under umbrellas and talk about their work and their duties in the world."

William, who had been a pudgy little boy when Erik Brummer had first gathered the friends together for his daughter, rubbed his face frantically. The palm of William's hand bore a shiny burn scar. William had a nervous tic in his right cheek.

Anna looked at William, then at Greta. If it took long for William to tell the story, Greta might get angry. William, Anna feared, had never been to a beach, had never seen a lake, because William's family had been poor.

"William," said Greta. Anna felt her shoulders pinch. Her lungs hurt in the heat and

hurt in anticipation of what might happen if
William could not think of a story. She grit
her teeth. Panic swirled in her gut, and she
fought it down. In a gentle motion, Margarette leaned over and squeezed William's
hand.

"There was a lake," said Margarette.

"There was a lake," said William, and
Anna's lungs heaved a burst of air in relief.
She prayed to the god of yesterday that the
sigh was quiet and Greta did not hear it.

"A big lake and with a lot of water," said
William. "And a lot of fish." He rubbed his
face again. It was stretched and scarred with
so much rubbing. His eyes were rheumy with
torment. "There was a family, a big family
with lots of children, very pretty children in
nice clothes. They all went to the lake on a
hot afternoon and sat down and took off their
shoes."

Anna looked at Greta seated on her low
chair. The girl's lips were pursed, but she
didn't seem dissatisfied with the story. If William told a good story, and a long story, Greta
would be happy and would go back downstairs to her family and leave the friends
alone. If William did not tell a good story and
made Greta angry, she would teach a new lesson to the class. It was the angry lessons that
had, just days before, made Joseph climb into

the tiny open window where the flies and the gnats and the smoke and the mockingbird song came in and try to squeeze himself through to fall to the dog-guarded yard four stories below. Only Margarette could talk him back inside by promising him silly but lovely things when the bad days were over and they could go home again.

"The children went swimming and they swam for a long time," said William. And then he stopped. It was obvious he couldn't think of what to say next. He did not know the beach of the lake and could not even imagine it well. William rubbed his face and looked around the circle at the friends. Susanne looked at the empty bookcase. Joseph licked his lips and folded his hands. Anna looked at William for a moment before looking away. She knew about lakes but was afraid to speak up and help William with his story. William's burned hand was the result of a music lesson Greta had given one morning. William had no rhythm, and Greta had insisted on all the friends clapping to her song. Try as he did, William could not keep the rhythm. When Greta had come back with the friends' daily meal, she had also brought one of Erik Brummer's cigars. William still could not clap in rhythm, but now he bore the rightful sign of the failed lesson.

"And what then?" asked Greta.

William's eyes squeezed into red slits.

Margarette's hand went up. Greta turned to her, the smile gone. "Now what, little girl?"

"Please, I'd like to tell some of the story, too." Greta crossed her ankles like her mother must have done. Her eyebrows strummed a rhythm of irritation across her brow, and then she said, "All right."

"They liked to go fishing, these children," said Margarette.

"They caught many colors of fish, red and blue and green and gold. Some they caught with nets and some with hooks."

Greta said, "Did they eat the fish?"

"Oh, some of them they did. Some they cooked and ate on the beach. They made a fire and cooked them, and the smoke went up as high as heaven. Everyone sang songs. There was a girl named Greta, and she could sing better than any of the other children."

And the story went on. It wound around the air of the hot attic, in Margarette's lilting, little-girl voice, laced with distant bits of Margarette's memory, embellished with daydreams.

After some time, Greta held up her hand to halt the tale, and she left the attic. She promised, in reward for the story, to come earlier with the daily meal. The dust and soot swirled where her footsteps had been. The door closed with a click. No one spoke. Margarette closed her eyes, and shivered.

Then Joseph said, "Thank you."

All the friends looked at Margarette and whispered, "Thank you."

Anna said, "I'll give you half my meal," although she knew Margarette would refuse, and she knew that was part of the reason she offered.

The friends stayed in the circle for a while longer. Then, slowly, they fell apart, moving to their own spots on the attic floor where they rested between lessons and dreamed their own dreams and fought their own nightmares. Anna curled up beneath the tiny window and looked at the crude beams of the ceiling. Outside, the mockingbird sang the tunes of the robin, the jay, the crow, the sparrow.

After a few minutes of silence, Joseph said, "The children sang. They sang as they sat with their parents in the boats and fished. They sang the same song as their parents, and there was no harmony, just melody."

William grunted as he turned to face Joseph.

"The fish were not different colors," Joseph continued. "They were all the same, silver and blue, like shining gems. But some were big and some were small. Some had twisted fins, and some were blind. The parents drew the fish in on the lines and put them into buckets. When they got to shore, they put the buckets on the muddy bank."

Anna turned her head slightly, her nostrils blowing the soot on the floor beside her, listening.

Joseph's voice was tight, and it trembled. He said, "The parents only fished for sport, to see the creatures struggle out of the water. The big fish with no flaws were sorted into one bucket. The fish that were not perfect went into another. The baby fish were taken from the parent fish and given to the children as pets."

Margarette said, "Joseph, I liked my story better."

Joseph said, "This is a good story. So listen. The fish with flaws were tormented, then set afire. The fish with no flaws were kept longer, but were set afire as well. The smoke did not rise to heaven, it was so thick it hung under the clouds and made the sky stink with soot and death. The little fish were tormented by children, and flopped in the buckets, trying to find the air they needed."

Susanne, by the empty bookshelf, whispered, "Margarette's story was about fish, Joseph. Don't do this to us."

"And my story is about fish. Haven't you learned the listening lesson? I am telling about fish. This is a little story about people at the beach. People playing and having fun, nothing more."

Anna stared at Joseph. The badly cut hairs of his head were wild beneath the linked fingers of his hands as he lay on the floor. He looked like a prophet; he looked like a mad lion.

"No more story," said Susanne.

"Please," said William.

"I want to kill her," said Joseph.

No one answered. Anna lay, listening to her heart, listening for the bird that had grown silent, watching the fine mist of gray gossamer smoke drift through the window over her head.

Margarette began to sing a nursery rhyme, and Anna faded into sleep.

The opening door woke them all on cue. They sat abruptly, having learned the lesson of quick attention. Anna's head spun but her eyes were open wide to appear alert. Greta was in another dress, this one blue with a white collar. She had brushed her hair up and back, and it was secured in silver. She sat down on her low chair, and the friends scurried to their places in the circle.

"Good news!" she said.

The friends waited.

"My father has found a new friend to join us. He is a little boy, younger than you, Margarette. I had asked my father for a little boy, but my father is a very busy man. But this morning he said he'd found a nice one during the selection, and shall bring him to us tonight after he's been checked over."

The friends watched and waited. Obviously Greta had forgotten her promise of bringing the meal early.

"Are you happy?" asked Greta.

All the friends nodded.

Joseph's fingers slid upward along his neck, found the ragged ruins of his hair, and began to play with them. Anna glanced at him, then looked quickly back at Greta. Joseph's good eye had been hard, bright, and twitching.

"Today's lesson will be a math lesson," said Greta.

"I have cards here that I borrowed from my uncle." She pulled white cards from the pocket of her blue dress. "I'll hold up the cards and you will tell me the answer to the problem."

Anna balled her fists in her lap. She was not good at numbers. If Greta would only give her an easy problem.

"You," said Greta to William. She held up a card that read "5 + 12." "Tell me, what is the answer to this?"

William rolled his lips in over his teeth. The tick in his cheek was vivid. Then he said, "Seventeen."

Greta had to check the back of the card, and said, "Yes, good." She put that card down and held up the next. To Susanne she said, "Tell me this answer."

Susanne looked at the card. It said, "18 − 9."

"The answer is nine," Susanne said immediately. She was good with math.

Greta checked. "Fine," she said. Then she looked at Joseph. "Your hair looks nasty."

Anna looked at Joseph. His hair, where his fingers had clutched and pulled, sat up in pointed strands. Joseph flinched and began to rub it down again.

"No, no, no, no," said Greta. "I think it needs doing again. I think you've played with it and ruined the cut. I best cut it over."

Joseph rubbed harder, trying the flatten the spikes against his scalp. The bright twitching of his eye had become a nervous flutter. His mouth opened as if to say, "No," but it closed again then, silently.

Margarette said, "I can do a problem. Please show me one."

Greta stood, the cards falling to the sooty floor. She said, "Joseph, come here and I'll do your haircut again."

Joseph looked from Anna to Greta to Margarette. His teeth began to clap together.

"Please let me do a problem," said Margarette.

Greta opened the chest by the window and took out the sewing kit. She lifted the lid and stared inside.

Joseph licked his lips. William's tic picked up speed. Susanne looked in confusion between the friends. Margarette folded her hands, in a near attitude of prayer. Anna's heart leapt into a fear-driven arrhythmia.

Greta stared into the open sewing case. Then she slowly lowered the lid. She turned to face the friends.

Margarette said, "Please, let me do a problem. I like numbers."

Greta said, "You have all been my friends for several months. I've brought you good food, and I have taught you good lessons." She pressed her fingertips together into a steeple of consideration and control. "Music lessons, art lessons, things other children of your station would beg for."

Greta walked to her low chair and sat, smoothing down the hem of her blue dress with the white collar. "If not for me, you would not have learned to listen, you would not have learned manners at a meal. I have been a good teacher." Her face clouded over then, darkening storms growing at the corners of her eyes. She said, "But oh. You are still very selfish, selfish children."

Anna needed to cough, but she swallowed it down. The hairs on the backs of her hands were prickled and alert. She looked at the window and back at Greta.

"My father has told me that I shouldn't expect very much of you. I don't want him to be right."

Joseph began to groan. It was a soft growl that, by the twist of his face, Anna could see frightened even him.

"Joseph," said Greta. "Is it you who has been selfish?" Joseph's growl grew louder, a pinched animal sound almost musical in its intensity. Susanne put her hands over her ears; Margarette held a hand up as if to quiet him.

"Joseph," Greta said. "I asked you a question. Answer. Is it you who stole from me?"

And Joseph stood suddenly, driving his hand into the waistband of his filthy short pants and pulling out the hair scissors. He screamed and lifted the scissors into the air, pointing them at Greta. His good eye was wide and ready. Greta stood from her chair and backed up a step.

Joseph took a step forward, the scissors poised.

Greta said, "Children, if he hurts me none of you will eat for a week. And you know I never lie. I was taught not to lie. Lying is a sin."

Joseph took another step forward, but Greta did not move. She knew she was safe now. At once, William, Susanne, and Anna were up, taking Joseph's arms and wrestling them down. William pulled the scissors from Joseph and presented them to Greta like a kitten presenting a prized mouse to its owner.

Greta brushed a tiny strand of hair from her face. She went to the chest and returned the scissors to the kit. Susanne and William and Anna sat down in the circle. Margarette took Joseph gently by the hand and helped him sit.

With her hand on the rough wall, Greta stood for a moment and looked out the tiny window. Anna looked at Greta, at the slice of shed roof outside the window, at the dark tops of the smoke stacks beyond the yard of Greta's home, at the smoke that hung, like the smoke in Joseph's story, too thick to reach heaven.

Greta went to the door. She did not turn back as she whispered, "Selfish children."

When she was gone, Margarette said, "This won't be forever."

Anna did not sleep for a long time that night. She listened as William and Susanne tossed restlessly on the floor. She listened as Joseph buried his face in Margarette's little-girl arms and, with her words and lullabies, she tried to soothe the insanity away.

Morning came with rain outside the tiny window and stale, humid air in the attic. The mockingbird's call was faint, as if he had found shelter from the rain in the branches of a distant tree, somewhere outside the yard. Anna lay awake for a long time. Her neck ached from the hard floor and the change of weather. No one spoke. Joseph was up, standing by the empty bookshelf with his face pressed against the slat of one shelf. His eyes were closed. Susanne and William were still asleep, or trying to be asleep. Margarette was making play shadows in the gray, rain-shrouded light on the attic floor.

The door opened and Greta came in, wearing a smile and a yellow dress with big front pockets. She did not push the door shut, but stood in the center of the room and put her hands on her hips. The friends moved quickly to their circle spots.

"A new lesson and a new friend today!" Greta said. She smiled individually at each friend on the floor. Her hair was in yellow ribbons. "First the new friend! Michael!"

The friends looked at the partially ajar door. They saw tentative movement, and then a small boy was standing in the doorway. He was no more than five. His dark eyes huge and numbed.

"He was to go with his mother, but my father brought him to me! My father is a good man to do this for us. Michael, sit with the others. We have many lessons in the circle. Susanne, make room there for Michael."

The little boy did not move. Greta's smile faltered.

Margarette said, "Michael, come sit with me." She patted the floor. Michael shuffled to her, and she eased him down. Margarette touched his hair as if in apology.

"I have a new lesson today," said Greta. She sat on her chair. "The selfishness yesterday was a surprise to me, though father would say I shouldn't be surprised. And so today the lesson is learning to give. I have given to you many things, and unselfishly so. Today you will learn to give to me."

No one spoke. The bird outside the window, far away in its tree beneath the rain, changed tunes from bluebird to wren to starling.

Greta pulled a revolver from one deep dress pocket. She made a sweeping circle, pointing it in turn at each of the friends. Then she trained it on Joseph. "You were very selfish yesterday. Ah, such a bad boy you were, Joseph. Today, you won't be. Today you will be good, and unselfish. I want you to give me something you treasure."

Joseph's good eye blinked at the revolver.

Greta then took a small white-handled pistol from her other pocket. She smiled and held it out to Joseph.

"Take it," said Greta.

Joseph's lips twisted into a silent, numbed grimace.

"Take it," Greta said.

Joseph took the pistol.

Greta said, "Give me who you love most, and I will forgive your selfishness."

Joseph stared at the pistol. His hand did not shake. "Give me who you love most," said Greta. She nodded at the revolver in her own hand. "And if I think you want to turn it on me, if it even looks as if you are thinking of turning it on me, I will use this on everyone here. Now, give me your treasure."

Joseph turned the gun toward his face and lowered his mouth to the barrel.

"Ha!" Greta barked, leaning over and smacking Joseph on the side of his head. "You don't love yourself! Look again. I know your silly little heart, boy, and know what you love. You cannot fool me. And if you act incorrectly, all here will suffer for your stupidity."

Joseph looked around the room. His good eye batted crazily, as if a gnat had gotten inside. Then, he raised the gun to Margarette, across from him in the circle.

Greta clapped her free hand to her smooth cheek. "Yes! Give me who you love most."

Joseph did not pull the trigger.

Greta said, "If you don't give her to me, I will kill her and then Anna and William and Susanne and you. My father sees hundreds just like you every day. I can watch from my bedroom window what goes on beyond our house, beyond the high fence. Many silly, weeping children are sent off with their parents, passed over by my father and gone in the blink of an eye. There are more friends if I need them. More than would fit here in the attic. I can have as many as I want. There are always more of you to be found under any stone."

Joseph slipped his finger into the trigger loop. Anna put her hands to her ears, her face into her knees. There was a crack, and a squeal of delight. Anna drove her face into the hairs on her legs; her jaws ground together.

Then Greta said, "Cleanliness! Haven't you learned? Clean up this mess and I'll teach you some new ballads and you can clap with me."

Anna lifted her face. She went with Susanne and William to the chest where the rags were kept. They wrapped up the mess and put it outside the attic door. Joseph spit on the floor to wash up the stains. It was futile, but the effort seemed to please Greta.

Back in the circle, Greta sang new songs to the friends. Michael threw up and cried, but Greta, for the moment, was too happy with her songs to notice. She would see it after the music was done. For the moment, however, she was the magnanimous queen in a pretty dress and the friends the willing servants of her humid court.

Even William clapped, his enthusiasm almost masking his inability to keep a beat.

And Anna sang her heart out. Her voice was forceful and clear. It took the damp air and sailed out to the yard among the flies and the gnats and the smoke. Her melodies skipped effortlessly from one to another, and the mockingbird had met its match.

Fisherman Joe

Katie Flory had gone on ahead, her Toyota's backseat crammed full with groceries, lighter fluid, matches, and target pistols. She knew where they had planned on camping, and by the time Bill Flory and friends Joshua and Melinda Asterton had finished packing the van and caught up with her, she had promised cleared tent spots, gathered wood, and a cozy campfire blazing. It was obvious to Melinda that Katie needed to do this to prove she was okay, that she was at least on the road to becoming okay.

"Just wait 'til you see it," Katie had said. "I wasn't a Girl Scout for nothing."

She left a full hour before the other three had found the lanterns hiding behind the Easter baskets in their garage. By the time all was secured and ready to roll, it was past three o'clock.

The camping spot was isolated, a good forty-five-minute drive from the city, back in the mountains where roads no longer qualified for paving and there could be a mile or more between houses. Most of the homes along the steep, graveled roads were small and colorless, sitting in the wire-fenced yards with cows and goats grazing nearby.

"It's Americana," said Melinda with a chuckle to Bill and Josh as the van groaned into another gear. "I wonder how many of these people all look mysteriously like each other." Bill glanced in the rearview mirror at Melinda in the back. His eyes, nervous and twitching, blinked several times before he spoke. "Quite a few, I'd bet," he said. "I've seen them come out of the mountains to the emergency room, and the resemblance to each other is amazing."

Josh, seated next to Bill, took a bite out of the Hostess cupcake he'd bought at the service station.

The two couples had discovered the camping spot on a Sunday afternoon drive just weeks before. Miles away, cresting a foothill into the mountains and just inside the boundary of the National Forest, they had found the site. It was off the road several hundred feet, down a dirt path. There was a creek, a canopy of sycamores and oaks, and across from the creek, a sheer cliff of rock that seemed to beg to be climbed by weekend vacationers. Large patches of humus would make great spots to pitch tents. A central dirt area could be honed into quite the place for a fire.

"Turn here," said Josh, his mouth full of cupcake. Bill steered from the main road onto the unpaved stretch. Melinda settled against the door as the van began its climb up the foothill. Sunlight winked through the branches of the tall pines and deciduous trees. It was a beautiful afternoon, just as Melinda had hoped. They all needed a beautiful afternoon, but for Katie and Bill, it was more a necessity than a luxury. Katie was managing, it seemed. But Bill, sweet little chubby Bill, a nurse at St. John's Memorial Hospital, was still struggling with every fiber, it seemed, to hang on to his sanity.

The van hit a bump. Josh said, "Hey, I dropped part of my cupcake!"

"Sorry," said Bill. His voice was suddenly soft and anxious.

"No problem," said Josh, leaning over. "I'll brush it off."

"Katie said she was going to make us a snack," said Melinda. "It'll be ready when we get there. Baked apples with raisins. Banana boats with nuts and chocolate and marshmallows. Maybe deep-dish peach cobbler, cooked in the coals."

"Katie's a good cook," said Bill. "She never could teach me how, but she tried, bless her. She was teaching Gillian, though, and Gillian was getting pretty good."

Josh said nothing.

Melinda didn't know what to say, so she said, "That's nice, Bill. That's really nice."

Not having a child of her own, Melinda couldn't fathom the anguish at the death of a child. Gillian Flory, seven years old, had been killed by a drunken, hit-and-run driver who had slammed into her on the sidewalk in front of the Florys' house six months ago. No one was ever caught or convicted. Katie still grieved, but her stoicism helped keep her rational. Bill's grief, however, had the man walking an edge that was sharp and dangerous.

It was Melinda who had talked Bill out of suicide the week after Gillian's death.

Melinda poked Josh in the shoulder. "You aren't going to have room for Katie's snack after eating that."

Josh swallowed a bite of the chocolate cup-cake, turned around, and grinned. There was chocolate on his tooth. "I always have room."

"Watch to the left," said Melinda. "The dirt path to the site will be here any minute."

They watched. The van bumped along, spraying gravel dust out behind it, dipping around curves and smacking potholes. Suddenly, a man stepped in the road. He turned and stared as if he were a deer caught in headlights. His black hair was greasy, his eye-brows as bushy as a bear's. Over one shoulder was a fishing pole and tackle bag. In the other arm was an ax.

Bill stomped the brake and laid on the horn. The van shuddered and skidded to a halt.

Bill's head shot from the window. "Get the fuck off the road, asshole!"

Melinda's heart jumped at Bill's shout.

The man in the road squinted, then saun-tered off into the trees.

"Goddamned moron," Bill said. His shoul-ders began to shake; his voice was tremulous. He sounded close to tears. "Goddamned in-bred insipid moron. Why don't people look?" All three sat for a moment. Bill's breathing was heavy and loud, like a steam engine roar-ing. His neck was flushed red. Josh caught Melinda's hand and gave it a squeeze. After a long moment, Bill said, in a near whisper, "I'm sorry."

"No problem," said Josh.

"It's okay," Melinda managed. *Goddamn it.*

"I want us all to have a good time," said Bill.

"So do we," said Josh. "We're going to have a good time. I promise."

"Thanks for being our friends," Bill said. "I've never had such good friends as you two."

Melinda said softly, "You're welcome." *Goddamn it, we don't need any scares this week.*

Bill pressed the accelerator; the van moved on.

And then the dirt path was there. Bill slowed the vehicle. "Ah," said Josh. "My bet is banana boats. Please let them be banana boats."

"I forgot my camera," said Melinda. She smacked Josh on the shoulder. "You let me forget my camera!"

"Nothing to take pictures of, 'cept lions and tigers and bears."

"Oh, my," said Melinda.

Bill tugged at the steering wheel. The van pulled onto the dirt ruts that made the path. The branches above were quite low, and Melinda, instinctively, dipped her head a bit as they drove under them.

The van stopped beside the trunk of a wide sycamore. The three friends popped the doors, hopped out, and stretched. A fire burned in the center dirt spot. A pile of wood was gathered and laid beside the fire. Two spaces had been cleared of twigs and rocks.

"Hey, nature girl really does know what she's doing," said Melinda.

"Katie?" called Bill.

"Open the back," said Josh.

Bill reached in and popped the hatch, still staring out among the trees for Katie. His hands crawled slowly into his pockets. "Katie?"

Melinda walked past Bill to the campfire, picked up a stick, and lifted the lid of a large pan that was nestled within the glowing logs. Above, a small breeze rustled the leaves and a red-winged blackbird squawked.

"No banana boats," she said. "It's peach cobbler."

"Okay, that's the next best," said Josh.

Bill walked to the back of the van, pulled out his blue tent case, and carried it to one of the raked tent spots. "I wonder where Katie is."

"Probably taking a nature break," said Melinda. She put the lid back on the pot, then walked to the other raked tent spot, where Josh had already dumped their red tent bag.

"Well," Bill said, dusting off his hands. "I don't remember how to set this thing up."

"Just wait a few minutes and we'll help you," said Melinda. Josh untied the strings and flipped the tent open on the ground. Melinda picked up the stake bag. Bill looked around, his eyes drawn up in concern. "I'll find Katie. You have your own tent. We can certainly do ours."

Melinda shrugged. She dumped the stakes onto the pine needles by her foot.

Bill walked through the spiny branches of young dogwoods and disappeared down the knoll that lead to the creek.

"I think the weekend will be fine," Josh said to Melinda.

"Yeah," said Melinda as she picked up a tent pole and unfolded it to snap it into place.

From down near the stream, they could hear Bill calling, "Okay, Katie! Finish your business. Your man is a wimp in the woods and needs your cunning to put up the tent!" Then he howled like Tarzan.

"God, I'm glad to hear a little humor coming back to him," said Josh. "Remember his sense of humor? He used to have us rolling in the aisles." Melinda nodded.

Down at the creek, Bill belted out another Tarzan howl. "Listen to him. Maybe we're going to loosen him up a little too much," said

Josh. "He'll want to go in to work Monday with a chimp and a loincloth. Won't the sick people just love that?"

"Would it be considered sexual harassment?"

"Depends on how bad Bill looks in a loincloth, I guess." Josh helped Melinda thread the first pole through the tabs on the tent, then poked the ends through the metal rings into the ground. The tent swayed like a kite.

"Get that other pole," said Melinda.

Bill howled again.

"He won't be fit to live with," said Josh.

Melinda stopped, and tilted her head in the direction of the creek. The howl was longer this time and didn't end with the traditional wavering Tarzan vibrato. It held in the air, guttural, clear, and loud.

Melinda dropped the pole.

"What?" Josh asked.

Bill's howl cut off, then resumed. It was not a shout of playfulness.

"Oh, God!" said Melinda. She stepped forward toward the small trees, her mouth caught in her hand.

It was a cry of torment.

Melinda raced toward the trees, batting branches away and skidded down the knoll to the creek. Behind her, she could hear Josh drop the tent stakes and call after her.

"Bill!" she shouted. She looked up the creek, where water swirled around rocks and logs, carrying leaves and minnows down its course. She looked down the creek and saw the top of Bill's head above a jam of logs on the bank.

"Bill?"

Bill looked up at her over the top of the jam.

His face was the stretched face of a haunted, demented clown. Melinda made herself walk to the jam. She looked over. Katie lay on the creek bank. Her neck, face, and chest were covered with gaping wounds. Blood covered her clothes and body like a slick coating of dark, nearly black oil. Her eyes were open to the sky, but she was beyond seeing. Her red hair was matted in dried gore.

Melinda dropped to the bank in the sand, her knees instantly soaked. She threw back her head and screamed.

"We have to call the police," said Josh. He had pulled his hair up from his head. His eyes twitched madly. Bill had loaded the semi-automatic target pistols and was filling his pockets with clips.

"We have to call the police!" Josh screamed.

Melinda stood, holding on to the branch of an oak, the remains of her breakfast spattered on the toes of her shoes.

"We're the law now," Bill said. His voice cracked, broke.

"Bill, I'll drive," said Josh. "Come on. God, let's get the police and find the murderer!"

"We're the fucking law," said Bill, his words barely audible. He turned and pointed the pistol at Josh and Melinda. "These uncivilized people don't know the law."

"Don't point the gun at us," said Josh.

Bill licked his lips. "I'm sorry." He held the gun down. "You're my friends. Help me."

"Bill," said Josh. "We'll help you. Let us drive you to town now. The sooner, the better."

"Why?" screamed Bill. "She's dead! What do you mean the sooner the better? I have to go find him now! No one else cares! No one else will care! I've seen how it fucking works! Help me, please!"

"We'll help you," said Melinda. She scuffed the vomit from the toe of her shoe and looked up at the men. She knew Bill was right. She knew if they didn't find the murderer, no one would. Gillian was unavenged. Katie couldn't be left the same way.

Bill winked, a mad, appreciative move. "Thanks," he said.

"Give us the other guns," Melinda said. Bill handed her a pistol and clip; she loaded it and held it out. Josh hesitated, then picked up the third gun and jammed in a clip.

"Bless you," Bill said. He sobbed once and wiped his hand beneath his eyes, leaving a long, dark streak of soot. He turned then, and led the other two on foot up the dirt path toward the road.

The murderer had not gone far. He was sitting, blood smearing his jeans, on a boulder just across the road from where the van had almost hit him. He was eating a sandwich from his tackle box; his fishing pole and ax were propped against his foot. The ax had dried blood on the head.

He looked up as the three approached him. He raised one hand as if in greeting. His mouth was lopsided.

He's retarded, Melinda thought.

And before the reality of the situation could register on the man's face, Bill was on him.

It took very little for the three friends to subdue him and drag the man and ax back to the campsite, his legs kicking, his sandwich forgotten in the dirt.

"Time for court," Bill had whispered to the man before he had jammed a handkerchief into the screaming mouth. *Yes*, thought Melinda. *Let justice be done this time, please God.*

*   *   *

The man doubled over with the blows of Bill's boot. Then Bill lifted the man and threw him against the sycamore tree. His new strength was astonishing, and Melinda stared with wonder.

"Help me!" Bill called to Josh. Josh held the man up on the tree, seeming not to want to look at the man's face, as Bill cut a length of nylon rope. Then he lashed the man to the trunk with a rope around his neck, waist, and knees. The man coughed and opened his eyes. They were red and wet and wild.

"Caught me an uncivilized asshole murderer! Caught a redneck Fisherman Joe!" shouted Bill. He balled his fist and drove it into the man's jaw. There was a crack. The man cried out. Bill swung his boot out and caught the man squarely in the crotch. The man screamed.

Melinda drew her hands into her pockets. Her heart thundered. *Let this be done quickly*, she thought. *Justice can be swift, I heard somewhere.*

"You like this, don't ya, Fisherman Joe?" said Bill. He leaned in to the man on the tree and pulled the wadded handkerchief from the man's mouth. Bill's teeth clacked together; he was beyond anything but the job at hand. "You like this? I'm a creative son of a bitch, more creative than you were with Katie. You haven't seen the first of it!"

"Bill," said Josh. "Please. Don't you want to reconsider? You've caught him now; he's tied up. The police won't have to go looking. We can drive him in to the station, for Christ's sake."

"Got to do the justice ourselves," Bill said. "Got to be judge and jury. There's no justice in the justice system."

Melinda felt Josh's eyes turn on her. She didn't look back but said, "Bill's right. He'll be free in a few years. Katie will never be free now. But Bill, please, do it quickly." *Justice can be swift.*

Fisherman Joe struggled violently, back and forth against the nylon rope. "Please don't! What you doin' this for?"

"Katie said that, I bet!" laughed Bill, ignoring Melinda. "No, Katie yelled it, I bet. She screamed it, begging for her very life, I bet! 'No, don't! What you doin' this for?' Did it make you hard, you fucking redneck bastard?" Bill stepped up to Fisherman Joe and almost pressed his lips against those of the bound man. "Did you get hard when you cut my wife into ribbons?"

"I didn't do nothin'!"

"Shut your fuckin' mouth!" Bill cried. He picked up a stick and slashed it across Fisherman Joe's mouth. The skin split apart on contact, leaving the man with a wide, bloody grinlike wound. Joe sobbed.

"Now," said Bill. He began to pace back and forth before the tree, rubbing his chin. "Let me see if I can recreate this little scene for you. Stop me if I leave out any important details. You found Katie building a campfire, and she looked like a good piece of ass. Yes?"

Joe, blubbering, shook his head. Tears, blood, and spit ran down his face to his shirt.

"I thought so," said Bill. "Good-looking piece of ass that would have nothing to do with an uncivilized thug from the backwoods. So you throw down your fishing pole and go for her. Hey, pussy tastes better than trout any day, doesn't it!"

"I never seen her!" screamed Joe. "I killed . . ." Bill hurled his fist into the man's face. Fisherman Joe coughed and sputtered.

Bill strode to the campfire. He felt around inside the utensil bag until he found long-handled barbecue tongs. From the fire he fished a glowing, bright red piece of wood. He went back to the sycamore tree. "Open his mouth," he said to Josh.

Josh said, "Bill, good Lord, would you let the law—!"

"Open his mouth, Josh! Let's have it done!"

"No!" cried the man on the tree. "Stop it! I killed . . ."

"I fucking know you did!" screamed Bill. He slapped Joe's bloody, drooling mouth.

Josh went to the tree and pried Fisherman Joe's jaws apart. The man gasped and gurgled, tossing his head back and forth. Bill shoved the burning coal into the mouth. The cries covered the sounds of sizzling, although Melinda could see steam rising from between the lips and out both sides of the bloody gash.

Bill dropped the tongs. "Man was perjuring himself," he said. "Can't have that in a court of law. Now, the evidence will continue."

Melinda felt her gorge rise, but she couldn't look away. *Kill him if you're going to*, she thought. *Get it over with!*

"She struggled, not wanting you to put your filthy claws on her," said Bill. "And so you picked up your ax and gave her a few chops. That old, trusty, rusty ax."

Fisherman Joe cried, coughed, and shook his head. Melinda glanced at the man's ax on the ground, at the dried blood and the black hairs stuck in it.

Katie's hair is red, she thought.

"Sliced her good and left her to die on the creek bank," said Bill. "You know, I'm trained to heal people, but I bet I can't heal Katie. You think I can, Joe?"

Fisherman Joe's head wavered, his eyes rolled in the sockets.

"I'll give you what Katie got. A little pain before you must be going." Bill took the pistol from his jacket pocket, and aimed at the man's foot. He pulled the trigger. Joe's shoe exploded with red. The man howled around his ruined tongue. Then Bill shot the man's other foot. Joe slumped, no longer able to keep his weight up.

"Do it, get it over," said Melinda.

"I love you guys," said Bill, looking over his shoulder. His face softened for a moment.

"Kill him," said Melinda.

Bill shot Joe's knees out, then put bullets through both of the man's palms.

"He looks too much like Christ that way," Bill said. He shook his head. "Can't have that. This man is no Christ." He picked up the ax, lifted it, testing the weight. "Nice tool. Sharp and heavy." He walked to the tree and with a grunt, swung the ax at Joe's left hand. It smacked through the flesh and bone and buried into the wood of the tree. The hand dangled half-off, spurting red. Joe's eyes rolled, pure white now. Bill loosened the ax and struck again. The hand dropped to the ground. He swung the ax at the man's right hand, catching both the hand and the man's thigh. The hand twitched like a dying spider, pinned on the bloody flesh of the man's jeans.

Josh groaned.

"Damn," said Bill. He pulled the ax free and grabbed the hand. With a few jerks, he pulled it off and held it up. "No more Christ."

"No more Fisherman Joe," said Melinda. Bill looked up at the man's face. He was indeed, dead. His mouth hung open. His eyes were glazed globes.

"Hmmm," said Bill. "And I had some other ideas." Beside Melinda, it was Josh's turn to lose control. He doubled up and barfed bile into the leaves.

Bill took the ax to the campfire and dropped it in the center of the flame. He collected the three pistols, wiped them off, and put them back into the van. "We were never here," he said to Melinda and Josh. "Get the tents, put them away. Douse the fire, stir it up. I'll take the Toyota, you two the van. We found Katie's body in the ghetto. You understand me? Then the justice system can begin its tailspin."

The tents went into the van, all traces of camping packed and swept away. Fisherman Joe remained tied to the tree.

"If he can feed the buzzards," said Bill, "then his life wasn't a total waste."

"Now," said Bill as he closed the hatch of the van. "Let's get Katie."

As the three walked through the dogwoods and down the knoll to the stream, Bill caught both Melinda and Josh's hands and gave them a squeeze. "Thank you. Greater love has no man than he who will help take a life for a friend." Josh and Bill gently lifted the butchered body from beside the jam of logs and leaves. One shoe fell from the dead woman's foot into the water. As Bill and Josh carried Katie up the bank toward the van, Melinda followed along side the creek to catch the shoe and take it back with them. No evidence could be left. Melinda grabbed a stick from the bank and tried to reach the shoe but it floated on, just out of reach.

The creek made a sharp turn around the rock shelf on the other side. Melinda, holding branches so not to fall in, went around the turn, watching the shoe.

She stopped.

She dropped the stick she was holding.

From somewhere behind, up at the campsite, she heard Josh call, "Melinda! We have to get out of here!"

Katie's shoe was snagged on a small creek rock within reach. Several yards beyond the shoe, lying on the creek's bank with its head split open was a black bear. Melinda took several steps closer. Her lungs were caught on the spikes of her ribs.

The bear's paws were splayed out, one on the ground, one across its chest. The ax-sharp claws were clotted with blood. A hank of red hair was tangled in one set of claws.

Katie's hair.

Melinda stepped into the stream and picked up the shoe. She hurried back to the campsite, where the van and car were turned around, engines revving.

As she climbed into front seat she was careful not to glance into the back where Katie lay wrapped in a tarp. But she did look at Fisherman Joe on the tree, mouth open and still, his expression one of terror and righteousness.

I never seen her!

"Let's go," Melinda said to Bill.

I never killed her, I killed . . .

She leaned against the door and closed her eyes. The van hit the road and sped toward the city.

Thundersylum

It is the first time Jeff has invited anyone to his home to visit. At least, the first time since he was quite young and his daddy had given in after much hoopla and said Jeff's friend Danny could come over to see the new Christmas toys. Later, after Danny had been taken back home, Jeff's daddy had pulled Jeff aside and said, "It builds up in there. It builds *up*, I don't know why I hadn't seen that before now! Everything must go somewhere, and it just *builds up* and unless you're giving out, you're taking in!" Jeff had listened as attentively as he could, the words meaningless and strange to his eight-year-old ears, and he tried not to cry too much for Danny.

But Danny is of the past now, long past. Jeff is twenty-six now. He understands what his daddy's words meant. He accepts the life of isolation his daddy taught him. But isolation and fear can be challenged. And hope of love is a strong contender.

The girl works in the office building where Jeff is a custodian. She is not beautiful, but she is intelligent and compassionate. She always speaks to Jeff first, sometimes holding the elevator door while he wrestles his buffer and carpet sweeper through the opening, sometimes inquiring on his health if he happens to have a case of the sniffles or if his already light-toned skin seems a shade paler.

Jeff has inquired casually among the other members of the janitorial stall and discovered that her name is Nancy and she is on the secretarial pool with Bowers and Brown on the fourth floor. Jeff is initially cautious, and harshly self-critical, fervently tossing out thoughts as they work their way into his brain. But with each new contact with Nancy, each new stirring at the base of his chest, he begins to allow himself the pleasure of dreaming that maybe, *maybe* she might see him as more than the cleaning man. Maybe he could let her come home with him for a visit. If the good Lord is willing and the creek don't rise.

If the good Lord is willing and the sky don't rain.

It is July, and extremely hot. The sky is cloudless and such a faint blue that it looks nearly white. Jeff opens the front door, jiggling the key and throwing his hip into the heavy, weathered wood. Nancy smiles pleasantly, holding her macramé clutch purse to her stomach, a peach tank top revealing her tanned and freckled arms. Her straight dark hair is swept back into a damp ponytail. She wears tiny pearl earrings, nothing flashy or loud like the other secretaries wear. These are elegant and simple. Jeff thinks the earrings are wonderful.

The door gives, and the two step across the threshold into the entrance hall. Jeff snaps on a portable radio on the foyer table, but it is only music and so he ignores it. He then launches into a string of nervous apologies for the condition of the place, although he spent a day and a half preparing it for her visit. The hardwood floors shine with polish; the fingerprinty door frames have been scrubbed and scrubbed again, and the entirety of the house has a radiant airiness that catches even Jeff by surprise.

". . . but you've got to understand," Jeff says, his forefinger and thumb twirling the

Elizabeth Massie

house keys around and around like a miniature drill, "I've lived by myself for almost three years, since my father passed away. I guess people let the slob come out when there's no one else around to complain."

Nancy laughs and touches his arm gently. "You're clean by profession, Jeff," she says. "I couldn't imagine you as anything else. This place looks wonderful. If you want to talk about slobs, you should see my apartment!" She raises one eyebrow.

"Well," Jeff begins, and then shrugs and gestures down the hall toward the kitchen and dining room. "I've got dinner ready for whenever we are. I fixed everything this morning. Are you hungry?"

"No, not yet."

"Oh, well . . ."

"Why don't you show me around the house? If you don't mind, that is. I love old homes."

Jeff hesitates. "I guess I could," he says. "There's not a whole lot to see. Antiques and things."

Nancy's face brightens and her nose wrinkles, ever so slightly. She obviously likes antiques. So does Jeff. He feel his heart squeeze, just a bit.

He takes her on the tour, embellishing descriptions with corny jokes and more unintentional apologies. Nancy appears to enjoy it all and follows willingly with questions and compliments. Jeff takes in her pleasure, feeling warmed and comforted and glad that he risked her coming. After all, he reassures himself, he is an adult, and he has taken the necessary precautions that were not taken in the long past.

On that long-ago day when Danny had come to visit.

As they step down to the first-floor hall again, Jeff tips his head toward the radio, listening. National news. Jeff turns to Nancy and says, "I hope all this exploring has made you hungry."

"It did," she says. "Lead on, McDuff." Jeff feels a sudden urge to put his arm around her shoulder, but he shakes it off.

They take the hall to the back of the house, Jeff leading, Nancy following. Suddenly Nancy stops and says, "And what is this?" The sharp jingling of a lock drives a spear through Jeff's gut. He turns back.

Thundersylum! he thinks, but manages to say, "Oh, nothing really. Just a place to store junk."

"A cellar, is it?" Nancy runs her hands along the small, narrow door in the wall beneath the stairs. "And I doubt junk. Sometimes the best treasures in an old house are hiding out in the cellar."

"No," says Jeff, watching the lock, counting his breaths and trying to keep them in check. "It's not a cellar. This house has no cellar. We always stored the nicer things in the attic. That's just an old . . . closet." *Thundersylum, Jeff, there's a storm coming, get to Thundersylum!*

Jeff looks at Nancy. One eyebrow is drawn up into a questioning, inverted *V*. "Are you okay?" she asks.

Jeff nods. "Sure. I'm fine. I was just hoping I'd remembered to put the mousse back in the 'fridge this morning. Chocolate mousse. If I forgot, I'll have a sea of chocolate all over the counter."

Nancy sighs dramatically. "If that be the sea, then let me drown!" She winks at him. He tries to wink back, but it feels dry and forced.

In the dining room, at the rear of the house next to the kitchen, the table is set and ready. Plain bone china is laid out, accented by the newly polished silver. Cloth napkins are coiled inside carved Polynesian napkin rings. The chandelier reflects light from the open windows. The curtains on the windows hang still and heavy.

Jeff pulls out an armed chair for Nancy. "Here you are," he says, and she sits. Jeff then goes to the stereo on the bookshelf by the window and clicks it on. The familiar voice of FM 93's George Bruce blasts instantly through the silence. Jeff fingers the knob to turn it down.

"I wish it would rain," says Nancy over George Bruce. "Anything to cool down this heat."

Jeff wipes his hands absently on his thighs, and says, "I'll get dinner."

He lifts the tray of cold cuts, pâté, crackers, and vegetable sticks from the refrigerator and carries it back to the dining room. Nancy watches him, smiling from her captain's chair.

"I thought cold foods would be best," Jeff says. "I don't know about you, but I can't stand a big meal on a day like today." *But maybe she expects more,* he thinks. *Maybe this is not the kind of thing you serve to people who visit . . .*

But Nancy folds her hands together over her plate, and she shakes her head. "That's perfect," she says. "You're quite a host, Jeff."

"And next," says George Bruce on the stereo, "we'll have state and local news, and then the weather."

Jeff centers the tray on the table. He takes dishes off and arranges them systematically about the table. Then he sits next to Nancy, quite pleased with his presentation of the food. For a moment he thinks maybe he should sit across from her because that might make talking easier, but now that he's seated he knows it would make him look indecisive to get up and move. So he stays put. Nancy smells good, like sandalwood.

Nancy smiles as Jeff pours a glass of wine and passes it to her. He fills a second glass and holds it shyly out in her direction.

"To friendship," he says.

"To all that friendship can become," Nancy adds before her lips close around the rim of the glass. Jeff wishes it was dark and he could kiss her.

And then George Bruce says, "It looks like we'll be getting that cooling spell after all. My latest report shows a cold front moving rapidly into our area, off course slightly from what was originally expected."

Jeff's eyes cut sharply to the stereo.

"This pâté is marvelous," says Nancy. "Have you ever thought of becoming a chef?"

". . . and we can expect a thunderstorm to arrive soon. So, boys and girls, forget that picnic you were planning, and let's be grateful to Mother Nature for her little quirks! Now, let's hear a tune to celebrate our luck. How about a blast from the past with Johnny River's 'Summer Rain'!"

"No . . ." whispers Jeff.

"No? Well, you should, you know," says Nancy. "You're great with food. You could start a catering business, or open a café . . ."

Jeff stands and moves quickly to the window. He presses his palms to the sill and stares up at the sky.

"Is there someone out there?" Nancy asks. "You know, with an apartment I'm used to lots of people, lots of noise. But I guess here, with all this space, noises seem all the louder."

Jeff spies the distant, rolling clouds, moving from behind the mountains like a dark and nightmarish tidal wave. "No, it's nothing, it's nobody," he mumbles. Faint thunder chuckles, and Jeff swallows with difficulty.

"Come on, Jeff." The voice is trusting, vulnerable. "Sit down, please. Let's eat. My stomach is growling." She laughs lightly.

The clouds spread across the sky, closing in. Jeff turns back to Nancy. "Yes, eat," he says. "But we have to hurry."

"Hurry?" Nancy pauses, cracker in hand. "Why do we need to hurry?"

Jeff goes back to the table and sits. He lifts a carrot stick in a trembling hand and tries to smile. "There are . . . problems here when it rains. It gets messy. The house. I mean the roof. It leaks. It's not a great place to be when it rains, believe me." He snaps off a bit of carrot in his mouth, but he cannot chew it.

"The whole roof leaks? Come on, now," says Nancy. "Maybe we could eat where it doesn't leak? The kitchen? Or living room? I promise not to spill anything on your carpet." Her eyes crinkle in humored doubt, and Jeff feels an unexpected anger rise at the test.

"Please finish," he says around the carrot. "I'm sorry, but you are going to have to leave very soon."

Thunder cracks again, and it is as though a fuse has been lit in Jeff's chest. A frantic, painful buzzing courses erratically, seeking his heart. Jeff coughs the carrot out into his hand. A soft warmth closes around that hand. It is Nancy.

"Jeff, please, I'd rather not go." Her voice is soft and sweet. "I've been looking forward to tonight so very much. I don't mind a leaky old house. Heck, I could even help you put out the buckets. We can share a tarp and sit on the sofa."

Jeff pulls his hand out from under Nancy's. "No, you don't understand—" And the thunder splits the darkening sky outside the window. Jeff flails backward, knocking his chair to the floor on its back and sending himself to his knees.

"Nancy, you can't stay! You've got to get out! Now!"

"Jeff, I *don't* understand, that's true! I . . ." Her voice trails as she stands over him, her hands spread in a gesture of confusion, her lips trembling. She watches him as he stares, horrified, at the open window, and as he begins to pull himself from the floor with floundering grasps at the table.

And then she says, "Ah."

Jeff braces his feet beneath him and in the grumbling of the oncoming storm he can hear the voice of his father, echoing inside the base of his mind.

It will kill us, Jeff! We can't be where it can get us, hurry, hurry, hurry to Thundersylum before the storm can reach us!

"You're afraid of thunderstorms, aren't you, Jeff?" asks Nancy.

"You don't want to be here!" cries Jeff.

Safety in Thundersylum, peace in Thundersylum, lose our fear in Thundersylum!

"Jeff." Nancy touches his arm but doesn't comment on their shaking. "Jeff, everyone is afraid of something. I can't stand heights. My best friend won't get into an elevator. Maybe I can help you through this. Okay? I want to stay."

Jeff finds his balance and rushes to the window. He throws a fist in the air and bellows, "This was not supposed to happen tonight! It wasn't supposed to storm! I listened! I took that precaution!"

"Jeff . . ."

He whirls on Nancy then, his eyes wild. "Please don't be here for this!"

But it wasn't raining, Daddy! It wasn't even raining when Danny came to our house! I don't understand what happened to Danny!

"Jeff, I care about you," Nancy was saying. "I hope you don't mind me saying so, but I do! Please, let me stay. You shouldn't have to face this fear alone."

Jeff stumbles for the kitchen, and Nancy hurries after him. On top of the refrigerator he fumbles for a glass mug in which are coins and pens and broken bits of plastic. The mug falls, sending the contents in a mad spray. Jeff dives for a key that bounces from the broken mug and flies under the kitchen table.

The fear comes out from us, Daddy had said. *We give it out, we get rid of it in Thundersylum. Fear is a force, Jeff, and it builds up. And unless you're giving out . . .*

Jeff runs into the hall with the key, to the narrow door in the wall beneath the stairs.

. . . you take in. Fear is a most powerful force, Jeff.

"Jeff!" cries Nancy from behind. "What are you doing?"

The key is jammed into the lock. The tumblers turn and click.

Daddy, where is Danny? He said he wanted to play hide and seek, but I can't find him? Where did Danny hide from me?

Jeff pulls the lock from its hook. The lock clatters to the polished hardwood floor.

"Go, Nancy! Go! The storm is coming!" Jeff screams. He claws his fingers around the door handle.

Daddy, I found Danny! He hid inside Thundersylum! What's wrong with him? Why is he crying and screaming and tearing his face open with his fingernails?

The narrow door squeals open.

"Go away, Nancy!"

Jeff, Daddy had said, *Danny wasn't afraid. He wasn't giving out, and so the force went in. Do you see? It went right in him like a vacuum. Sucked right in him, filled him like a sponge, poor, poor boy!*

Jeff falls through the door into the darkness that was Thundersylum. He can hear a voice from outside. "Jeff?"

Daddy, Danny won't be back at school. The teacher told us so. She said he had to go live in a special place now. What kind of special place is that, Daddy?

Never, never invite anyone else here again, Jeff, do you understand me? Never! It isn't safe, it isn't right!

I won't I won't I won't!

The voice from outside in the hall comes again, pinched, far away. "Jeff, please come out and talk to me!"

Jeff curls up in the corner of the tiny room. Energy flows, tension and fear move, concentrating and seeking their way out. Moving, draining away. Jeff clutches an old blanket that has been part of Thundersylum forever. He pulls it about himself, drawing deeper into the firmness of the black corner. Fear and anguish going out, going into the walls, safely held, safely kept.

The voice speaks again, this time from just above the security of the dark corner.

"Jeff, I'm not going away. I want to help you. I want to . . ." The voice stops abruptly, and there is a chilling silence.

Jeff looks up at the silhouette inside Thundersylum. Against the light of the hallway beyond, the silhouette seems to be shaking.

Tears well up in Jeff's eyes. He wipes at them with the edge of the blanket.

"Nancy, no," he whispers, knowing it is too late. "Please go away."

Nancy screams, a scream that is full of terror and insanity and incomprehensible hopelessness; a scream that muffles the harsh laughter of the thunderstorm outside.

Elizabeth Massie

Wire Mesh Mothers

It all starts with the best of intentions. Kate McDolen, an elementary school teacher, knows she has to protect little eight-year-old Mistie from parents who are making her life a living hell. So Kate packs her bags, quietly picks up Mistie after school one day and sets off with her toward what she thinks will be a new life. How can she know she is driving headlong into a nightmare?

The nightmare begins when Tony jumps into the passenger seat of Kate's car, waving a gun. Tony is a dangerous girl, more dangerous than anyone could dream. She doesn't admire anything except violence and cruelty, and she has very different plans in mind for Kate and little Mistie. The cross-country trip that follows will turn into a one-way journey to fear, desperation . . . and madness.

___4869-8 $5.99 US/$6.99 CAN

Dorchester Publishing Co., Inc.
P.O. Box 6640
Wayne, PA 19087-8640

Please add $1.75 for shipping and handling for the first book and $.50 for each book thereafter. NY, NYC, and PA residents, please add appropriate sales tax. No cash, stamps, or C.O.D.s. All orders shipped within 6 weeks via postal service book rate. Canadian orders require $2.00 extra postage and must be paid in U.S. dollars through a U.S. banking facility.

Name_____
Address_____
City_____ State_____ Zip_____
I have enclosed $ _____ in payment for the checked book(s).
Payment <u>must</u> accompany all orders. ❏ Please send a free catalog.
CHECK OUT OUR WEBSITE! www.dorchesterpub.com

Welcome Back to the Night
Elizabeth Massie

A family reunion should be a happy event, a time to see familiar faces, meet new relatives, and reconnect with people you haven't seen in a while. But the Lynch family reunion isn't a happy event at all. It is the beginning of a terrifying connection between three cousins and a deranged woman who, for a brief time, had been a part of the family. When these four people are reunited, a bond is formed, a bond that fuses their souls and reveals dark, chilling visions of a tortured past, a tormented present, and a deadly future—not only for them, but for their entire hometown. But will these warnings be enough to enable them to change the horrible fate they have glimpsed?

___4626-1 $5.99 US/$6.99 CAN

Dorchester Publishing Co., Inc.
P.O. Box 6640
Wayne, PA 19087-8640

Elizabeth Massie
Sineater

According to legend, the sineater is a dark and mysterious figure of the night, condemned to live alone in the woods, who devours food from the chests of the dead to absorb their sins into his own soul. To look upon the face of the sineater is to see the face of all the evil he has eaten. But in a small Virginia town, the order is broken. With the violated taboo comes a rash of horrifying events. But does the evil emanate from the sineater...or from an even darker force?

___4407-2 $5.99 US/$6.99 CAN

Dorchester Publishing Co., Inc.
P.O. Box 6640
Wayne, PA 19087-8640

Please add $1.75 for shipping and handling for the first book and $.50 for each book thereafter. NY, NYC, and PA residents, please add appropriate sales tax. No cash, stamps, or C.O.D.s. All orders shipped within 6 weeks via postal service book rate. Canadian orders require $2.00 extra postage and must be paid in U.S. dollars through a U.S. banking facility.

Name_____

Address_____

City_____State_____Zip_____

I have enclosed $_____ in payment for the checked book(s).

Payment <u>must</u> accompany all orders. ☐ Please send a free catalog.

CHECK OUT OUR WEBSITE! www.dorchesterpub.com

The Horror Writers Association presents:
THE MUSEUM OF HORRORS
edited by Dennis Etchison

A special hardcover edition featuring all new stories by:

PETER STRAUB
JOYCE CAROL OATES
RICHARD LAYMON
RAMSEY CAMPBELL

*And: Peter Atkins, Melanie Tem, Tom Piccirilli,
Darren O. Godfrey, Joel Lane, Gordon Linzer, Conrad Williams,
Th. Metzger, Susan Fry, Charles L. Grant, Lisa Morton,
William F. Nolan, Robert Devereaux, and S. P. Somtow.*

"The connoisseur of the macabre will find a feast on this table."
—Tapestry Magazine

JOHN SHIRLEY
Black Butterflies

Some nightmares are strangely sweet, unnaturally appealing. Some dark places gleam like onyx, like the sixteen stories in John Shirley's *Black Butterflies*, stories never before collected, including the award-nominated "What Would You Do for Love?" These stories are like the jet-black butterflies Shirley saw in a dream. They flocked around him, and if he tried to ignore them they would cut him to shreds with their razor-sharp wings. Shirley had to write these stories or the black butterflies would cut him up from the inside and flutter out from the wound . . . into the world.

__4844-2 $5.99 US/$6.99 CAN

ATTENTION
BOOK LOVERS!

Can't get enough
of your favorite **HORROR**?

Call **1-800-481-9191** to:

— order books —
— receive a **FREE** catalog —
— join our book clubs to **SAVE 20%**! —

Open Mon.-Fri. 10 AM-9 PM EST

Visit
www.dorchesterpub.com
for special offers and inside
information on the authors you love.